The Calorium Wars

Also by Dennis O'Flaherty

King of the Cracksmen

The Calorium Wars

AN EXTRAVAGANZA OF THE GILDED AGE

Dennis O'Flaherty

Night Shade Books
NEW YORK

Night Shade books may be purchased in bulk at special discounts for sales promotion, corporate gifts, fund-raising, or educational purposes. Special editions can also be created to specifications. For details, contact the Special Sales Department, Night Shade Books, 307 West 36th Street, 11th Floor, New York, NY 10018 or info@skyhorsepublishing.com.

Night Shade Books™ is a trademark of Skyhorse Publishing, Inc.®, a Delaware corporation.

Visit our website at www.nightshadebooks.com.

10 9 8 7 6 5 4 3 2 1

Library of Congress Cataloging-in-Publication Data

Names: O'Flaherty, Dennis, author.
Title: The Calorium wars : an extravaganza of the gilded age / Dennis O'Flaherty.
Description: New York : Night Shade Books, 2016.
Identifiers: LCCN 2016018017 | ISBN 9781597808811 (paperback)
Subjects: | BISAC: FICTION / Science Fiction / General. | FICTION / Fantasy / Historical. | FICTION / Fantasy / General. | GSAFD: Steampunk fiction. | Alternative histories (fiction)
Classification: LCC PS3615.F534 C35 2016 | DDC 813/.6--dc23
LC record available at https://lccn.loc.gov/2016018017
Print ISBN: 978-1-59780-881-1
Ebook ISBN: 978-1-59780-888-0

Cover design by Jason Snair

Printed in the United States of America

This book is for Mel, my *sine qua non.*

"...modern chemistry only starts coming in to replace alchemy around the same time capitalism really gets going. Strange, eh? What do you make of that?"

Webb nodded agreeably. "Maybe *capitalism* decided it didn't need the old magic any more.... Why bother? Had their own magic, doin' just fine, thanks..."

—Thomas Pynchon, *Against the Day*

New York City and Environs
October 31, 1877

Chapter One

ere it was, 9 a.m. on the hottest Halloween since Hell opened for business, and Billy Garrity and Finn McGonigle were stuck humping a brokedown peanut cart from the Manhattan Gas Light Company to Union Square, slogging their way down 14th Street from the East River with the temperature somewhere in the nineties, the right front wheel loose on its bearings and ready to come flying off every time they hit a crack in the pavement, the sweat pouring down them from nerves and the Indian summer swelter, and the both of them so jumpy they were ready to pee their pants just thinking about the secret compartment under the mountains of bagged peanuts, crammed full of hot-off-the-press anti-Stanton rags that could get them shot where they stood.

Billy threw a rebellious glance at Finn, wondering how he could have been such a chump—saying he'd help without thinking twice. If he'd told Finn to sling his hook he could have been cooling off in the river right now, floating on his back and watching the clouds drift by instead of trudging along baking like a potato in his Sunday shirt and pants and boots and the air so thick and heavy with river mist and steam-engine smoke and horse crap you could cut it with a knife. He spat into the street, trying to clear the taste out of his mouth.

"That's it," Billy announced, "I need a breather."

He let go of the push bar and took a slug out of their water bottle before passing it to Finn.

"Just look at this!" Billy said indignantly, wiping his face on his sleeve and waving his hand towards Third Avenue. "Somebody die, or what?"

14th and Third was usually teeming with people and vehicles, but right now it was dead as a doornail, the only action in sight being one of those puke-smelling giant cockroaches they'd been seeing around—this one bold as brass and dragging a dead dachshund towards an alleyway.

"What's the big deal?" Finn asked, raising an eyebrow and making a show of what a cool fish he was.

"It ain't normal," Billy muttered, "that's what." He wiped the sweat off his freckled ten-year-old mug. "Where's all the people at? Where's the buses? Where's the steam jitneys? Where's the *noise*?"

"Leapin' jeeze!" exclaimed Finn, two years older than Billy and a chunky, red-haired scrapper already tapped for promotion from the Little Whyos to the main gang. "Ain't you got no sense? Where *would* they be once the coppers and the Johnnies rounded up everybody they could lay their mitts on and dragged them over to the Square?"

A swelling roar rose up in the distance, its tone ambiguous, and its volume even a couple of blocks away suggestive of some caged monster goaded beyond endurance. Despite the crazy heat Billy shivered and crossed himself.

"I don't like it," he said.

"You don't *gotta* like it," Finn said, "you just gotta remember what Danny D said—do this right and you can move up just like me. You wanna spend the rest of your life with the babies?"

But Billy had stopped listening, turning instead towards a weird galloping sound coming down the Avenue towards them: *THUMP thump, THUMP thump, THUMP thump,*

2

accompanied by a stentorian, twanging bellow: "*HAHN*, hoo hree, *HAHN*, hoo hree, *HAHN* hoo hree horr hahn hoo hree . . . *HAHR LAYOO!*"

"Shite on a *kite!*" groaned Billy. "*Johnnies!*"

"*Can* it!" Finn snapped, grabbing Billy's arm so hard he yelped. "Don't you move a damn *muscle*," he hissed out of the corner of his mouth, "they ain't after us, just make like a cigar store Indian and you'll be OK!"

That was an easy one—Billy was already paralyzed with terror, only his eyes following the detachment of Gendarmes as they double-timed down the Avenue towards 14th Street with their nickel-plated weapons glinting in the sultry October sun. Every one of them a hulking thug at least six feet tall, sprung from the Tombs or Sing Sing to fulfill the martial fantasies of their boss, Horatio Willard ("Willie") Pilkington, chief of the Department of National Security's Secret Service, and all of them kitted out in the uniform of draft-dodging Willie's favorite outfit: the 5th New York Volunteer Infantry, Duryee's Zouaves, blooded at Bull Run, Fredericksburg and Chancellorsville.

Like all the "zouave" volunteers on both sides, Duryee's regiment had copied the uniforms of the French North African troops, with their short open-fronted jackets, baggy trousers, sashes and oriental headgear, but the New Yorkers' uniforms had been particularly sumptuous—the jacket and trousers midnight black with red trim, with a red fez, gold ornaments (including a gold tassel for the fez), white canvas gaiters and black leather leggings over spit-shined cavalry boots.

Willie, not content with mere historical realism, had improved on it by issuing all the men brilliantly nickel-plated weapons: Remington pump shotguns, long-barreled Colt Frontier six-shooters, razor-sharp Bowie knives and massive spike-studded brass knuckles, the whole glittering ensemble finished off with a crimson-and-gold cloisonné shield on each man's breast pocket showing a flaming sword clenched upright

3

in a mailed fist and a crescent of gold letters underneath: NYMCG, for New York Metropolitan Corps of Gendarmes.

All of which was just icing on the cake for Willie, who prized the Johnnies above all for the gleeful zeal with which they followed his orders to execute anyone and everyone guilty of "sedition." Since this crime was never defined with any precision and since the Johnnies themselves were mostly none too bright, they quickly claimed more victims than the Great Cholera Epidemic of 1849 and seemed set to keep at it till either New York was sedition-free or the giant cockroaches took over St. Patrick's, whichever came first.

Meanwhile Billy just scrunched his eyes firmly shut and kept saying "Hail Marys" under his breath as the *THUMP! thump!* of the double-timing Johnnies thundered past and started to recede.

"There they go," murmured Finn.

Billy's eyes popped open and he followed them as the detachment wheeled right onto 14th and headed briskly west. Billy shivered again.

"They're heading for the Square," he said with a tremor in his voice. "What if they catch us with the papers?"

"How many times I gotta tell ya?" said Finn brusquely, as much for his own benefit as for Billy's. "It's a lead pipe cinch—just hand out the papers along with the peanuts and first thing you know we're outa there. Now button yer lip and let's get this junkheap rolling!"

○—╥

Three blocks west, on Union Square, the crowd surged and heaved, sloshing around like a patch of ocean working itself up for a hurricane. Hemmed in on three sides by tall limestone buildings and on the fourth, Broadway side by the ruins of the Department of National Security's New York Headquarters (dynamited a few months earlier by Liam McCool's gang The

Butcher Boys and currently being rebuilt by order of Edwin M. Stanton, the all-powerful Secretary of National Security), the mob of spectators had been herded off the streets at gunpoint by Stanton's "Eyes" and the NYPD. Teachers on the way to school, bartenders opening their saloons, shoppers with their purchases, sailors on liberty from the Brooklyn Navy Yard, journalists, sales clerks, pickpockets, teenagers playing hooky—50,000 or so sullen, sweating, absolutely unwilling eyewitnesses all jammed cheek by jowl around the periphery of the square, leaving a vast rectangle in the middle vacant for the ceremony.

A horde worthy of Genghis Khan, mused Department of National Security Plain Clothes Officer Hiram Pennywhistle, *and if I had my way I'd hang them all if it took a week.*

Tall, pudgy, luxuriantly-moustached, his pale gray eyes as glacial as chunks of Hudson River ice, the DNS man strolled back and forth slowly along the front ranks of the mob, peering down his patrician nose at them, his hands clasped behind his back and his chin held aloft by the wings of his brilliantly white starched collar.

Just look at them! sneered Pennywhistle to himself. *City trash! A treasonous rabble, the sweepings of all the gutters of Europe and Asia, the scum of the world whether they're dowagers from the so-called Social Register's 400 families or barflies from the shebheens of Five Points!*

He swallowed hard, fighting down the gorge that rose in his throat at the mere sight of them. Pennywhistle was a Virginian, a country gentleman, forced by circumstances to take a job with the Federals during Lincoln's war and mired fast now in the toils of the bureaucracy by a spendthrift wife and a relentlessly growing family. Too senior after all these years to even think about giving up that pay packet, he was as much a wage slave as any petty clerk. So when Stanton detached him from the Department of National Security in Washington (and his nearby Virginia home) in order to work for Willie Pilkington's faltering DPS in New York, there was nothing he could say but "Yes, sir! Of course, sir! Delighted, sir!"

An angry growl swept through the crowd on the 17th Street side of the Square, and as Pennywhistle turned to watch, the ranks of spectators grudgingly parted to admit a huge black steam van approaching from the Broadway corner, its panels displaying the mailed fist and flaming sword of the Department of National Security's Social Harmony Subcommittee in glittering scarlet and gold. Pennywhistle greeted it with an acid little smile. A prison transport—almost time for the main event, and none too soon. Venting a giant gout of steam, the van pulled up next to the structure in the middle of the Square and screeched to a halt. At the sight of it the crowd abruptly went silent, and in the dead hush the clang of the van's rear doors flying open was appallingly loud.

For a moment or two, it seemed as if everyone in Union Square had frozen in place. Then, incongruously, a piping voice cut through the silence: "*Peanuts! Five cents!*"

⚷

Billy and Finn were pushing their cart into the crowd from the 14th Street corner of the Square. Billy looked around, wondering what was going on—everybody was just standing there like a bunch of dummies. He picked up a bag off the top of the heap and waved it overhead with a raucous shout:

"Getcher fresh roasted *PEANUTS!* Nickel a bag!"

There. That seemed to wake them up. People shook themselves like snapping out of a trance, laughing and shouting at Billy and Finn:

"Hey kid! Over here! Gimme a bag! Gimme *two* bags!"

"Let's make this fast," Billy muttered to Finn, "whaddya say we wrap each bag in a paper and see if we can't get the Hell *outa* here!"

Finn didn't like the feel of the place either. "Yeah, good," he muttered back, "all's Danny D said was, make sure to move all the papers."

Suiting the action to the word, they threw open the door to the secret compartment and started wrapping each bag of peanuts in a folded broadsheet, the papers and the peanuts moving so fast that they were more than half gone in a couple of minutes. The calls for more peanuts were slowing down as the crowd around the boys began to get involved in reading the papers and Finn looked around impatiently:

"We gotta get going—let's move up closer to the front, there's people waving at us."

The crowd parted around Billy and Finn slowly, buying peanuts as they went, and by now people were pushing up to the cart and asking for the papers without the peanuts.

"What's *in* this rag?" Billy asked, frowning at the broadsheet as he spread it out to wrap another bag of nuts.

"Gimme a break," snorted Finn. "I can't read no more'n what you can. Danny D said President Lincoln writ a letter from where he's hid out saying Stanton's a bum."

"He can say that again," Billy said firmly, and as he wrapped bags of peanuts the front ranks of the crowd flowed back towards the boys, opening a view across the vacant rectangle in the middle of the Square.

"Aw, *jeez*," Billy exclaimed, dismayed.

It was one thing to hear about it, it was a whole other thing to see it with your own eyes. The scaffold squatted there, towering and oily-black like it was made out of old railroad ties instead of regular lumber, with the floor of the platform, where the trapdoor was, standing a good ten feet off the ground. The crosspiece stood another ten feet higher, for sure a couple of railroad ties this time, mounted across two thick columns of cut-down telegraph pole. One of those new "brainy" police Acmes (you could tell by the little hump on their head where they had the dynamite charge, plus they were enameled shiny black all over except the gold flaming-sword badge on their front and Danny D said they cost 50 *grand* apiece which was plain nuts) was busy looping the ropes over the middle of the crosspiece and tying them in place—two hawsers as thick as Billy's arm, spaced six feet apart with a trapdoor under each, the nooses already tied on the ends and hanging down long enough so the huge coiled knots lay right on the trapdoors.

Meanwhile, another "brainy" Acme was climbing out the back of the DPS van carrying a big bucket of sand; Billy had heard about that one, they always tied it to the rope now to test the drop, ever since the one snapped with that geezer from the Railroad Workers' Union and they had to hang him all over again with a new rope and him already turning black in the face and pissing his pants . . .

"That's the last paper gone," Finn said, breaking into Billy's thoughts. "Let's scram!"

Billy slammed the secret compartment shut and started to wheel the cart around, scanning the crowd nervously for the clearest path.

"What's *in* that damned paper? Can't you make out the headline?"

Secretary of National Security Edwin M. Stanton was starting to get irritated, and the sweat broke out on Secret Service chief Willie Pilkington's forehead, fogging the eyepieces of his fancy Zeiss Porro-prism binoculars and forcing him to wipe his face on his sleeve. With a disgusted exclamation Stanton snatched the field glasses out of Willie's hand and moved up closer to the window. Willie and Stanton and "Great Detective" Seamus McPherson, Acting Head of the giant Pilkington International Detective Agency and onetime scourge of the Mollie Magees, were watching the preparations from the windows of the Agency's HQ on the corner of 14th and

Fourth, and with good binoculars the crowd below them could be seen as close up as if they were in the room. *There it was, by Gad, he could read it as clearly as a theater marquee!*

"DAMNATION!" shouted Stanton.

"Sir?" quavered Willie, who lived in permanent terror of his master's bad moods, like a pilot fish convinced that its shark might suddenly turn on it and eat it for dessert.

"Mr. Secretary?" brightly queried McPherson, a born survivor who could have out-toadied Uriah Heep.

"It's that same infernal issue of *Freedom*," Stanton growled furiously, "the one with that scurrilous 'Lincoln Letter'." He spun around and kicked a wastebasket at McPherson with furious force, forcing the Great Detective to leap back into Pilkington and capsize them both. As they scrambled to pick themselves up, Stanton continued his tirade, his voice rising dangerously:

"A letter, mind you, that would never have come into *being* without you two for its moronic midwives! Lincoln was *totally* in my power, locked in a sub-basement of the Smithsonian Institution! I had paid that Russian scoundrel Lukas a fortune to remove Lincoln's brain and install it in one of those fancy Acmes of his! Lincoln was the Man in the Iron *Body*, by Gad, and he would never have been seen or heard from again without YOUR HELP!"

As Pilkington and McPherson cringed on the floor, Stanton clapped the glasses to his eyes again, balefully registering the crowd's amusement as they devoured the huge black headline and the story that followed: "BOW DOWN TO TSAR EDDIE!!!" The writer had had the temerity to laugh at Stanton's new Emergency Regulations, by far the most draconian version yet and designed by Stanton to fill the public with fear and trembling, not to mention an awestruck reverence for his new title: "*Pro Tempore* Director of all U.S. Armed and Police Forces." It looked like *Freedom* was being handed out by a couple of ragamuffin peanut vendors . . . where in Tophet were the Johnnies? Where was that worthless NYPD? Ah . . . *there* was somebody he could count on—that fellow Pennywhistle that he'd sent up here to keep an eye on Willie and report on his foolishness.

"*Shoot the little bastards!*" he shouted, clenching his firsts and *willing* his subordinate to obey.

0—ᴛ

It was almost as if Pennywhistle had heard his master's command. A moment earlier he had snatched a copy of the broadsheet from a spectator's hand and skimmed the lead story, his face darkening with anger as he read the poisonous thing. Where had this filth *come* from? 'Freedom' indeed! As if freedom were meant for anyone except those who could *afford* it, who had learned to temper the exercise of freedom with the responsibilities of *property*!! His eyes narrowing, his teeth grinding cholerically, he looked around with such ominous intensity that the crowd melted before his glare as if they'd been made of wax, leaving Billy and Finn—their retreat slowed by the awkward bulk of the peanut wagon—exposed near the 14th Street corner.

"HALT!" screamed Pennywhistle.

Billy froze in place, too terrified to breathe. Finn, made of tougher stuff, took off like a miler, shouting back at Billy as he went:

"Run, shite-wit, RUN!"

That snapped Billy out of his trance and he turned and started after Finn, just not quite fast enough. Before he had even reached the corner, Pennywhistle was already pulling a pocket pistol out of his waistband and aiming carefully as he thumbed back the hammer. A moment later the thing went off with an earsplitting *BANG!* and Billy leapt into the air as if he were reaching for an invisible brass ring only to fall to the ground on his face, dead as mutton.

Pennywhistle stared at the inert bundle on the pavement with a frown, as if he were surprised by the result of his shot. A moment later a growl of rage ran through the crowd as they registered the killing and started moving towards the DNS agent with the obvious intention of ripping him limb from limb.

"Get back!" screamed Pennywhistle with a touch of hysteria. "Get back before I shoot!"

But the mob that had flowed towards the peanut-sellers and their forbidden papers had no more individual reasoning power than a school of piranhas swarming a wounded tapir; without even a hitch of hesitation they poured over and around Pennywhistle, who could be heard screaming insanely for a moment or two before he went silent.

Not soon enough to escape the notice of the "brainy" Acmes though, as they raised their left hands—the "Gatling arm" for them as for the earlier-model "curfew" Acmes—and fired a rattling warning salvo into the air. Immediately the crowd fell back all around the Square until they were standing on each other's feet, pressed as tightly against each other as if they were sardine-tinned into one of Beach's Pneumatic Transit subway cars. For a long moment of total, breathless silence, spectators and Acmes alike seemed to freeze in place, contemplating the tangled lump of bloody clothing that had been Hiram Pennywhistle, until one of the Acmes—apparently satisfied that the threat of disorder had passed—clomped down the scaffold stairs and clanked its way across the pavement to the back of the prison van.

As it waited outside the van's open doors, another Acme appeared in the opening with a human prisoner in tow, a clean-shaven, muscular-looking young man of average height, his curly auburn hair cut short and the sprinkling of freckles across his nose standing out clearly against his jail pallor before they lost themselves in an ugly purple-and-yellow bruise that spread from his cheekbone to his jaw. His hands

11

were manacled and he walked haltingly, his steps hobbled by a short chain joining the leg irons locked around his ankles; but despite all the dungeon trappings he had a spring in his step and an ironic twinkle in his eye. He looked around at the jam-packed mob with a grin:

"Look at that, will you? My public's come to see me off!"

"LIAM!" shouted a man's voice. "LIAM MCCOOL!" shouted another, echoed by one voice after another as he slowly mounted the scaffold towards the gallows: "MCCOOL! MCCOOL! MCC*OOOOOOOOO*L!"

Liam raised his manacled hands overhead like a boxer saluting his fans and shouted back, his voice echoing from one side of the Square to the other:

"BAD 'CESS TO EDDIE STANTON AND TO ALL HIS DIRTY VILLAINS!"

At that an inarticulate howl went up from every corner of the Square, the sound as vast and terrifying as the roar of a cyclone:

"MCC*OOOOOOOOOOOOOOOOOOOOO*L!"

Liam grinned cheerfully and turned towards the Pilk-ington Agency, as certain as could be that Stanton and the rest of his gang were up there in the Old Man's office, watching. His grin broadening, he raised his manacled hands towards the office, jamming the thumb of his right hand between his first and second fingers, a hand signal his supporters responded to with a thunderous breaker of laughter and a renewed bellow:

"MCC*OOOOOOOOOOOOOOOOOOOOOOOOOOO OOOO*L!!!"

Chapter Two

ow *dare* he give me the fig? *Damn* his impudence!" Stanton was glued to the window, transfixed with fury as he glared down at Liam through the binoculars, his curly gray beard bristling and jutting with outrage, the deep, disapproving grooves that normally tugged the corners of his mouth downwards growing still deeper and more censorious, the wrathful frown dragging his bushy eyebrows down over the top of his glittering little pince-nez, the heavy gold chain across his black brocade waistcoat rising and falling like a mooring line in a storm as his maddened wheezing jiggled a paunch whose growth had kept pace with the steadily increasing grandeur of his titles.

He spun around and lowered the glasses, turning his rage on Pilkington and McPherson, wagging a porky finger at the two of them as if he wished it was a club:

"I blame this whole business on your incompetence, both of you."

Fanatically attuned to his master's needs and fancies, Pilkington had imitated him not only mentally but physically, with the result that a natural plumpness had turned into full-fledged corpulence, his body wreathed and garlanded with fat and his face bloated until his eyes were tiny sparks of feverish anxiety shining out above the suety mounds of his cheeks.

Unfortunately the new, fatter Willie Pilkington sweated twice as much as the old one, especially when he was worried, and by now he was absolutely dripping with perspiration.

"But, sir!" cried Pilkington in despair. "My men and I have worked day and night to find these villains!"

McPherson, a big, beefy roughneck with sandy hair and whiskers and the fiery red nose of a man who liked his first whiskey with breakfast, edged away unobtrusively from Pilkington. Partly, of course, to get away from the smell of his boss' muck sweat, but at least equally to emphasize the absolute *gulf* that separated his own fine work from Pilkington's lamentable errors and miscalculations.

"Sure, now, yer honor!" groaned McPherson, slipping into a pained brogue. "My Agency's operatives have been turning over every stone in the city, and I'm willing to bet it was them breathing hot on his trail that turfed out the informer who gave you McCool."

"Don't you flannelmouth me, you cretins, you egregious nincompoops!" Stanton was so infuriated that flecks of saliva flew with every word. "Let's not even get *started* on what just happened to poor Pennywhistle and the fact that you two are supposed to be responsible for public order and decency in this mutinous Sodom—which as far as I can see hasn't developed a thimbleful more order *or* decency since the Draft Riots. No, let's just talk about that vile thug down there with the rope around his neck!"

Stanton sneered at his cringing lieutenants with ferocious sarcasm. "One man! Imagine my surprise when I saw they were leading just one man out of the van to be hanged. *Surely* there must have been at least forty or fifty of him to be flimflamming you two at every turn and setting all your efforts at naught, but no! Just one scrawny little Irish rogue, the very same Liam McCool I sent the pair of you to arrest in Washington not six months ago. And did you arrest him? Did you, hah! He and that damned female scribbler Becky Fox knocked

14

you senseless, stripped you to your long johns, tied you up and bathed you with Chinese rotgut, and then proceeded to free Lincoln and see him safely into hiding! And how did you pay them back, eh? Tell me that!"

Stanton glared daggers at the cringing duo: "*You* . . ." he stabbed a finger at McPherson, ". . . let him and that creature break into this very room, rifle your safe and publish documents exposing the crimes you committed to conceal the bastard *he* . . ." the stabbing finger swung around to point at Pilkington ". . . fathered on one of our spies, and while McCool and his *hetaera* pulled *that* off they amused themselves by blowing up *your* brand-new, million-dollar office building!"

Stanton clenched his fists at his sides, his face almost black with rage, and bellowed at them:

"Was *ever* any patient, long-suffering statesman burdened with such gormless, contemptible *imbeciles* for helpers? Who knows how many more heinous crimes that swine might have committed if I hadn't been lucky enough to receive the anonymous denunciation that led my operatives right to him! And you haven't even been able to locate the informant so that I might shake his hand and pin a medal on him!"

Pilkington set his jaw and did his best to look intrepid and determined, looking in spite of himself more like a schoolboy who has just been soundly thrashed by the principal.

"I promise you, sir," he said earnestly, "every Secret Service operative in the country is on the track of the informant. Clearly, the man is hesitant to claim the credit his public-spirited act deserves for fear of a cruel revenge at the hands of the seditionists, but the *instant* we discover his identity I promise we will seize him and force him—uh, *encourage* him—to tell us *everything* he knows about the Freedom Party!"

"Indeed, sorr," McPherson asserted, his brogue fighting his best efforts to suppress it, "and every Pilkington detective who could be pulled off other jobs is out beating the bushes under orders to stay on the job day and night till they discover where these damned Freedomists make their lair— when we know *that* we'll root them out with fire and the sword, I swear to yez on me mither!"

"Hmph!" snorted Stanton, slightly mollified. "Just see that you do, and don't be dithering on about it forever—I want to see every last one of those vermin dangling from the end of a rope by Thanksgiving!"

As if in response, a vast, muffled groan rose up from Union Square: *"NOOOOOOOOOOOOOOO!"* Stanton turned back to the window, raised the glasses and saw—with absolutely delicious clarity—one of the "brainy" Acmes fitting a black hood over Liam's head and then sliding the noose down over the hood and pushing Liam roughly towards the cracks in the planking that outlined the waiting trapdoor.

"Ahhh!" breathed Stanton with a rapturous smile. "Words cannot *begin* to express the beauty of that picture— Liam McCool wearing a hangman's knot for a cravat!"

"Indeed, sir," said Pilkington eagerly. "And if ever there was a well-merited . . ."

"Be quiet, you fool," snapped Stanton, "*I'm* the one who finally managed to trap him and I've earned the right to enjoy this in peace!" Still peering through the glasses he chuckled spitefully, hugging the hard-won triumph to himself and gloating over the shackled figure on the scaffold: "You thought you could make a fool of *me*, you foul little shanty-Irish pustule? Make a mockery of Edwin M. *Stanton*, the architect of the new *America*?" He bared his teeth in a feral grin. "You *contemptible* little mongrel! In a few moments it's *you* who'll be twitching at the end of a rope and soiling your pants!

He lowered the glasses and turned back to the others, the very thought of McCool's execution filling him with such a blissful sense of expectation that he couldn't help giving Willie and McPherson a jovial Santa Claus chuckle. Stanton's helpers returned his smile warily, so taken aback by his sudden festive mood that their expressions made him think of a little dog he had beaten with a hairbrush when he was a boy. Stanton shook his head ruefully. The poor simpletons looked terrified; clearly, the moment called for a touch of magnanimity.

"Let's drink a toast, boys!" He gave the Great Detective a hearty clap on the back. "Come now, McPherson, you must still have a drop of that special rye!"

Relieved beyond measure, McPherson bustled over to an ornate mahogany sideboard, grabbed a bottle and some glasses and poured out three healthy shots.

"Right, then!" cried Stanton, raising his glass. "Here's to the destruction of the Freedom Party, may they be ground to atoms and scattered to the four . . ."

Before he could finish, a swelling uproar from the crowd of spectators turned into a bedlam of shouts, catcalls, boos and scattered applause. Stanton frowned, tossed off his drink and hurried back to the window, raising his binoculars to see what was happening.

In the Square below, a private steam phaeton with brilliant midnight-blue lacquer-work and brass fittings polished to a golden luster had pulled up next to the DNS van. A pudgy, pleasant-looking middle-aged man wearing clerical garb, his wavy gray hair hanging to his shoulders and his substantial Roman nose probing the air questioningly, like a gopher checking for foxes, was standing next to the car peering around as the chauffeur held the door open for him.

Stanton clapped his hand to his forehead with a groan: "Damnation! Rev. Beecher's already here and we're still missing one of the prisoners!"

Pilkington almost squeaked with panic: "You mean the Man in the Iron Mask? But sir! I *ordered* the jailers . . ."

Stanton interrupted in an ominously low voice: "Then you had better get on the voicewire at once and find out what's happened to their van . . . before I send *you* down there to take his place!"

Turning abruptly back to the window, he waved energetically at the Rev. Beecher until he succeeded in catching the attention of the chauffeur, who tugged on his employer's sleeve and pointed up at Stanton.

        ⊙━

"Ah, Edwin! *There* you are!" exclaimed the Rev. Henry Ward Beecher, his perennial smile of mild amiability widening as he followed his chauffeur's gesture and caught sight of the gesticulating figure in the window. The uproar in the Square had grown so strident that the clergyman was getting uneasy about drawing out the delay much longer. True, he still had plenty of supporters—especially in New York—but that plaguey adultery trial had stirred up a great deal of totally unfair censure, especially among the Irish and the other hordes of immigrant Papists, and he would just as soon be back in his peaceful Brooklyn parish as quickly as possible.

Resorting to pantomime, Beecher pulled his watch out of his waistcoat pocket, held it up for Stanton to see, then put it away and turned towards the gallows, gesturing at the empty spot on McCool's left. Spreading his hands and raising his eyebrows, he sent Secretary Stanton a message as plain as any billboard: "*What should I do now?*"

Stanton hesitated for a moment, then shrugged and made a rolling motion with both hands, saying with equal plainness: "*Get on with it!*"

Relieved—if a little uneasy about how to include the missing prisoner in his homily—Beecher turned and climbed the stairs to the scaffold, followed by his chauffeur and one of the giant "brainy" Acmes who flanked him protectively as he moved to the railing to address the crowd, his smile a beacon of gentle affection.

"My dear brothers and sisters!" he intoned, spreading his hands in welcome. At once the volume of the catcalls, whistles and applause jumped to an alarming level and a visible wave of unrest ran through the throngs that lined every side of the Square. Beecher blenched a little but kept the loving smile firmly in place and raised his speaking voice to open-air Chautauqua volume:

"Now some of you may feel that you wouldn't have me as a brother, not for all the tea in China . . ."

A roar of laughter, some derisive and some amused, echoed across the Square, and canny orator Beecher seized the moment to turn the crowd's emotions and bring them under his sway:

"But no matter what faith you profess or what politics you espouse, we are all brothers and sisters in the face of this poor young man's suffering . . ."

At that, Beecher turned and gestured dramatically towards the hooded figure standing on the trapdoor next to him:

". . . and we all must ask ourselves how a promising and vigorous youth became the contemptible wretch we see before us."

This time the catcalls and whistles were fewer and farther between as Beecher turned back to the suddenly solemn crowd and spoke out with the fire that had made him one of the most popular speakers in America:

"The answer is all too simple, my friends—it is the age-old tale of the foolish youth setting up his own pennyworth of cleverness against the vast, accumulated wisdom of his elders and betters, who know that God himself has ordained and sanctioned the gulf between the palace of the millionaire and the cottage of the laborer . . ."

o—r

On the roof of the building next to the Pilkington Agency's HQ, Harold Nakamura, alias Harry the Jap, a wispily-bearded young man who was the Butcher Boys' chief artificer and the bosom pal and jiu-jitsu partner of Liam McCool, listened with a bemused smile to Beecher's oration and the bedlam of shouted comments that interrupted it.

These *gaijin* were great talkers, Harry mused, but they were short on efficiency. He pushed the background noise out of his mind and went back to his task, peering through the Malcolm Telescopic sight atop his rifle and making a minute adjustment to the windage. Harry's weapon was a Sharps Creedmoor Model 1874 lever-action falling block target rifle, and Harry had tweaked and tuned it till it could punch the middle out of a silver dollar at 1000 yards. The distance from Harry's shooting platform to the scaffold was scarcely a hundred yards, but there was no such thing as paying too much attention to accuracy, and he studied the flapping of the flags and banners on the buildings around him as minutely as if he were on the 1200 yard firing point at Wimbledon.

Finally satisfied, Harry pulled away from the scope and looked towards the block of buildings at the 17th Street end of the Square, waiting for his signal and thinking that their collaborators from the Whyos gang seemed to be shaving this one a little bit too close. He had been worried a while ago when the detachment of Johnnies showed up at the 14th Street corner, but fortunately they weren't as brave facing a huge angry mob as they were when they were shooting one or two terrified "seditionists," so they had double-timed straight on down 14th Street and out of sight. Now, however, the anointed champions of the Swell Set, the toffs of New York's own 195th Light Infantry, had shown up at the Broadway corner of the Square, all set to keep the plebeians in line and supported (from behind, where else?) by none other than the detachment of Johnnies. That was too many rifles for civilians to face, and if the Whyo sentinels didn't send their signal soon . . .

Harry looked towards the top of the building on the Broadway corner, but so far the Whyos were keeping out of sight. He could feel the irritation and anxiety seeping into his thoughts like sediment stirring at the edges of a limpid pool, and he forced himself away from them into the clarity of *zazen*, watching the movements below him without any thought of their meaning or content, his breath steadying and slowing until at last he could . . . *aagh!* The serene moment popped like a bubble as a huge black DNS steam van tore into the Square, its gruesome pneumatic siren loud enough to make your ears bleed. "*Now what?*" muttered Harry. He raised the Malcolm sight to his eye and peered down towards the gallows, where the van had screeched abruptly to a halt, venting billows of steam.

As the rear doors of the van clanged open, the Rev. Beecher brought his oration to a practiced dramatic pause and turned to watch as two more of the "brainy" Acmes dragged another hapless figure down the van's steps and up the stairs towards the scaffold. Where McCool had seemed quite fit and cheerful apart from his bruises and abrasions, this prisoner seemed scarcely able to walk, having to be supported by one of the "brainy" Acmes while the other slipped the noose over his head and settled it around his neck.

It wasn't the man's physical condition that disturbed Beecher most, however, it was the ghastly metal helmet whose front half was pierced like a jack-o'-lantern with holes where eyes, nose and mouth should be and whose back half was joined to it and locked shut by a series of tiny padlocks set in holes drilled all the way around its circumference.

For once completely at a loss, Beecher reached out as if to touch the man, stopping himself with a jerk as he suddenly realized what he was doing. The clergyman cleared his throat instead and raised his voice to be heard above the pandemonium caused by the masked prisoner's arrival:

"Ah . . . are you all *right*, sir?"

The answering voice was clear and British-crisp if a bit weak and oddly echoey: "Am I all right? Am I *all right?* Let's see, now—I've been beaten and kicked regularly for days and jolted with enough electricity to run a trolley and then there's this tin pot locked onto my head and I'm about to be hanged, but apart from *that* I suppose everything's really quite splendid! Are *you* quite all right, sir? You seem to be suffering from the last stages of terminal idiocy!"

At that, McCool burst into a peal of uproarious if somewhat muffled laughter and Beecher—stung into momentary speechlessness—just stood there with his jaw hanging open until a faint sound of shots and screams reached them from the direction of 17th Street.

"Great God," Beecher muttered in a distraught voice, "I don't think I can stand much more." He looked across the Square towards the ominous racket and unthinkingly moved around behind the comforting steel bulk of the "brainy" Acme.

⊙━

Up in his rooftop aerie, Harry was tracking the same worrying noises, swinging the Malcolm sight around towards 17th Street and trying to make sense of the hubbub of armed men and terrified spectators milling around the corner of Broadway and 17th. Fortunately, his confusion was ended a moment later by the arrival of the long-delayed signal from the Whyo sentinels on top of the building at the Broadway corner: a triple mirror flash that said "They're coming!"

Harry nodded, smiled, checked the row of shiny brass cartridges waiting in a neat row on the lid of his rifle case and set his sights squarely on the "brainy" Acme that was standing in readiness to pull the lever and drop the trapdoor under Liam's feet.

Harry put another click or two of windage on the telescopic sight. There, perfect! His bull's-eye would be the little

22

hump that the British mechanician Royce had set at the point where the Acme's neck joined its head. It had been meant to discourage his competitors from screwing off the thing's head to find out how the "brainy" part worked and it bore a label stating clearly that any tampering would set off a small charge of dynamite, enough to make the tamperer regret his nosiness.

For Harry, however, the hump was simply a handy aiming-point. Emptying his mind of distractions, he began applying a gentle pressure to the Sharps' trigger, slowing his breath until his lungs were barely moving, thinking that however solidly Henry Royce may have crafted his "brainy" Acmes, he couldn't have planned for the colossal slug mounted on the end of a Sharps .44-90 cartridge—more than an ounce of lead flying at 1300 feet per second. A bullet like that could punch its way through a half-dozen Acmes and still knock bricks out of a wall . . .

BLAM! The shot had fired without any conscious control by Harry, and an instant later there was a second and louder explosion on the scaffold as the carefully measured dynamite charge blew the Acme's head to smithereens. Without a moment's hesitation, Harry swung the barrel of the Sharps towards the "brainy" Acme standing ready to drop the trapdoor on the second prisoner, simultaneously levering open the breech, inserting a fresh round, and still on his Zen plateau of perfect calm, firing again, then, finally, as the second Acme's head disappeared in a cloud of smoke and some sort of disgusting bloody goo of brains and wires, repeating the entire operation smoothly and nervelessly as he blew the third Acme's head into fragments and then the fourth and the fifth as Beecher flattened himself on the floor of the scaffold, screaming hysterically as he tried to wipe the brains off his jacket, and then gave up and covered his head with his hands.

Pandemonium swept through the crowd, screams and cheers and excited shouts sweeping from one side of Union Square to the other as Liam tugged at his hood. Then, once he had torn it off, he grinned up towards the roof of the building that Harry had fired from, mouthed "Thanks!", and lowered his manacled hands to his neck, grabbing the noose, wrenching it open and dragging it back up over his head. Liam looked around the Square urgently . . . *there!* He breathed a huge sigh of relief as more screams and a crackle of gunfire came from the Broadway corner, the crowd making way hastily as a nightmarish-looking steamer appeared and raced towards the scaffold.

It was as if someone had taken one of the old Civil War ironclads and put it on wheels—a vehicle as big as the DPS prison van, but with sloping sides made of boiler plate and vertical gun slits on three of its sides, plus a Gatling gun in a revolving turret on top. As one of the gentlemen warriors from the 195th shouted for his men to fire at the strange machine, the turret spun around and fired a rattling volley back at them, making them drop instantly to the pavement and cover their heads in terror.

Definitely time to hoof it. Liam leapt to the other prisoner's side, opened the noose and pulled it up over the weird "iron mask" with its border of tiny locks, started to help the man walk towards the steps, then changed his mind, dropped to his knees, jerked his manacled hands as far apart as they would go, pulled the man up across his shoulders for a fireman's carry and took off towards the stairs at a staggering run.

o—⌐

"No, damn it! No, no, no!"

Maddened with fury and frustration, Stanton pounded with both fists on the sealed window of the Pilkington Agency office, totally oblivious to the danger of smashing the glass and cutting his hands.

"You can't! You mustn't."

But Liam McCool was already lurching down the stairs from the scaffold to the pavement of Union Square, his burden precariously balanced on his back with his manacled hands stretched back over his shoulders and the chain between them pressing into his own throat.

As Stanton watched, nearly dancing with wrath, the ironclad steamer screeched to a halt in front of Liam and an armored door clanked open, disgorging a cheerful young man with blond hair and the pug nose and wide cheekbones of his Russian muzhik ancestors. The man ran to Liam and relieved him of his burden, passing the prisoner on to an armed man who had followed him out of the steamer and then throwing his arms around McCool.

0—π

"I don't believe it!" roared Stanton. He shook his fist crazily at Willie: "You miserable wretch! You told me you had *captured* Mike Vysotsky!"

"We *did*," whined Pilkington, "but somehow he managed to escape again!"

0—π

Liam and Vysotsky—his oldest pal and co-chairman of the Butcher Boys—were embracing happily when a thought seemed to strike Liam. He broke away from Mike, talking urgently, and pointed up towards the window from which Stanton and the others were watching.

"DOWN!" shouted McPherson as the significance of the gesture sank in. He grabbed Stanton and Pilkington and pulled them to the floor, ignoring their indignant cries.

In the Square below, Mike was leaning into the open hatch of the ironclad, giving orders, and a moment later, the turret on top of the vehicle moved smoothly around and the

25

barrel of the Gatling gun rose slowly to a 45-degree angle. Then, with a deafening roar of .45-70 cartridges exploding in a non-stop stream of fire, the Gatling delivered a couple of hundred slugs through the window where Stanton, Pilkington and McPherson had been standing a moment ago.

"There!" Liam said with a laugh. "That'll give them a little something to remember us by . . . now let's get rolling!"

He and Mike jumped into the steamer, and a moment later it spun around as gracefully as a couple of tons of armor could manage and tore rapidly back across the Square. As it disappeared around the Broadway corner, a vast cheer rose up from the shanghaied crowd, and as the men of the 195th, the detachment of Johnnies and a miscellany of NYPD personnel—both humans and automata—rashly raised their weapons and fired into the air to intimidate them, the crowd abruptly threw all caution to the winds and poured over their tormentors like a tidal wave, reminding them—even if only for a few painful moments—of the immemorial truth that it doesn't do to push New Yorkers too far . . .

Chapter Three

here was a giant hurricane moving towards New York from the Caribbean and the ocean off Long Island's South Shore was already showing a stiff two-foot chop, but Captain Billy Grogan and his steam launch *Straight Up* had run the blockades in the Civil War and weather like this just made the old river pirate grin in his bushy white beard.

"A tempest in a teapot, Liam me lad," he chuckled as he got Liam and Mike and their mysterious companion settled belowdecks. He held out a bottle of Old Bushmills. "Here, a drop of that'll set you right as rain. And as for that poor fella," Captain Billy clucked sympathetically and shook his head as he inspected the Man in the Iron Mask, "youse had best be gettin' that tin pisspot off his head and the rest of that Bushmills into him, he don't look too good!"

Throwing them a salute, the old river pirate headed back up the ladder to the pilot house while Liam and Mike struggled to get the mystery man into a bunk, a frustrating task with his long arms and legs flopping around bonelessly like a giant marionette.

"*Chort!*" Mike cursed in Russian. "He don't weigh much but he must be a good six-six when he's standing up."

With a final heave-ho they managed to get him into the bottom bunk of a rack of three, but not without banging his helmet into the bulkhead with an awful, hollow *clonk!* The man groaned painfully and started a strident harangue in some language neither Liam nor Mike could make head nor tail of.

"Red Indian?" Mike asked. "One of those Iroquois rebels maybe?"

"I don't think so," said Liam, "I've heard it before but . . ." He bent closer to the hole in the mask, listening with a frown; then he stood up, smiling a little. "You have, too," he said, "on Mott Street."

"What, he's *Chinese?*"

"Unless *wángbādàn* means something in some other language. It means 'bastard' in Mandarin. You have your picks on you?"

Mike grinned. "Does Michelangelo have paint?"

He reached into an inner pocket of his smart glen plaid Norfolk jacket and pulled out a roll of morocco leather the size of a small salami, unsnapped it and rolled it out onto a table bolted to the floor next to the rack of bunks. The morocco wallet had been divided into a row of miniature pockets by stitching, each pocket about big enough to hold a pencil but holding instead several dozen slender tools, some like a dentist's probes, some like screwdrivers with tiny teeth, some clearly improvised and corresponding to nothing any hardware dealer would recognize. Liam examined them judiciously, picked out two and set to work on the mask's tiny padlocks as the mystery man maintained a non-stop obbligato of incomprehensible muttered conversation, broken by loud shrieks and curses.

Mike looked pained: "What'd they do to this poor geezer?"

"If it was the same pair that worked on me you don't want to know," Liam said with a wry smile, "it would ruin your digestion." He squinted at the lock he was working on with total concentration, his tongue clenched between his teeth as he probed with a long, springy pick. Suddenly there was a barely audible click and the lock popped open.

"Hah!" cried Liam triumphantly. "Gotcha!" He held it up for Mike's inspection. "See that, the little letters next to the keyhole? '*Toledo*.' That's Toledo, Spain, Misha, not Ohio—this mask thing is one of the toys Willie Pilkington's Spaniards brought over in their luggage. I bet Stanton is mad as a hornet that we snatched this bird before he could string him up." He set to work on the next lock, humming a little now that he'd plumbed its secrets.

"Spaniards?" Mike said.

"Mm hm," Liam said in an abstracted tone. "They were a present from Stanton to his blue-eyed boy Fat Willie, all the way from the Old Country. First-class professional persuaders—their ancestors cut their teeth on heretics back in the Inquisition."

"Heretics," Mike muttered dubiously.

"Yeah," Liam said with a little grin, "you know, witches, foreigners, birds that carry lock picks in their jacket pockets."

The second lock popped open and as Liam pulled it loose a panel sprang free in the lower half of the mask and revealed the prisoner's mouth, which was badly bruised and cut. Whether it was a change in temperature or light or something else, the man suddenly went crazy, screaming wildly, tearing at the mask and at his prison tunic, thrashing in the bunk and howling as Liam and Mike tried to hold him down, then suddenly bellowing in English:

"NO! NO! NONONONO*NOOOO!* NO CALORIUM! *NOOO* CAL*OOO*RIUM!"

"Whiskey!" barked Liam, and instantly Mike grabbed the Old Bushmills and uncorked it. "I'll pry his jaw open, you pour!" Liam said.

A moment later they were filling the man like a tea kettle, pouring whiskey until he finally started sputtering and shaking his head.

29

"Okay." Liam said. "That ought to do it." And in fact, the man's thrashing slowed down and his gibbering and shouting weakened until they finally gave way to exhausted, ragged breathing. Mike wiped his forehead with the back of his hand and tipped up the bottle, finishing it off.

"Holy jeez," Mike said in a strained voice, "willya *look* at him?"

The man had torn the prison tunic to shreds in his frenzy, exposing a kind of nightmare relief map: a continent of purple, green, and yellow bruises intersected by a black-and-crimson topography of old wounds—scabbed-over lash-marks, poker and electric-shock burns and meandering gouges dug by unidentifiable instruments. Liam examined him for a long moment, his expression going totally opaque, then shook his head briskly and jerked a thumb towards the small galley:

"Check out the cupboards and get us some more whiskey, will you?"

While Mike rummaged through the ship's stores Liam went back to work on the locks, moving fast now that he knew their secrets, his expression distracted as his hands worked instinctively and his thoughts wandered. After a few moments, Mike returned with another bottle of whiskey:

"Now what?"

"Hang on," Liam said. Another second or two of gentle tweaking and the final lock clicked open and fell into Liam's hand. "There," he said. He scooped up a dozen or so of the little locks and dumped them into his trousers pocket. Mike raised a curious eyebrow:

"*Nu, chto, Lyovushka*," he said, "I never seen you keep souvenirs before."

"I never ran into anybody like the Spaniards before," Liam said with a cryptic smile. "One of these days I'm going to see them again and then we'll figure out some other things you can do with little locks."

He raised the mystery man's torso off the bed a few inches: "Give me a hand with this, will you? We have to get these rags off him and clean him up."

Undressing the man was pitifully easy: his whole wardrobe amounted to the ragged tunic and a pair of threadbare denim pants. Liam threw them into a trash barrel, then soaked a corner of the blanket with whiskey and used it to swab the man's wounds. As the alcohol stung the open sores the man groaned and muttered drunkenly.

"Lucky we got some of this booze into him first," Liam said, "he'd be howling like a banshee."

Mike wiped the sweat off his forehead with the sleeve of his jacket. "I seen a lot," he said hoarsely, "but never nothing like this. You gotta promise me, when you find the Spaniards I get a piece of it."

Liam nodded. "Sure." He grinned: "If there's any left when I'm done. Now . . . get a good grip on his upper arms, I want to take the upper half of his mask off but he may go crazy again."

As Mike held the man down Liam inspected the mask carefully, tapping and pulling at it gently here and there. The front half fit into the back half with the seamless precision of a fine pocket watch, but Liam couldn't see any reason it shouldn't just lift off now that the locks had been removed. Crossing his fingers mentally, he inserted his fingers into the gap left by the panel that had sprung loose a few minutes ago and pulled upwards gently; there was a momentary resistance, almost as if the join was sealed by a vacuum, then it let go and the remaining portion of the front half came free.

"Whaddya know," Mike said in a hushed whisper, "he really is a Chinaman after all. What's Stanton got against *them*, anyhow?"

The man's face was long and hollow-cheeked, with a prominent patrician nose and a wide, thin-lipped mouth framed by a drooping moustache; even bruised and bloody

31

and distorted by delirious grimaces, it was an aristocratic face, suggesting a strong will and a sharp intellect.

"I'm guessing Stanton doesn't care about Chinese people one way or another," Liam said, examining the man's face thoughtfully. "Willie's pet Inquisitors didn't do me over half as bad as they did this fella—they were just playing with me till it was time to send me to Union Square for the long drop. But five will get you ten our friend here was sitting on some valuable information Stanton would have given his eye teeth for, so you just know they tried everything they could think of before they finally gave up trying to crack him and sent him to keep me company."

"They were wasting their time," Mike said with a note of approval. "Just look at that face. He's got a jaw like my old man, stubborn as a mule. There's no way this geezer's ever breaking, not even if you put him on the rack."

Liam smiled as he thought of Old Vysotsky, a bank robber who'd marched the three thousand miles from Moscow to Siberia in chain gangs *po etapam* three different times without ever giving up so much as his name.

"Pick him up again," he said to Mike, "I want to get the rest of this junk off him."

As Mike lifted the man's upper body away from the bunk, Liam freed the back half of the mask and tossed it into the trash barrel. Then he pulled the sheet and blanket up over the man's naked chest and tucked him in.

"I reckon that's it for now," he said. "We must have poured a pint of Bushmill's into him. It'll be a while till he sobers up. Let's go see what's going on up topside and find out if we can get him some duds from Cap'n Billy."

o—┰

Once they were out under the sky again Liam and Mike moved as far forward as they could go, finally seizing hold of a couple of stanchions so they wouldn't fall down every time the bow of the *Straight Up* slammed into a trough. Standing with his feet spread, the tails of his borrowed slicker flying straight out behind him in the wind and his eyes squinted half-shut against the constant spray of icy salt water, Liam could feel the pent-up bitterness of the past couple of months washing away like layers of dirt.

"You have to hand it to Stanton's boys," Liam said, shouting over the wind, "they know how to run a clink. How many times did you try to spring me, anyway?"

Mike made a disgusted face: "Five times in three months, and we couldn't even get close to the part where they were keeping you. Only other place I know that good is the Shlisselberg Fortress in St. Petersburg."

"Look at the good side," Liam said, "I would have hated to miss out on the Spiggoty Twins with their dainty little pimp moustaches and their shiny fingernails." His eyes narrowed as he slipped back into his memories: "Adalberto and Fulgencio. Very polite boys, a couple of really dedicated artists."

Mike looked at his friend sharply, weighing Liam's tone with a concerned look. "*Nu, nu, starik,*" Mike said in a soothing tone, "don't let it get to you, we got some real artists in the Butcher Boys, too." He grinned. "Maybe not so polite, but hey, whaddya expect, they're city boys."

Liam had just opened his mouth to answer when the front of the boat lifted high over a crest and slammed into the trough of the wave with a crash like a cannon shot, throwing back a washtub-full of cold sea water that knocked him to the deck and left him coughing and spitting up salt water and laughing helplessly:

"Okay, I needed that," he sputtered. "Listen, Misha." He scrambled to his feet and grabbed his pal's arm with his free hand: "Listen to me. If you see me starting to feel sorry for myself again just pour cold water on me. You get into bad habits in solitary, all you can do is think about your poor dear self and how miserable you feel, but now I'm out that's over. We got a lot to do and I don't want to waste time on silly stuff like the Buenos Días Boys and their tricks. They're just trained animals, bad dogs—if I see them in the street they'll be sorry they didn't stay home pulling the wings off flies, but that's it. Let's leave revenge to the Count of Monte Cristo, OK? We've got bigger fish to fry."

"Yeah?" Mike looked interested. "Like what exactly?"

Liam bent closer and raised his voice, as the wind howled around them:

"You remember what I said about Stanton back in July, after Becky and I came back from Little Russia?"

"Sure." Liam could see the wheels turning as Mike tried to guess where he was going with this. "You said Stanton was on his way to putting together a big-money strong-arm gang like nobody heard of since Genghis Khan, with the Army and the Navy and sixteen different kinds of coppers for muscle, so we had best be keeping our heads down until we figured out how we were going to deal with them."

Liam nodded. "That's what I said all right, and you can forget I ever said it. We don't need to lay low, we need to *organize* and get *moving*. Right away! Us, the Whyos, the Dusters, the Rabbits, the Bowery Boys, everybody who's in the life."

"Whaddyou mean, everybody?" Mike was shaking his head as he tried to absorb the idea. "Even the Chink tongs? Even dodos like the Molasses Gang? You get all these birds together in one room there'll be blood coming out the chimney."

"I said everybody, I mean *everybody*," Liam said flatly. "If we don't move fast, start working together, start hitting Stanton and the rest of those jokers every time they turn around, it's going to be too late. He means to polish off every last one of us as fast as he can. Us and anybody else that isn't saying 'Yessir, yessir, three bags full!'"

Mike gave an incredulous snort: "Are you serious?"

"Is getting your neck stretched serious? Are the Hasta la Vista Twins and their blowtorches serious?" He gave Mike a level look and poked him in the chest for emphasis: "For you and me and our boys and the Rabbits and the Whyos and every other all-right guy in this town and in every other town where there's crooks and coppers—there's one job and one job only: *Dust Stanton!* And once *he's* gone we croak everybody that was in his pocket and then we bust up whatever's left of their tea party and chuck the pieces into the East River. *Then* we can relax and drink a beer and get back to how things used to be."

Mike grinned broadly, reached into his sleeve and took out a short, narrow-bladed knife. He made a quick incision on his palm and passed the knife to Liam, who followed suit, then grabbed Mike's hand and squeezed their palms together in a hard handshake.

"War to the knives," Mike said.

"To the knives," Liam echoed.

They held the handclasp for a long moment, then let go and turned back to watching the waves, Liam feeling a touch of discomfort as he reflected that for once he hadn't been 100% honest with Mike. When it came to the question of revenge it was true they had to make sure all their boys got the message that getting rid of Stanton came first and foremost. But he did have his own private score to settle alongside the big one, a purely personal question that was bound up part and parcel with solving the problem of "Tsar Eddie."

As questions went, it was simple enough: *Who had betrayed him?* Who was it that had hated him enough to give his name to Stanton's Eyes, knowing that there was only one place it could lead to: Union Square, with him standing on the gallows wearing a rope around his neck?

He shuddered as he remembered Union Square and his first sight of the gruesome fist-thick coil of hemp hanging from the crossbeam. The nightmare vision of that rope had almost sucked the air out of him during those endless weeks in solitary. Deep underground, in total silence, without light except for the sporadic visits of Adalberto and Fulgencio, Liam had begun to appreciate how much the thought of the *future* had fuelled him and how fragile that faith was. That's how those bastards twisted the knife in you when you were in the hole: how could you live if you stopped believing in the future?

Liam shook the thought off and let the icy ocean spray clear his mind. Now, thank God, his life was his again and he could see his dreams as clearly as if they were right here in front of him. One of them was a warrior's dream: he looked forward almost gleefully to battling Stanton and his armies— though he wasn't about to admit it to Mike or anybody else, he saw himself as Vas'ka Denisov in Count Tolstoy's *War and Peace*, leading a relentless guerilla force that would nip at Tsar Eddie's flanks until every one of his thugs and murderers had been chewed up and spit out, just like Napoleon's armies in Russia.

And the other beacon he'd held onto through the endless darkness of solitary was a lover's dream. Liam smiled wryly and shook his head. There it was, right out in the open and no ducking it: he had to go to Shelter Island and see Becky before he went to war on Stanton and find out whether his future was going to include her or not.

He'd seen some strange visions after he'd been in the cooler for a while—monsters and demons and things it was going to take him a long time to forget. After a while he even had a hard time remembering what familiar things really looked like. But the one thing that kept him more or less sane was the unchanging vision of Becky as he'd first seen her in Mrs. Clark's little restaurant in Henderson's Patch, the Pennsylvania coal town where Pilkington's Detective Agency had forced him to spy on his fellow Irishmen in a secret miners' defense group, the Molly Magees.

As famous as she was for her sensational news reporting, she'd come all that way out in the sticks just to interview Liam's sweetheart, Maggie, for a story on the impending mass hanging of ten Molly Magee "terrorists." Maggie, however, had been murdered the night before, so Becky had come looking for Liam to see if he could tell her anything about Maggie's death. And the truth was, if Becky had asked him his own name that first moment he saw her he would have been at a loss, since all he could think of was her face . . .

. . . A high and serene forehead, just fringed by a bang of auburn hair; eyebrows and lashes thick and all her own, free of any kind of war paint; eyes a blue as deep as a mountain lake, steady, fearless, ready for anything; a straight, strong nose, no cute little upturn; a wide, humorous mouth, half-smiling even in repose, the lips full and without a hint of rouge; chin—firm, forthright and determined . . . a picture as perfect and indelible as any Liam had ever seen, and she made him feel like some ragamuffin from the slums of Five Points with his nose pressed against the outside of Delmonico's restaurant window looking in at the swells eating ice cream.

He'd caught himself a moment later and tried to talk to her without falling over his own tongue, but the damage was done—if he'd never seen her again he would never have forgotten her. And as it was they'd ended up having more adventures together in a few days than he'd had in years . . . and more passion than he could think about peacefully. But always he found himself wondering just how long an extraordinary woman like Becky could stay interested in a shanty-Irish cracksman—even one good enough for his peers to call him the King of the Cracksmen—whose old man had died drunk leading a mob in New York's Draft Riots and whose greatest intellectual achievement to date had been reading Pushkin's poetry and Count Tolstoy's novels in Russian . . .

A dozen yards or so ahead of the *Straight Up* a seagull was beating its wings doggedly in a vain effort to fly into the gale-force winds, advancing a foot or two and then being pushed back, over and over again until finally it wised up, dropped down to wave-top height and sped away. Liam watched the little drama intently, a grin spreading across his face until he burst into laughter: he was no Roman augur, but even he could read those auspices—come Hell or high water, he was going to fight for Becky until he found a way to make her his own for good and all.

And as for who it was that had squealed on him to Stanton and his merry men, he'd just hold that one close to his vest and keep his eyes peeled. Somebody out here on Shelter Island had it in for Liam McCool bad enough that they'd tried to turn off his future like a gas tap, and when he figured out who it had been there would be a reckoning.

Chapter Four

he chilly southeasterly wind buffeting the lee shore of Shelter Island might as well have been blowing on another planet as far as the average New Yorker was concerned that sultry Halloween afternoon. Tomorrow, perhaps, when the hurricane finally came ashore, the city would cool off. Right now, though, surrounded by two rivers and an ocean and simmered gently at ninety degrees or so on a granite and asphalt frying pan, the heavily-dressed and densely-packed city dwellers were cooking as surely and as unwillingly as any mossbacked old pincher in Shanley's lobster palace.

But however miserable and stupefied they might be, none of them was too addled to ignore the hissing and clanking monstrosity that was rumbling its way north along Tenth Avenue. Built for Stanton by the Pullman Palace Car Company, eighty-five feet long and tall as a double-deck omnibus, it was lacquered a glossy, iridescent black with no apparent windows, its ominous midnight look broken only by an even more ominous symbol: a flaming sword clenched upright in a mailed fist above a crescent of gold letters: NYMCG, for New York Metropolitan Corps of Gendarmes.

Inside, ensconced in plush armchairs on loan from the Harvard Club and watched over by stolid "brainy" Acmes and an honor guard of dress-uniformed Johnnies holding their chromed shotguns at port arms, were "Tsar Eddie" himself, Secret Service chief Willard (Fat Willie) Pilkington and Great Detective Seamus McPherson, all earnestly puffing cigars and nipping at a bottle of fine old Kentucky Bourbon as they tried to erase the shameful memory of how they had shrieked and writhed on the floor of the Pilkington Agency office while a firestorm of Gatling Gun slugs tore the paneled walls of the room into kindling.

"We're running out of time, gentlemen," grumbled a thoroughly jaundiced Stanton. "On New Year's Day—and that's a scant *two months* from now—we will be declaring war on Little Russia and our preparations are woefully incomplete!"

"But sir," Pilkington said with an anxious grimace, "surely there can be no great hurry about it—Little Russia has been dozing peacefully on the other side of the Mississippi since Jackson sold our western territories to the Tsar in 1835. Even with Dr. Lukas or Prince Yurevskii or whatever his name is taking over in New Petersburg and getting the Japs to help him build airships our agents say nothing's changed. Why not let the declaration of war wait till spring, when we'll have all our preparations in place and the weather's more favorable?"

"Willie, Willie, Willie," Stanton chided reproachfully, "right now the forces of the Russian Empire are fighting tooth and nail against the Turks in Bulgaria. Every spare soldier, every serviceable airship, every possible resource is being bent to the task of crushing the Ottoman Empire. You know perfectly well that swine Lukas turned out to be Prince Nikolai Aleksandrovich, the Tsar's son by his morganatic marriage to Princess Yurevskaia. You think Daddy's just going to sit in St. Petersburg playing tiddlywinks if we attack his offspring? If we don't conquer Little Russia before the Turks surrender to Tsar Aleksandr, the next thing we know the Balkan War will be over and his airships and soldiers will be free to come pouring across the Atlantic to defend his subjects in Little Russia. If that happens we can say goodbye to the idea of taking back our lost territories. Indeed, the Tsar might use it as an excuse to invade the United States!"

McPherson squared his shoulders and put on a bellicose scowl: "Just tell me what you need me to do, sorr! Sure I'll lay down me life, bedad!"

"I need you to stop being such a feckless moron," Stanton snarled. "And start doing your job! And you too, Willie, you insufferable *pudding*! It would be bad enough just trying to put the country on a war footing without having to contend with the so-called Freedom Party. But thanks to the two of you we must *also* deal with Lincoln hiding out somewhere issuing slanderous manifestoes when what I had *wanted* to see was him standing trial for treason, a big, gala trial with daily newspaper reports full of shocking details completely discrediting him and the Freedom Party. And if Lincoln weren't enough, now that incendiary scum McCool is on the loose again plotting God alone knows what subversive mischief!"

Pilkington and McPherson nodded uneasily, puffing their cigars hard and praying that the smoke screen would obscure them enough to make Stanton think of someone else to blame for his troubles.

Stanton, who knew these two better than their own mothers did, greeted their pusillanimous game with a disgusted grunt and turned to stare out at the passing scenery. Though no one could see into the "Black Coffin" as it steamed along on its enormous hard-rubber tires, Stanton could see out easily through the two-way glass windows and for some unaccountable reason it irked him to the point of fury to see frightened passersby scurrying away like mice at the sight of the Department's armored bus.

"By the Lord Harry," muttered Stanton, "there'll be no skittering down your rat holes once we introduce the Table of Ranks! We'll know *precisely* where to find you!"

Both Pilkington and McPherson, courtiers more attentive than any bird dog, went instantly on point at the sound of a new idea from their master:

"Sir?" queried Pilkington, his dewlaps quivering with eagerness to please. "Table of Ranks?"

"A table of ranks, begorrah!" McPherson exclaimed, slipping back into a brogue in his uneasiness. "D'ye mean like the Tsar of Roossia, yer Honor?"

Stanton rolled his eyes: "I trust the public will be more go-ahead than you two stick-in-the-muds. Look here!"

He levered his corpulent body up out of the armchair with an involuntary grunt and crossed to a roll top desk which he unlocked with a small brass key. Rolling back the tambour of linked wooden slats he pulled out a long scroll and unfurled it in front of his subordinates.

"Have a look at *that!*" said Stanton proudly. He gestured at three densely-packed columns of print spread across a sheet of white oilcloth the size of a folded-out newspaper. "And count yourselves privileged to be among the first witnesses to the Magna Carta of a new America."

Trying in vain to make sense of the thing, Pilkington nervously dabbed his forehead with a handkerchief. "It's ah ... amazing!" he said.

McPherson was leaning forward in his chair, peering intently at the scroll as he chewed on his lower lip: "There's to be civil ranks?" he said dubiously. "Plus military ranks and Federal Government Ranks? Mr. Secretary, sorr!" he exclaimed. "Ye mean to say we're all to be assigned ranks starting from Warrant Officer and Collegiate Assessor and ending with Privy Councilor and Field Marshal? It's pure Roossia, sorr, no American's going to stand for it!"

Glaring at Pilkington and McPherson with eloquent disgust, Stanton rolled up the scroll and put it back in the desk.

"Stand for it or not, it will be the law of the land beginning on the first of December!"

Stanton dropped back into his armchair with a protesting squeal of springs and finished off his bourbon as the others hastily followed suit, gulping down the liquor as if it might be their last earthly comfort. Stanton shook his head, watching them with a bleak eye:

"The Russian Tsar may be an enemy, gentlemen, but that shouldn't stop us from taking good ideas where we find them. We are entering a time of great unrest, of war and sedition and economic uncertainty. If our manufacturing and commerce are to flourish and triumph over our competitors in the world market-place Americans must act together, without pulling in different directions, and that's the beauty of the Table of Ranks. Every single white male citizen will have a rank within the body politic, with all the corresponding duties and rewards. Everybody will have his place in society and keep to it on pain of death, so that everyone will know whom they must obey and—with the exception of the lowest rank, who must obey *them*. Not to mention," he added with a self-satisfied smirk, "the assignment of fixed addresses for men of every rank, to be changed only by application to the proper authorities!"

Pilkington cleared his throat desperately: "But what if some refuse to comply, sir, what if they're happy not having a rank and a fixed address, what if they'd rather just be . . ." he waved his hand helplessly . . . "you know, private citizens?"

Stanton sat back in his armchair, his eyebrows arched in disbelief: "*Private* citizens in a time of national emergency? Are you serious, Willie? There are no such creatures—in a time of emergency everyone must serve the common good! As to what you should do if someone refuses to obey a lawful Government order, you'll *shoot* them, of course! *Pour encourager les autres!*"

43

Pilkington nodded distractedly and looked towards the ceiling as if he were hoping for it to melt away and let the winds sweep him up to heaven, like Elijah.

"Right," he muttered weakly, "of course."

Stanton looked back and forth from Pilkington to McPherson and rolled his eyes. "If only I could get Tesla to wire your heads together perhaps you two might have one good brain between you! It's all about *timing*, gentlemen! Our success will depend on perfect timing, with no room for slip-ups or trying again! That's why we need the Table of Ranks: we must have order and discipline if we are to end up being the ones holding the knife when the time comes to carve up the world's wealth!"

As he spoke the last word a bell rang in the front of the bus and a window opened in the partition behind the driver, who sang out:

"*We're at Tenth and Boorman, Mister Secretary!*"

Wreathed in smiles, Stanton pulled himself to his feet again, gesturing to the others to follow him.

"I've been looking forward to this for weeks," he said, "having this factory in production is going to be the keystone of our future plans!"

The Johnnies snapped to attention and executed a smart "Present arms!" as Stanton moved past them to the open door of the bus, followed—with somewhat less enthusiasm—by Pilkington and McPherson. As Stanton stepped down onto the street ahead of them, Willie turned to McPherson and muttered urgently:

"What the devil is this place, do you know?"

McPherson, his ruddy complexion noticeably paler than usual, crossed himself and spat over his shoulder for luck: "Sure, yer Honor, whatever it is I'm startin' to wish I'd never left County Kerry."

○━

Outside, the hazy Indian summer sun illuminated a huge red-brick Gothic building with mock battlements, conical spires with slate roofs topped with greenish brass lightning rods and weather vanes, and innumerable rows of small windows suggesting a colony of monastic scribes in dusty brown robes. Previously, the rambling structure had in fact been a Catholic priory but Stanton had disestablished it and transferred all the monks to an engineer battalion engaged in building defensive earthworks around Washington, D.C.

Now, as the Secretary of National Security and his henchmen approached the entrance, a tall, soberly-dressed man with a military bearing and a pronounced limp appeared from a dimly-lit archway and hobbled towards them.

"Mr. Secretary!" he called out. "Welcome to Federal Calorium-Engine Works #1!"

"Sergeant Longfellow! Or perhaps I should say *Engineer* Longfellow." Stanton said as he took the man's hand and shook it warmly. "It's a pleasure to see you again!" He gestured towards the others: "These gentlemen are my assistants, Mr. Pilkington of the Secret Service and Mr. McPherson of Pilkington's International Detective Agency."

"Welcome, gentlemen," Longfellow said with a half-bow towards the others. Pilkington murmured something noncommittal while McPherson nodded curtly, observing the man's red nose and rivers of sweat with the sharp eye of a fellow tippler, and the suspiciously heavy lump in his right jacket pocket with the equally sharp eye of a seasoned street fighter.

None of this seemed to bother Stanton, who clapped Longfellow on the shoulder and gave him a benevolent smile. "Longfellow lost his leg at First Manassas when he was accompanying me on a reconnaissance of the Rebel positions, and we have stayed in touch ever since he returned to NYU to become a mechanical engineer. A brave man and a loyal soldier! Well, Mr. Longfellow, is the factory ready for our inspection?"

"We have put our backs into it, sir," Longfellow said, "both my staff and the laborers, and though there may be a rough spot or two, I judge we're ready for you! If you gentlemen will just follow me, I'll be glad to give you a guided tour." With that, he turned and hobbled towards the entrance, flanked by Stanton and followed grudgingly by Willie and McPherson.

As they walked through the arch and approached a substantial gate of brass-bound oak, a smartly-attired black doorman saluted them and pulled it open to reveal an astonishing vista: walls had been knocked down to make one vast space out of the sanctuary, the refectory where the monks had once dined, and the library, so that as Stanton's party stood at one end they could barely make out the far end despite bright carbon-arc lamps hanging from the rafters fifty feet above them.

In the open space itself, hundreds of men—all of them black, and all of them wearing identical denim uniforms, each with an identification number stenciled front and back—labored next to what looked like three miniature copies of an elevated railway, the rails set at waist height and approximately two feet apart. But instead of miniature railroad cars, what moved between the rails was a tambour of metallic slats similar to the wooden slats on Stanton's roll top desk. And the tambours were kept rolling endlessly forward by a steam engine at the end of each line that turned a roller at a steady, deliberate speed as its gears engaged the gears on the slats of the moving belt.

The purpose of the stately speed of the belt became obvious as Stanton's party watched: a sort of metal shell, roughly the size of an Acme's torso and split open to reveal its interior, was progressing in front of the workers, each of whom performed a single, repeated operation with screwdriver or wrench or hammer, adding one more part to what was destined to be the power plant of a finished Acme before the shell moved on to the next worker. And despite the fact that each of the men was working in deliberate, sullen silence, staring down at his work without looking from side to side, the clamor of the steam engines and the clatter of the moving tambours and the clanking and banging of the men's tools on the metal shells created such an uproar that it was almost literally impossible to think.

Beaming like a proud parent, Stanton turned to his old comrade-in-arms: "Excellent, Longfellow, excellent! How many finished units do you reckon you can turn out in a twenty-four hour period?"

"At present, sir, working in two 12-hour shifts per day, we can produce around 400 torsos completely ready to be fitted with heads and limbs and put to work. But . . ."

The engineer's face darkened and his lips tightened angrily as he hesitated.

"What is it, man?" Stanton broke in impatiently. "Speak up, I can't read your mind!"

"Just this, sir," Longfellow blurted, trying not to let his frustration turn to fury as he vented a long-standing grievance. "I improved on your original specifications weeks ago and we could have been producing *twice* as many units if I didn't have to work with this rabble. If you had seen fit to leave me with the experienced white workers who were originally assigned to me instead of drafting them all into the Army and saddling me with a gang of ignorant niggers . . ."

Stanton gave Longfellow a warning look and answered sharply: "Now, Longfellow, you know better than to let your personal feelings interfere with your duty! These decisions were made for strategic reasons and are not subject to discussion."

Then, as he saw the hurt look in Longfellow's eyes, Stanton softened his tone: "However, since you are an old comrade, I *will* point out that without an army big enough to seize from Little Russia (which is an enemy determined to deny us so much as a teaspoonful of this precious substance) the raw

47

calorium that we need to *power* these new Acmes, all your work on these automatons will be for naught. So, Longfellow, I advise you to take care of your assignment and let us take care of strategic questions. If all goes as I intend it to, by a year from now all of your present laborers will be replaced by tirelessly efficient calorium-powered robots which won't require the draining expense of wages, food, lodging, medical attention and the myriad other vexing burdens imposed by human workers."

But before Longfellow could answer, one of those anonymous figures suddenly turned away from the belt and stepped directly in front of Secretary Stanton.

"Sir!" the worker said in a resonant, cultured voice. "Are you Edwin M. Stanton, Secretary of National Security?" Despite an ill-fitting denim uniform stenciled front and back with the number 47, he was clearly no laborer, but an educated, self-confident middle-aged man used to being treated with respect. Stanton, however, was so taken aback by having this faceless laborer come to life and confront him that he licked his lips nervously and backed away a couple of steps.

"What's it to you?" he asked in a harsh tone.

"Just this, sir," the man said patiently, "if you are indeed the director, *pro tempore*, of our nation's destiny, I should like to lodge a protest with you."

Stanton, totally unable to deal with any of this, cleared his throat desperately, which the man took for a reply.

"The reason is not far to seek," the worker said with painful self-control. "I am Dr. Leander Stubbs of the Harvard University School of Medicine, and I have been shanghaied—kidnapped in broad daylight and imprisoned at forced labor—while on my way to deliver a lecture at Columbia University!"

"Well . . . ah . . . Number 47," Stanton replied, grating the words out with obvious effort, "I am very sorry for the inconvenience, but I'm afraid that emergency conditions dictate . . ."

"Dammit, Eddie," roared Longfellow, "don't make excuses to this black bastard!" He turned on Stubbs and bellowed even louder: "I fought to free you worthless trash and took a rebel Minié ball for my pains, so don't you sass *me*!"

Stubbs gave him a disgusted look and addressed his answer to Stanton: "Tell me, sir, do your 'emergency conditions' stipulate that one of this country's leading cardiac surgeons must endure the ravings of a creature like this drunken buffoon?"

"*BUFFOON?*" screamed Longfellow, and before anybody could react he snatched a short blued-steel pistol out of his pocket and shot Stubbs six times, as fast as he could pull the trigger, *BLAMBLAMBLAMBLAMBLAMBLAM!!!*, the impact of the bullets lifting the hapless surgeon off his feet and hurling him backwards into the nearest production line. The workers dove for the nearest cover, yelling hysterically, while the broken belt snapped back into the steam engine with a clatter and tossed Acme parts in every direction, the empty steel torsos clanging and banging like a truckload of washtubs.

McPherson, who had fallen into a wary crouch the moment Longfellow reached for his gun, muttered distractedly:

"Huh. Must be that new double-action Colt . . ."

. . . While Pilkington, who had thrown himself flat on the ground, wriggled towards the exit with desperate speed, totally oblivious to Stanton's shouted commands to stand up and come back.

Exasperated almost beyond endurance, Stanton turned on Longfellow: "I am *very* disappointed in you, Longfellow, I had no idea you were such a fool! Just tell me this, how much production will we lose while you repair the belt and find somebody to take that fellow's place on the line?"

"I'm sorry, sir," muttered Longfellow sulkily, "I'll get the doormen to take the body away and clean up. One of them can stand in for him till we get a replacement."

"Well, see that you do," snapped Stanton, "and be quick about it. We have deadlines to meet! And just in *case* you should find yourself tempted to harm any more of our precious labor resources, please remember that you were *not* wounded in a war to free the slaves, you were in fact wounded in a war to break the Southern planters' death grip on American business and free it to lead the world in production and profits. Keep this up and you'll be helping the planters to claw their way back to power!"

With that, he turned on his heel and strode towards the door, fuming, pausing only long enough to deliver a mighty kick into Pilkington's plump backside, which elicited a heart-rending shriek that made Stanton draw a deep, bracing breath and smile.

He bent over and yelled into Pilkington's ear, "Get up, you brainless hippopotamus, before I have Longfellow shoot you as well!" Humming to himself, he headed for the exit feeling better than he had all morning. Sometimes all it took was a bit of excitement to get a man's juices flowing and brighten his outlook . . .

⚬—┱

As Stanton headed for the black omnibus followed by a limping Pilkington and a severely stressed McPherson, a Johnny jumped down to the street and ran towards Stanton waving a piece of paper and shouting:

"Wireless voicewire, sir, sent on from the office urgent!"

Stanton snatched it out of his hand without comment and read it, glaring at first, then slowly smiling and finally breaking into a delighted chuckle. He turned back towards Pilkington and McPherson, waving the message triumphantly:

"I *told* you, by George! I said the man would finally see his duty and step forward!"

"Sir?" queried McPherson uneasily, ready for anything by now.

"Mr. Secretary?" croaked Pilkington, making sure to lag behind a little so that McPherson stood between him and Stanton.

"It's the Informer!" chortled Stanton. "He's ready to give away the whereabouts of the Freedom Party *and* Liam McCool as long as we can agree on terms, and he'll be calling us again at 5 p.m. for a little chat!"

Chapter Five

ike had finally gotten tired of the howling wind and the freezing spray and gone below for a couple of fingers of Old Bushmills and a lie-down, but Liam was a long way from getting his fill of the outdoors. Then too, the closer he got to seeing Becky again the more his mind kept going over and over their last day together on Shelter Island, the carefree innocence of the hours before he set out for the city to carry out what felt like a suicide mission—cracking a crib at the personal request of President Lincoln.

The day had started so happily, waking up with Becky in his arms in the big, sunny room overlooking the lawn that swept down to the sea wall and the sparkling whitecaps of the Bay, making happy love and daydreaming about endless long, sunny days together . . .

And then heading downhill so fast after they brought him Lincoln's gentle summons: could Liam possibly join the President for breakfast? If it had been anybody else but President Lincoln, he would have said no the minute he learned the reason why. For one thing, the crib Lincoln wanted Liam to crack was a government archive, which meant armies of guards. And for another, Liam hadn't even the glimmer of a chance to case the target first. He had only done that once before in his whole working life, a job to help Mike's Uncle Tolya, and it had ended with Liam being thrown into the Tombs and sprung only to find himself in the clutches of Old Man Pilkington, forced to spy on other Irish workingmen in the Pennsylvania coal fields. Not the best of precedents.

But he was stuck: how could he say no to his former Commander-in-Chief? Between his memories of the desperate battle on Little Round Top and the day a few months later when he and a bunch of other convalescing soldiers had heard the President give that unforgettable address at Gettysburg, Liam would follow the man anywhere, whether his voice came out of the custom Acme in which the scheming Dr. Lukas had installed his brain or out of a burning bush.

But the worst part of the whole business, the most unforgivably stupid part, had been letting himself get suckered into discussing the job in front of a roomful of strangers, those nice square-John civilians from the Freedom Party who couldn't possibly be nursing a secret viper in their bosom, oh no.

He had tried to tell President Lincoln that the fewer people who knew, the better. But the President just swiveled that impassive automaton head back and forth in an unmistakable "no" and said that he'd spent too many years in back-room politicking when he was in Washington—now he wanted to be sure everything was done right out in the open so everyone had a chance to take part in making the decisions.

And when Liam got stubborn about it, naturally Becky had had a conniption fit: how could Liam mistrust these splendid brave people who were risking everything to fight the evil ogre Stanton, etc., etc., indeed how could he even *imagine* that one of these citizen-heroes might be a secret turncoat?

Liam winced, remembering. In spite of himself, he had raised his voice a bit at that. Well, maybe more than a bit. Splendid brave people or not, would *she* tell these nice citizens what she was writing in one of her exposés before it was safely published and on the news stands? Like fun she would, she knew as well as he did that nobody could beat a nice citizen for pure blabbermouth gossiping and he'd already had one go at sitting in the Tombs twiddling his thumbs, *thank* you!

Then President Lincoln chimed in, in his gentle, chiding voice, and once Becky and the President had whittled Liam down to about an inch high and smarting all over, he had finally knuckled under and said OK, OK, he would sit there and keep his mouth shut while President Lincoln told the Party members what the plan was and wait for their decision . . .

Liam shook his head and snorted derisively: as if he'd ever had a chance of saying no! So there he had found himself a few hours later, transported back to the City by Captain Billy and—God help him—about to crack a crib with the democratic blessings of the Freedom Party . . .

○━┱

The streets were quiet, way too quiet for the East Side on a stifling, airless July night when you'd expect people to be out on the stoops in their shirtsleeves sweating and drinking and gossiping, and Liam was already wishing he was back in the wheelhouse of the *Straight Up* listening to Captain Billy's tales of life as a river pirate. And headed the other way, too—*returning* to Shelter Island with the job done and Becky waiting to welcome him.

He stopped as he came to a densely shadowed space between two buildings and moved back into the narrow alley so he could inspect the street at his leisure. The East River did a little dog-leg right around the point where East 17th Street met Avenue B, and Captain Billy had been able to put him ashore in a totally dark area just five blocks from the warehouse he was headed for.

Liam scanned the street again left to right, procrastinating. You really had to wonder about the way everybody and his brother was jammed in side by side in this city. From where he was standing right now it wasn't more than ten minutes' walk cross-town to the genteel purlieus of Washington Square Park, where all the swells lived and where Liam had discovered the pied-à-terre of Dr. Lukas, the criminal genius who had stolen Lincoln's brain, imprisoned Liam's Grandma and now ruled Little Russia as Prince Yurevskii, bastard son of Tsar Aleksandr II. Over there in the Village, a flash customer like Lukas didn't even get a second glance.

Here on the East River, on the other hand, the nearest park was in Tompkins Square, just two blocks south of tonight's burglary target and the scene of endless tussles between mobs of angry workers and the coppers and soldiers sent to clear them out. In fact, this was all solid working-class territory, from here on south to Liam's birthplace in Five Points, and the more he peered out into the streets where he'd spent so much of his life the more jarringly wrong the emptiness and silence seemed. Working-class people didn't go to the Opera or Delmonico's to entertain themselves, they went out into the streets. But the streets were empty. *Ergo* . . . Liam shook his head. *Ergo mind your eye, Liam me son!*

A movement from across the street caught the corner of Liam's eye and froze his blood momentarily. Then he relaxed, but only partly: it was one of those *über*-rats, a thing about the size of a small pig, with big yellow teeth like a beaver and glowing red eyes. It looked at Liam for a long moment, as if he might be dinner, but when Liam reached for the Colt Peacemaker in his waistband, the creature seemed to get the message and disappeared the way it had come, snorting and squeaking irritably.

Liam shuddered. Now that he'd teamed up with Crazy Horse and Custer in Little Russia and learned what The People were up to with their Sun Dances and all the other medicine that had produced this plague of giant critters, he at least understood what was going on. The united native tribes of North America were upping the ante in their struggle to get President Jackson's Indian Removal Act thrown out and their homelands restored, and their best weapon was their command of natural magic. But knowing all that only stretched so far—Liam was an old-fashioned city boy and rats of any size still gave him the willies.

All right, then, McCool. No more dithering! Liam forced himself forward out of the shadows and crossed the street briskly, moving on a diagonal towards the warehouse's alley entrance. According to the President, Stanton's people had managed to dig through the wreckage of their Union Square HQ and exhume all the files that had been buried by the explosion the Butcher Boys had triggered. Then they had loaded them onto a caravan of steam wagons and moved them here for safekeeping till the new HQ was finished. Liam's assignment was to find the files on the Freedom Party and either steal them if they weren't too voluminous or destroy them on the spot. Liam rattled a box of Lucifers in his coat pocket and grinned sourly, thinking that lighting one or two of these and dropping them in a drawer full of paper would work a lot faster than reading a bunch of files. That was one problem solved, anyway.

Once more, as he reached the side entrance on 12th and B, he paused for a moment and looked in every direction. Nothing. Even the rat had cleared off. Well, in for a penny in for a pound, right? He reached into the holster under his arm and pulled out the two-foot, hardened-steel jimmy which was going to make this a fast and dirty entrance. Wedging one end under the edge next to the lock plate he leaned on it and pushed with all his strength until the wood splintered with an appallingly loud crack . . .

. . . And suddenly, disorientingly, the harsh radiance of a dozen carbon-arc searchlights sprang up from rooftops bracketing the warehouse, whistles and sirens screamed their obbligato and a threatening basso profundo bellowed out from a megaphone somewhere nearby:

"Liam McCool! Throw down your weapons now! Assume a prone position and do not move until you are instructed to by an officer of the New York City Police Department! Do it now!!"

Liam shook his head disgustedly, dropped the jimmy with a clang and set down the Colt Peacemaker next to it, and then lay down gingerly with his face to the cobblestones. There were definitely times, and this one went right to the head of the list, when being able to say "I told you so" just didn't amount to a hill of beans.

Mr. Lincoln he could understand, in many ways he was really just too credulous and trusting to have spent all those years in the White House. Probably his advisers had done their best to insulate him from daily reality and no doubt that took its toll. But *Becky?* Becky was a smart girl, as fly as any of the Butcher Boys, and they were the sharpest gang of thieves, forgers and burglars in New York City. She'd spent years now seeing the world as it actually was and reporting on it for big-city readers who knew which end was up. Maybe her insisting on the public discussion of the warehouse job was just the effects of hero worship, like Liam's being willing to pull the job in the first place. Sure, she would probably go along with President Lincoln even if every alarm bell in her head were ringing to warn her against it . . .

"HEY! WAKE UP!"

Liam jumped as if a pistol had gone off next to his ear.

"Chto ty, durak, glukh chto li?"

Mike was bending close, making a megaphone of his hands and yelling as loud as he could. Liam stuck a finger in his ear and jiggled it:

"I *will* be deaf if you keep hollering in my ear!"

Mike gave Liam a knowing grin that was even more irritating than the yelling.

"Aw, *bednyi Liovushka, poor* little Liam! Wuzzums dweamin' about the pwetty lady?"

Liam's jaw set like granite and he drew back his fist warningly.

"*Edakii govniuk,*" Mike snorted. "C'mon little fella, I need some help to take care of a sick Chinaman."

He started back towards the aft companionway and Liam saw that Captain Billy was supporting the erstwhile Man in the Iron Mask outside the open hatchway that led down to the cabin. He was heavily wrapped up in discarded pieces of nautical uniform including a long navy-blue woolen scarf probably knitted by Mrs. Captain Billy that was wrapped around his neck until he could barely move his head. Whatever his basic skin color might be, right now it was a disturbing mix of tea and milk and enough India ink to give it a sickly grayish look.

"*Nǐhǎo,*" Liam said with a polite little bow.

The man examined Liam suspiciously, as if he were weighing the ulterior motives behind his "Hello." Finally he returned a grudging little bow.

"You're looking a little better," Liam said, "Irish whiskey must agree with you."

The man grimaced and glared at Liam without any sign of having understood. After a moment he spoke, in a sort of music-hall sing-song:

"Chinese man very bad English, but hab fashion, no can help."

"Is that a fact?" Liam asked in a mildly derisive tone. "And here I was telling my friend how smart you were." He looked towards Mike and gave him a broad wink, which seemed to make the man uneasy. He looked back and forth between Liam and Mike with his eyes narrowed to slits, plainly wishing he could peer into their heads. Finally he shrugged and gestured towards the deck:

"Thisee chop boat, what name him sailing to?"

58

Liam rolled his eyes and laughed. "Mister, I don't know what you do for a living but unless you're a daisy at singing and dancing, I reckon you wouldn't last five minutes on the stage. Why don't you just drop the Dumb Chinaman wheeze and tell us how you ended up in Stanton's clink?"

The man shook his head angrily and bared his teeth as if were about to bite someone.

"OK," Liam said flatly, "you want to talk pidgin I can humor you."

He reached out and tapped the man on the chest with his forefinger, not hard enough to hurt but deliberately enough to get his attention:

"You wantchee catchee one piecee straight talk right now, you savvy?" He gave the man a hard little grin. "That's if you want to stick with us and stay clear of the coppers and the Johnnies and Stanton's Eyes. But I don't want to hear any more phony blather, *talk* to us! Like we say back in Five Points, 'no tickee no washee.'"

The man glared at Liam for another moment or two, and then finally shrugged and smiled a little:

"I suppose you must have been the prisoner with the black bag over his head? That would rather change things."

"Uh huh," Liam said with a touch of irony, "it means I heard your little chat with dear old Reverend Beecher." He turned to Mike: "Our friend here gave Henry the Rev a regular scorcher of a call-down, that whole Balliol College my-dear-sir turn. I was laughing so hard I almost tripped and hanged myself."

"New College, actually," the man said, "but if I may ask again without seeming ungrateful for your help—where is your vessel bound for?"

Liam shrugged. "How about a trade? You tell us who you are and what you were doing on the gallows with your head in a tin pot, then we tell you where we're going."

The man hesitated for a long moment, looking back and forth between Liam and Mike as if he were weighing them on some invisible scale.

"Hey!" Mike said indignantly, "Mr. McCool here just finished *saving* your dilapidated ass, so the least you can do is say thanks!"

"Liam McCool? And you are his coadjutor Mike Vysotsky?" All the man's indecision had vanished like smoke: "I have heard Stanton's people cursing you. Thank you! Thank you both!" He held out his hand: "Ambrose Chen, gentlemen, at your service."

The three exchanged energetic handshakes, holding onto bits of rigging as the *Straight Up* wallowed and bucked in the heavy weather.

Then Liam spoke again, "OK, then, Mr. Chen, time for question #2: why did Stanton's ghouls work you over so hard? What were they trying to squeeze out of you?"

Once again a kind of anxious evasiveness crept into Chen's manner: "That's a rather complicated, ah . . . you see, I had spent some time in Secretary Stanton's employ, and he finally decided to give me the sack. But . . . ah . . . he couldn't just let me go, the man's an absolute paranoiac, he was convinced I had some secret knowledge that belonged to him, knowledge I must reveal before he could set me free."

Liam and Mike stared at Chen thoughtfully.

"You're leaving something out," Liam said, "something big."

"Certainly not," Chen insisted heatedly, "it was nothing more than one of Stanton's delusions, a manifestation of his neuropsychopathy. The man is barking mad!"

Mike wasn't impressed. "What line are you in, Mr. Chen? What did Stanton hire you for?"

"That's a good question," Liam agreed. "Stanton may be crazy, but never enough to interfere with business. Either tell us what you have that he wants, or get lost—go ashore

60

where we're headed and keep going, or let Cap'n Billy take you along when he goes back to the city. Maybe you'll understand better if I tell you we're square in the middle of a *war*, so we need to make sure rescuing you wasn't a mistake."

Chen closed his eyes and raised his eyebrows, thinking something over. Finally he let out a heavy breath and opened his eyes again.

"Very well, gentlemen. I am by profession an alchemist, and I have discovered a simple way to refine calorium."

Both Liam and Mike were so nonplussed that they simply stood there and stared at Chen.

"Please believe that I am no charlatan. Chinese alchemy is an ancient body of knowledge, a science that had already achieved great sophistication when the highest achievement of Western science was striking pieces of flint with a hammer stone."

"I never even heard of calorium until they started using it to run Acmes," Mike said with a dubious frown. "What's the big deal?"

"If you run a steam engine on coal," Chen said in his most professorial tone, "you must pay constant attention to the replenishing of the coal—your machine is, in effect, tethered to its coal supply. Calorium, however, when properly refined (and this is the key, since it is a very dangerous substance to deal with) will produce the desired amount of heat for firing your boiler indefinitely, without being renewed. All you need worry about is replenishing the machine's water supply, and water is both cheap and ubiquitous."

Liam shrugged, "OK, but why would Stanton torture you over that? It looks like they already know how to refine calorium—what do you know that they don't know?"

Chen smiled, and this time the hint of smugness was unmistakable: "At present Stanton can only get ready-made calorium-powered Acmes from the British manufacturer Royce, and their refining process is unnecessarily complex and expensive. It's also proprietary and patented to the hilt. That's one reason those nice shiny black Acmes cost fifty thousand dollars apiece. The process discovered by Dr. Lukas is simpler than the British one, but still expensive and inherently dangerous, and is in any event being used by him to create an army of calorium-powered Acmes for the Little Russian Army. My process is both cheap and safe, but by the time I had completed my research I realized that Stanton was going to use having my formula as a pretext for invading Little Russia . . ."

Both Liam and Mike were nodding now and they finished Chen's sentence simultaneously: ". . . because that's where the raw calorium ore is."

"Bravo, gentlemen. In the former territory of Arizona, in the mountains of the Apacheria. True, there's some in Canada as well, but at this particular time it's a smaller challenge to take on Lukas than the British Empire. In any event, I would sooner cut out my own heart than help that swine Stanton in his plan of conquest."

Liam held out his hand and he and Chen shook emphatically. "Welcome aboard," Liam said, "it looks like you ended up in the right place. Now all we have to do is get everyone behind the idea of putting Stanton . . ."

Before he could finish there was a wild shout from the pilot house behind them:

"SHARK!" bellowed Captain Billy, "*SHARK!!*"

They jerked around in the direction of Captain Billy's shout, galvanized by an unfamiliar note of panic in the old sea-dog's voice. Captain Billy himself was standing on the stern deck frantically shoving fresh shells into the magazine of a pump-action shotgun, while an appallingly tall and thick shark's fin—its tip nearly as far above the surface of the ocean as the top of the pilot house—raced towards them through the waves leaving a wake like an ocean racer.

In what seemed like the blink of an eye, the creature was nearly even with the stern of the boat, its huge mouth with its terrifying array of teeth open as if to swallow the boat. Immediately Captain Billy began firing the shotgun, holding the trigger down so that it fired every time he cycled the slide, the *BOOM!* of one shot segueing into the next so that it sounded like one interminable *BOOOOOOM!* as Liam and his companions rushed to Billy's side, Liam and Mike with drawn pistols.

The shark, meanwhile, flipped its tail derisively, splashing the humans with cold sea water before leaping into the air in a dolphin-like exhibition of acrobatics that was even more frightening than its teeth, considering that it was easily as long as the *Straight Up* and considerably bulkier.

"Jehoshaphat, Billy," yelled Liam, "what were you using in that blunderbuss, birdshot?"

"Birdshot, Hell!" Captain Billy said grimly. "That was double-aught buck, enough to knock an elephant on its ass!" He fumbled more shells out of his oilskin pocket with shaking hands and as if at a signal the shark stopped showing off and headed directly for the boat, its wake higher than before.

"SHOOT, DAMMIT, SHOOT!" howled Captain Billy, at which Mike and Liam joined him in unleashing a fusillade that would have stopped a bus. The shark, however, seemed not to notice, and in one huge, horrifying *CHOMP!* tore the lifeboat off the stern davits and swallowed it whole.

"Jasus, Mary and Joseph!" wailed Captain Billy, crossing himself as the shark flipped away from the boat, putting on another display of gargantuan acrobatics.

"BILLY!" Liam roared into his ear, loudly enough that the Captain shook himself like a wet dog and started loading the shotgun again.

"Forget that," Liam continued, "you have some dynamite below decks?"

Captain Billy nodded emphatically and shoved the shotgun into Chen's hands before running back into the pilot house.

Mike was shaking his head somberly, looking as worried as Liam had ever seen him. "*Neveroiatno uzh yobanaia ryba!*" he muttered, stuffing fresh cartridges into his pistol.

"You can forget the popgun." Liam said, "If Billy's dynamite doesn't work we might as well call it a day."

Chen held out the shotgun, his forehead wrinkled with thought. "It can't work," he said, "it's not that kind of problem."

Liam shot him a questioning look, but before he could speak, Captain Billy ran back up on deck with a double handful of bundled dynamite sticks and a glowing cigar clamped between his teeth. At almost the same moment, the shark pulled one more somersault and headed back towards the *Straight Up* at top speed.

"Here!" yelled Mike. "Gimme one, I useta pitch for Cincinnati."

Liam nodded approvingly and lit a bundle before handing it over. Mike had, in fact, been with the Red Stockings for a season before he decided leading the Butcher Boys was more fun and came back to New York.

"There it comes," Billy sang out. The shark had closed to about fifty yards, its mouth open wide enough to swallow a hansom cab. At the same moment, Mike wound up as if he were on the mound and let fly with a perfect strike, which disappeared into the creature's maw like a dainty snack into a sinkhole. For a moment the creature looked distracted and then a tremendous explosion echoed out of its gaping jaws and a hurricane of half-eaten fish and other disgusting rubbish spewed all over the four men on the open deck. At that, the shark abruptly dove, disappearing from sight in a flash.

"I hope that thing is dead," Mike said, trying to brush off the bits of stinking garbage, "getting clean's going to take being towed behind the ship for an hour or two."

"I shouldn't count on it if I were you," said Chen with a morose shake of the head, at which the shark abruptly reappeared a couple of hundred yards ahead and turned grimly back towards the ship, gnashing its heart-stopping array of teeth with a grinding, screeching noise like a steam-powered tree shredder.

"*Akh, bozhe ty moi,*" Mike said faintly, "it's twice as big as it was!"

"I've seen that growing trick before," Liam said. "Back in Little Russia. Only back there I knew a geezer that knew what to do about it."

By now, Billy and Mike were both crossing themselves, Billy the Irish way and Mike the Russian way. Liam shook his head and turned to Chen:

"Well, Ambrose," he said as cheerfully as he could manage, "it looks like it's up to you. Is Chinese alchemy any good on supernatural sharks?"

Chen threw Liam an exasperated look and turned back to watch the shark, which was by now about twenty-five yards away and clearly mad as Hell.

"If it is," Liam added with a touch of stress in his voice, "now would probably be as good a time as any for you to *do* something."

Chapter Six

he supposed all underground political parties had the same problem—cut off from the rough and tumble of daily life, the members ended up making war on each other, forming factions and delivering speeches and sneaking around behind each other's backs as if they were living ordinary quarrelsome lives in some busy city, where they could speak freely and never have to think twice about informers and secret police. Becky had seen it all before with Mexican revolutionaries and Russian revolutionaries, and she certainly couldn't blame her fellow Freedomists for blowing off a bit of steam.

It was a *gilded* cage, to be sure, she thought as she strolled away from the main house. Banking mogul Abner Goodyear, a secret supporter of the Freedom Party, had been happy to offer them refuge in his family's summer mansion on Shelter Island, and his elevated social status had protected them from Stanton's snoopers ever since.

The main building—a blend of stone and slate and whitewashed clapboard—had been begun in the late 1600s and added to and modernized steadily ever since. By the end of the Civil War it had grown to more than a hundred pleasant, airy rooms, and less than half of them were filled now by Freedom Party members. If you simply *had* to go underground, it would be hard to pick a more agreeable hideout and Becky had spent a few especially memorable days—and nights—here with Liam in the days after their escape from Little Russia.

But, honestly—if she had to sit through one more Party conclave, endure one more maddeningly parliamentary, pernickety and oh-so-polite exercise in the democratic politics of Cloud Cuckoo Land, she would scream. And not just a single ladylike scream, either, but a whole uncorseted succession of them, piercing and soul-cleansing.

Gathering up her skirts she settled herself on a boulder at the edge of the sea wall, feeling the warmth of the afternoon sun on her face and watching the whitecaps march briskly across the surface of Little Peconic Bay only to dash themselves into foam against the stones.

Like this morning. A gentleman from Bridgeport had proposed that the Party approve a commendation of some sort for Liam in recognition of his brave attempt to retrieve the Party's police files and the suffering he'd gone through in consequence, but almost immediately that maddening fussbudget Mrs. Redingote had taken up her cudgels and the proposal had detoured—ever so politely—into a maddening argument over whether it was really proper for the Party to commend a convicted *felon*, and one who was not, moreover, a *member* of the Party.

As the barrage of polite barbs and empty phrases flew back and forth across the meeting room, Becky found herself thinking more and more forcefully of the trial of the Knave of Hearts in *Alice in Wonderland*, and finding herself more and more tempted to follow Alice in crying "Stuff and nonsense!", even if her fellow Freedomists were to rise up in the air and come flying down upon her like Alice's deck of cards.

"Stuff and nonsense indeed!" Becky muttered out loud, interrupting a sandpiper that had been pecking at a nearby patch of sand so that it cocked its head and peered at her inquisitively. "I hope you find more to sustain you here than I have," she told the bird crisply and took off across the lawn in the direction of the woods that bordered it.

The real trouble was, she admitted to herself, that what she had been doing with the *Freedom* broadsheet just didn't feel like journalism to her. For her, journalism had always meant travel, investigation, conflict, and interviews with all sorts and conditions of people, most of whom had no intention whatever of being honest with her and were as hard to unlock as any Chinese puzzle box. She missed it. She missed the *challenges*. Without them she could feel herself beginning to stagnate and she was afraid she was going to turn into a crotchety old lady without having had a real go at anything between youth and decrepitude.

Her work for *Freedom* really meant little beyond writing the occasional editorial based on someone else's risks and exertions and organizing the bits and pieces of political information picked off their far-flung grapevine telegraph, and the truth was almost any literate person could do as well as she'd been doing. After a career that had featured stories based on escapades like smuggling herself into Mecca during Ramadan masquerading as a deaf-mute beggar, riding with Mexican bandits trying to overthrow Porfirio Diaz and having herself thrown into New York's hellhole women's prison disguised as a drunken prostitute, letting other people sweat for her material was truly excruciating.

And even if she'd been able to resign herself to the deadly boredom of her work, the thought of Liam and her questions about Liam and what kind of future the two of them could make together simply wouldn't leave her in peace. She could scarcely claim to have led a sensible, circumspect life, but even for her the thought of linking her fortunes with those of a man who skated constantly along the thin edge between freedom and arrest seemed totally outlandish. On the other hand, she had to admit she hadn't experienced a single moment of boredom during the time they'd been together, and that was a fact too singular to be ignored.

One way or another, she'd simply had more of a rest than she could stand and she was beginning to feel a bit like the shrew she'd caught in a jam jar during a school picnic in Central Park. The poor little mite had almost gone mad jumping up the sheer glass walls and falling back to the bottom until she'd taken pity on it and set it free, and now at last she could truly appreciate what it had been going through.

But what could she do? President Lincoln and Mr. Clemens had begged her to take over *Freedom*, and since she and Liam had been given refuge here on Shelter Island after their recent adventures in Little Russia and *Freedom's* previous editor had just been swept up by Stanton's myrmidons leaving the paper with nobody at the helm, it had been impossible to refuse.

She stepped into the cool twilight of the woods with a sense of relief. Lovely silence. Birds singing. Little creatures rustling through the dried leaves. Becky sighed deeply, leaned her forehead against the cool moss on the side of a tree and wondered, finally, what it would be like to see Liam again. Mike had sent Captain Billy with a message three days ago, and she knew it was going to be soon . . . could it be today?

It was hard to believe how short a time they'd actually known each other, since it felt as if they'd already lived a couple of lifetimes together. They'd only met this past June, and in the space of a few days they had raided the basement storehouses of the Smithsonian Institution on a mission for the Freedom Party, unexpectedly discovering and freeing President Lincoln from Stanton's cells while retrieving Crazy Horse's captured medicine bag, which they then took to Little Russia to return to him and his sidekick Laughing Wolf, *né* George Armstrong Custer, so they could resume their leadership of the Indian liberation struggle.

Then (as if that hadn't been enough already), after joining forces with Custer and Crazy Horse they'd destroyed the HQ of the Little Russian secret police in New Petersburg, stolen the prototype of Stanton's new aerial battleship from the aerodrome of the Little Russian Aerial Navy and flown it back to New York just in time to liberate a concentration camp at Sing Sing, where they thwarted Dr. Lukas' plans to transfer the prisoners' brains to his growing army of human-brained automatons, and finally, almost as an afterthought, dynamited Stanton's new million-dollar HQ in Union Square.

Becky smiled, remembering the crazed, headlong pace of those days and then the sudden idyllic halt as she and Liam stole a long moment together in a peaceful Canadian meadow . . .

Then she shook her head and sighed, remembering how abruptly they'd come down to earth again once they'd found themselves here on Shelter Island. Too many conflicting demands and too many competing loyalties. All unbidden, a sharp picture of Liam popped up in the midst of her musings—his curly auburn hair and clear hazel eyes, his strong jaw and the boyish half-smile that tugged at the corner of his mouth and made him look too young to be a veteran of Gettysburg and the leader of a New York gang. It wasn't as if she'd never had a lover before, she thought with a flash of irritation, nor even as if she'd never had one she cared about deeply. It was just that she'd never before lost a piece of her independence, a big enough piece that she felt suddenly bereft.

Just then a faint, sweet sound of singing came to her from somewhere deeper in the wood, sending a shiver up her spine. It was one of the local legends that Captain Kidd had buried his treasure here in these woods, leaving it to be guarded by the ghosts of his murdered crewmen. Becky shook herself and looked around, trying to guess where the sound was coming from; it was a woman's voice, half-humming, half-singing, and it didn't sound like any pirate Becky could imagine. After a moment of hesitation she set off through the wood in search of the singer.

The sound of the woman's voice grew stronger and clearer as Becky walked further into the wood, and before long she realized the singing was in Gaelic and the singer's voice was familiar. There was really only one person it could be, and Becky smiled wider as she realized it was the one person among all the Goodyear mansion's inhabitants she actually felt like talking to just now.

Becky stood for a moment among the trees just beyond the edge of a small clearing, watching the woman who was singing as she worked, clearing all the underbrush and shrubs and thorny growths that clustered around the roots of a circle of tall, ancient white birch trees, a perfect circle formed of single trees, each as thick as a human body and smooth and white as an alabaster column. The woman herself was as slender as a sapling, small and rosy, not more than five feet high but strong as a man considering the ease with which she uprooted whole bushes and bound them up with vines. And her gray hair, knotted at the nape of her neck, didn't signal any dimming of her senses, as it wasn't a moment later that she stood up abruptly, looked towards Becky in her leafy hiding place and greeted her with a wide grin and a sparkle of green eyes:

"Becky, acushla! Sure, I thought for a moment you were a tree nymph, come to pinch me nose for disturbin' yer sleep!"

Becky laughed and moved into the clearing to give Liam's Gran a warm embrace. "What is this place, Gran? I've never seen such beautiful old birches. And why are you gathering up all the underbrush? Is there going to be a bonfire?"

Gran cocked her head and gave Becky an appraising little smile.

"What?" Becky asked, her curiosity piqued. "Did you find Captain Kidd's treasure?"

Gran laughed. "Don't I wish it, though? No, darlin', I'm getting ready for Samhain."

71

"The Irish Halloween?"

"Halloween, pah!" Gran snorted. "Samhain was already old as the stones when St. Patrick came to Ireland to worrit the snakes. Samhain belongs to the *old* religion from the ages before the druids and its time has come round again—I can feel it in me bones sure as you're a foot high."

She hugged herself as if she'd felt a sudden chill and cast a look at the darkness among the trees beyond the birch circle. Then she turned back to Becky and gave her a little smile:

"Here in New York I've been called a witch more than once, and most of the people who said it didn't know they were just speakin' the plain truth."

Becky frowned and shook her head: "Witch?"

The old lady answered with a wry smile and a shrug: "In Ireland it was just a part of life—in the countryside the old beliefs were always stronger than the new religions and the doubts that the English tried to teach us with their school-books. The women of my clan bore *cailleacha*—witches—as often as they did ordinary lasses, and Liam's people go all the way back to the grandest hero in our legends, Finn McCool. So you can take it as gospel, Becky dear: the old gods are stirrin' in their sleep, and wakin' again wherever enough believers call them back."

Becky was watching Gran with a dubious frown, looking uneasy enough to make Gran burst into merry laughter.

"It's not me mind that's goin', begorrah, it's me back! Lend us a hand will you, darlin'? Help me pile all this rubbish in the middle of the circle."

For a couple of minutes the two women worked in silence, gathering all the bundles of brush and windfallen branches, Becky darting the occasional glance towards Gran until she finally couldn't contain herself any longer:

"Tell me, Gran, do! Don't be mysterious—by old religions do you mean things like all the oversized creatures and the odd weather? When we were in Little Russia Chief Crazy Horse told us that Indian medicine had caused those. Are you expecting something *else*?"

Gram straightened up and stretched backwards until her spine popped, then wiped her forehead on her sleeve and grinned at Becky: "You're children of your doubtin' times, you and Liam, and him that ought to know better, descended direct from the great chieftan of the Fianna." She gave Becky a wry look: "It's been a long war, darlin' girl, the war of steam and money against the forces of magic and faith, but the tide's turnin'. It's like the wise man in the Bible says: 'To everything there is a season, and a time to every purpose under heaven.'"

"Come on, then," she continued briskly, putting her arm through Becky's, "I expect it won't be long till Cap'n Billy's boat brings Liam home to us, what do you say we take a little stroll down to the dock and make sure we're there to welcome him in case today's the day?"

Becky laughed. "I say you may be mad as a March hare, but every so often you have a really good idea!"

The two women strolled away out of the serene hush of the birch circle and back into the surrounding woods, and for a moment Becky had the oddest sensation of having crossed a threshold—as if she'd stepped from one world into another . . .

Chapter Seven

ell?" snapped Liam.

The only thing that kept him from smacking Chen to get his attention was the thought that the man had already been hit enough for a lifetime by Stanton's jailers. Still, he and Mike and Captain Billy didn't seem to have a clue between them about stopping the shark, which left things up to Chen's Chinese alchemy. Assuming there was anything more to that than ye olde Shanghai snake oil, that is.

The shark tore past them on the port side, its wake rocking the *Straight Up* as if the heavily-armored blockade runner were no more than a canoe, then paused for a moment a hundred yards aft of them to put on another stomach-churning display of gymnastics. Something told Liam that once it finished showing off, the creature's next run at the boat would be all business.

Chen was staring absently into the distance, for all the world as if he were trying to remember where he'd left his spectacles. Liam leaned closer, until he was a couple of inches away from Chen's ear, and bellowed at the top of his lungs:

"HEY!"

Chen jumped as if he'd been stuck with a pin and Liam pointed towards the shark, taking pains to speak calmly:

"Remember him? Ready to try some of that alchemy, or should I start saying my prayers?"

Chen glared at him and answered with icy British composure: "My dear Mr. McCool, I'm afraid you're labouring under a fundamental misunderstanding of . . ."

Liam wasn't listening. The shark had just performed what looked like a double somersault, raising a splash that would have swamped them if they'd been any closer, and now it was knifing towards them through the waves with terrifying speed.

"Oh, oh," Liam said in a hollow voice.

"If we get out of this," Mike said grimly, "I'm never eating another fish as long as I live!"

The shark was so close now that when it opened its mouth it looked to Liam like the Warren Street end of the Beach Pneumatic Transit tunnel.

"You got a hold of the wrong end of it," Liam said, "the question is whether this one eats *you.*"

"Here, dammit," roared Captain Billy, "somebody give me a hand with this sea anchor!"

He was wrestling with a peculiar contraption lying on the deck in the stern sheets, what looked like a pyramid of heavy cast-iron squares with a cast-iron rod skewered through their centers; a long coil of rope was attached to the narrow end by a ringbolt set in the rod. Liam leapt to help Billy and discovered that it was going to take the two of them just to pick it up, and that barely to chest level.

"Heave it down that thing's gullet!" shouted Billy, and a moment later he and Liam had pitched it over the side into the shark's gaping jaws.

For a brief moment, it seemed as if the shark had been stunned into immobility; then it snorted madly, thrashed around as if it were trying to cough the sea anchor up, and took off at top speed in the opposite direction. Liam watched as the coil of rope rapidly diminished and then shouted at the others:

"HANG ON TIGHT!"

No sooner had he said it than the rope went taut with a thrumming *twanggg!* and the entire vessel was jerked sideways so that the decks were instantly awash, Chen and Mike slipping in the water and crashing to the deck while Liam and Captain Billy had to fight to keep from going over the side. Then, before any of them could gather their wits, the monster shark changed course once more, now running ahead of the *Straight Up* and pulling it through the waves after it like a child's toy boat on a string.

"If we can't stop that thing," shouted Captain Billy, "we're going to founder!"

Liam shook his head grimly, pulled himself upright, snatched his Peacemaker out of its holster and fired at the swivel securing the end of the sea anchor's rope. Two of the big slugs were enough to smash it loose and with a keening whistle the rope flailed away after the shark.

For a moment all four men sat on the flooded deck in a sort of post-traumatic daze, and then Liam jumped to his feet and yelled furiously at Chen:

"No wonder Stanton threw you in jail, you charlatan! That Chinese alchemy of yours isn't worth a plugged nickel!" He bared his teeth in a furious sneer:

"I should have figured it out sooner: what kind of tenth-rate dud '*alchemist*' would let a bunch of thugs throw him in solitary and torture him without turning them to stone or walking through the wall or something? You're about as . . . as alchemistical as a stuffed *owl*!"

At that, Chen jumped up and wagged his finger at Liam so dementedly that Liam involuntarily backed away a step.

"How *dare* you, you . . . you *ruffian*! Those filthy people kept me in a drugged stupor from the moment they arrested me until they sent me out to be hanged, apart from the occasional *torture* break! As for my alchemistic abilities, I'll have you know that I am a *fully* qualified . . ."

Liam interrupted with a disgusted snort: "A fully qualified bunco artist, and *that's* the by-God goods, Mr. Chinese Charlie! I hope that damn fish eats *you* first, maybe he'll choke on you and we'll get a chance to clear out!"

It had been a very long day for Ambrose Chen, which was probably the only reason his normal icy composure totally deserted him, leaving him red and sputtering and hopping up and down slightly with barely restrained rage:

"You think so, eh? You *think* so, do you? Hah! Hah *hah!* By Jove, I'll show *you!*"

And with that, Chen bent over, took a double handful of the sea water which was sloshing back and forth through the scuppers, held it up to the sky while muttering furiously in Chinese, then doused the water over the top of his head, closed his eyes and stood immobile as a cigar store Indian while his lips continued to move soundlessly.

Captain Billy picked up a belaying pin and smacked it on his palm, eyeing Chen reflectively.

"What the divvil's he up to now, then?" the Captain asked.

"Beats me," Liam said, "maybe he's finally gone off his nut."

"For cryin' out loud," Mike said, pointing, *"look!"*

An area of glassy calm with the *Straight Up* at its center was spreading rapidly in all directions, and in less than a minute it had caught up to the monster shark, which stopped abruptly and turned back to look at the ship. But before it could make another move a boiling turbulence sprang up around the giant fish, within which it leapt about madly as if it were trying to escape. Now Chen began to hum, louder and louder in a kind of keening melody that sent a prickle of apprehension up Liam's back, and the turbulence around the shark grew more and more violent and chaotic until suddenly it began to rise from the surface of the calm sea, climbing higher and higher and spinning the colossal shark around faster and faster until it was so far from the watchers below that the shark finally looked no bigger than an ordinary fish.

"Ah, begorrah," cried Captain Billy in a quavering voice, "sure and we'll all be ending up in Hell tonight and that's the Divvil himself standin' right there singin' in Chinese!"

"Get ahold of yourself, Billy," Liam admonished, but at that moment the shark exploded with a thunderous roar and a flash like a lighting strike, and everyone but Chen threw himself flat on the deck and waited for the end.

After a moment Liam heard a kind of disdainful sniff and Chen said:

"If you'd had the *elementary* politeness to let me finish what I was saying . . ."

Liam got up and eyed Chen disgustedly as he tried to brush himself off.

". . . I could have explained that Chinese Alchemy is a very *specific* set of scientific practices dealing with the *five elements* of wood, metal, fire, water and earth and not at all what was called for to rid us of the shark. As it happens, however, I *am* a Taoist sorcerer as well as an alchemist . . ."

Chen spread his hands and gave Liam a superior little smile: ". . . and therefore quite competent to deal with 'supernatural sharks,' as you so quaintly put it. Contact with the seawater allows me to use my alchemy to control the waves, at least for as far as I can see them, and a bit of sorcery (which is, since you seem to require nursery-school definitions, a discipline quite separate from control of the five elements) allows me to put the shark in harm's way." He bowed: "*Et voilà c'est tout*: the shark is no more!"

Liam blew out a huge sigh and spread his hands in a gesture of resignation. "Ambrose," he said, "I'm not sure if I want to give you a medal or punch your head for you, but until I decide maybe I'll just compromise and get us another bottle of Old Bushmills."

Chen nodded judiciously. "I think you may be wiser than you look, Mr. McCool."

Mike headed for the hatch. "This one's on me," he said with a grin.

"Sure and the Hell of it is," lamented Captain Billy, "that everyone's going to think this is just another one of my sea stories."

Chapter Eight

u, Lyovushka," Mike said, "what's the plan?"

Mike and Chen and Liam were sitting on the poop deck of the *Straight Up* as she cruised slowly across Little Peconic Bay towards the Goodyear mansion's dock, soaking up the sun and enjoying the peace and quiet of the sheltered harbor after the bedlam on the Atlantic side.

"Plan?" Liam said. He had been drowsing and daydreaming about Becky and he wasn't happy about coming back.

"*Vstavai, durak,*" Mike said with a touch of asperity. "Like, whadda we do next, you know?"

Liam shrugged and yawned. "I have a couple of things to take care of here and then we can go home. Cap'n Billy says we should just about make it back to the city before the worst of the storm hits."

Mike folded his arms on his chest and gave Liam a look of heavy patience. "Go home and *what, govniuk,* play cribbage and take little naps till we get old?"

Liam grinned. "I could use a nap. It's hard work getting executed." He held up his hand to keep Mike from blowing his top. "OK, OK. Did you and the boys finish moving all our stuff to the tunnels?"

"There's nothing important left where Stanton's people can get at it. Every now and then I glue on a beard and walk past our old building on Bleecker and you can see they got Eyes coming out of the cracks in the walls." He shook his head and snorted derisively: "Sometimes they even station Acmes across the street, like they expect us to drop in to change our underwear."

Liam nodded. "Good. I hope the boys are all ready to live underground for a while, because we're going to have to stay invisible until Tsar Eddie and his gang are breathing dirt. That means we have to set up some kind of Crooks' Congress to get together everybody that's in the life and then sell them on fighting Stanton instead of each other. And by Congress I don't mean a gabble-shop like this Freedom Party either. I mean *organized*, like an army headquarters."

He turned to Chen. "How about you, Ambrose? Do you want to stay here with the Freedom Party people or do you want to go back to the city with us?"

Chen took a long pull at the bottle of Irish and then fell into a brown study, staring abstractedly at the label.

"You're not going to find the answer there," Mike said.

Chen nodded grudgingly and turned back to Liam: "Do you know anything at all about the properties of calorium?"

Liam gave Chen a narrow look: was all the Bushmills finally getting to him? "We're back to calorium?" he said.

"I'm not intoxicated," Chen said testily, "I need to know how much I have to explain."

Liam shrugged. "Well, if you took everything I know about calorium and stuffed it up a flea's bum you'd have plenty of room left over."

Chen made a face. "I rather thought so. Very well, then: calorium must be refined from a mineral called pitchblende and that involves two awkward problems. First, there are only three people alive who understand the problem well enough to have refined calorium from pitchblende *successfully*: Prof.

Faraday of the Royal Institution of Great Britain, who has formed a very profitable partnership with the English mechanician and Acme manufacturer Royce; Dr. Lukas, otherwise known as Prince Nikolai Aleksandrovich Yurevskii, Regent of Little Russia; and," here Chen bowed solemnly, "your humble servant."

Mike made a face: "If this bird gets any humbler we'll have to make a hole in his head to get the swelling down."

"You already told us all that," Liam said, "what's the second problem?"

Chen nodded grimly: "Simply this: if anyone without the necessary training and experience tries to extract calorium from pitchblende, the odds in favor of a disastrous accident are huge. Unfortunately, once Stanton realized that I was adamant about keeping my process a secret he imprisoned me and contracted with a former student of mine, Chiang Lee, to discover how to replicate my work. Lee—though somewhat talented—is unscrupulous, slipshod and greedy, and I shudder to think what may happen at any moment now that he's trying to reproduce my research. This is a problem that demands a solution without delay and I may need to turn to you for help."

"Just how dangerous is it?" Mike asked.

"'Dangerous' scarcely begins to describe it, Mr. Vysotsky. In the wrong hands (and I find it hard to imagine the right ones) the misuse of calorium could destroy all life on the planet."

Chen's tone was so flat and so final that both Liam and Mike were momentarily speechless. Chen mistook their silence for a criticism:

"I know, I know," he said grimly, "you're doubtless asking yourselves how I could have agreed to work on calorium at all for a swine like Stanton, but the answer is painfully simple: he had imprisoned my entire family in a camp outside Sing Sing, and threatened to execute them one by one unless I should show him the secret of refining calorium."

Liam and Mike exchanged a knowing look: "We know that camp all right," Liam said, "and I expect Stanton had you pretty well buffaloed. So why did you finally . . .?"

"I was fortunate enough to have important friends in the New York tongs," Chen said with a narrow smile, "and they managed to free my family and send them West in a stolen Navy flyer. To the best of my knowledge they are now safely in Los Angeles, the capital of the Bear Flag Republic, so in answer to your original question, I prefer to go with you to New York so that I may arrange to go West to make sure that my family are all well. As soon as that's taken care of, I must return to the East to solve the Lee problem. For all our sakes."

"How the Sam Hill do you expect to get from New York to the Bear Flag Republic?" Liam asked.

Mike was looking troubled. "Yeah, and what are you going to do about this other Chinaman? Sounds to me like we ought to put the business on him."

"Now that I'm free I'll find a way to California," said Chen, "and for that opportunity I thank both of you gentlemen with all my heart. As for Chiang Lee . . ."

Before he could finish Captain Billy threw open the wheelhouse porthole and shouted to them:

"Look lively, lads, there's the pier dead ahead!"

Liam froze, not quite ready to turn around and look. He felt a sudden pain behind his eyes as sharp as if someone had shoved an ice pick through his temple:

What if she's decided she won't have me? What if now she's had time to think it over she can't think what in God's name ever possessed her to take up with me?

o—⚷

The walk from the woods to the waterfront was idyllic, a broad, sunny sweep of soft emerald grass dotted with wild-flowers and accented by neat graveled paths with whitewashed stone borders, but both Becky and Gran were too preoccupied to notice it.

For Gran, there was the persistent and disturbing thought that making a fairy circle on Samhain was no party game, not remotely like playing with a Ouija board or table-rapping "spirits." It meant knocking at the door of the Land of Faërie, and no mortal could ever be quite sure what might answer the summons, no matter how many times they had dared it before. Not to mention that it had been a long time (too long?) since she had done it last.

For Becky, there was the painful litany of questions she'd been asking herself over and over again ever since Liam had set off on his mission for President Lincoln: *What if he hates me for putting him on the spot, for insisting that he let President Lincoln talk over the plan in public? I still don't know for sure that there was a traitor among us, but it can scarcely matter now to Liam whether it can be proved or not, the fact is he spent three months in Stanton's clutches no matter how that monster learned about it. Dear God, what if Liam turns away from me, won't even shake my hand? . . .*

"Good afternoon, Mrs. McCool, Miss Fox . . ."

Becky started as sharply as if the cordial greeting had been a bomb going off. Crossing their path on his way to the main house was a cheerful, rosy-cheeked young man with a tidy little waxed moustache and brown hair parted fastidiously in the middle, neatly turned out in a forest-green checked suit and tipping a matching cap towards Gran and Becky.

"Goodness, Captain Ubaldo," Becky said with a flush of embarrassment, "you startled me!"

Ubaldo grinned at them. "You certainly seemed to be in something of a reverie, Miss Fox. You must forgive me for intruding. Are you ladies coming to the meeting?"

Becky and Gran looked around, realizing belatedly that a stream of Freedom Party members was pouring towards the main house from various directions, talking and laughing and throwing curious glances towards the two women, who had been walking obliviously in the opposite direction.

"What meeting?" Gran asked with a frown.

"Why, to take a final vote on the question of whether or not the Party will approve a commendation for Mr. McCool's brave attempt to break into the Stanton archives!" Ubaldo examined them curiously, as if he couldn't imagine the two of them passing up a chance to cast their votes.

But Gran just burst into a peal of merry laughter: "Sure, the lot of ye are bad as a roomful of drunken Fenians jawbonin' about whether they should condemn the Queen's latest outrage! Come on now, Captain: fess up, are ye all secret Irishmen?"

Then, suddenly contrite when she saw Ubaldo's shocked expression she gave him a placating pat on the arm:

"There now, acushla, ye must forgive an old biddy blitherin' on, I meant no harm!"

"I'm afraid it's my fault, Captain," said Becky, "I'm a bit worn out from putting the new issue of *Freedom* to bed and Mrs. McCool kindly consented to keep me company while I get some fresh air."

"Certainly, ladies," Ubaldo said urbanely, tipping his cap again, "I'll be sure to find you after the meeting and let you know how it came out."

As he strolled away, Becky looked after him for a moment with a bemused smile. "Did I tell you he had proposed to me?"

Gran raised her eyebrows: "Did he, now? Well, he's a handsome lad, sure enough."

"Do you think so?" Becky laughed and started walking again. "I'm afraid he's not quite the sort of man I fancy, but I was at great pains to make him think I took his proposal seriously. He's a gentleman. And he's also a brave pilot who has put himself at risk for the Party many times."

"Mmm," Gran said noncommittally. "And Liam *is*, then?" she added with a twinkle of mischief.

"Is what?" Becky asked evasively.

"Is the sort of man you fancy?"

Becky rolled her eyes and sighed. "God help me, I suppose so."

Suddenly the two of them came to a halt, staring across the remaining stretch of grass towards the Bay, where the *Straight Up* had appeared as if by magic around a wooded promontory.

"Oh, dear heavens," Becky said in a faint voice, "there they are."

○—ᴛ

On the *Straight Up*, Liam was standing at the taffrail gauging the distance he'd have to jump if he didn't wait for Captain Billy to fool around with all the nautical stuff involved in tying up the boat. They were close enough now for him to see Becky plainly and he really hated to admit just how bad a state he was in at the mere sight of her. She was bareheaded, her long auburn hair gathered up at her neck with a simple ribbon and blowing in the ocean breeze. A sworn enemy of corsets and other "fashionable idiocies," she was dressed as simply as usual, in a soft blue frock with the bodice open at the throat, and the mere sight of that face was enough to make his heart squeeze up like a baby's fist.

"Dammit, McCool, just wait a minute!" Captain Billy shouted from behind him, but he was too late—Liam was already flying through the air, suspended for a split second over the water while everybody on both sides of the gap caught their breath . . . and then landing with a crash on the boards of the pier, off-balance enough that he staggered and had to run almost to the far edge before he regained his balance.

Watching from the *Straight Up*, Mike and Chen both shook their heads incredulously.

"Is he always that impatient?" Chen asked.

Mike smiled slightly. "It depends on the woman."

On the pier, Gran was studying Liam and Becky with a rapt expression and thinking that one of the best things about being old was being past craziness like this. The two of them were standing not more than six feet apart, absolutely transfixed by emotions they couldn't quite handle and apparently unable to move another inch closer. Liam opened and closed his mouth several times in futile attempts to say something and succeeded only in imitating a beached fish. Becky didn't even try to speak, but only stared at Liam with feverish intensity as if she were trying to see into his brain, her upper lip beaded with perspiration and a flush slowly mounting further and further up her throat and into her cheeks until she looked as if she'd run miles to get to the pier. It was Liam who finally broke the silence, clearing his throat desperately before he said:

"Good afternoon, Miss, ah . . ."

Becky looked at him for a long beat and then said: "Oh, *Hell!*"

At which both of them leapt towards each other as if they had been shot from cannons, melting into an embrace so intense that the rest of the world had clearly ceased to exist for either of them.

Chen and Mike had disembarked, leaving Captain Billy aboard to keep up steam, and they approached Gran and the embracing couple cautiously.

"I've read occasional accounts of spontaneous human combustion," Chen said in a low tone, "but I had always thought them rather silly. Still . . ."

"Yeah," said Mike, "I know what you mean." He gave Gran a quick hug and then turned to Chen. "Ambrose, this is Liam's grandmother." And to Gran: "Mrs. McCool, this is Ambrose Chen, a new pal and, uh . . ." he smiled a little uncertainly, ". . . a big-time Chinese sorceror."

Chen bowed deeply, then took Gran's hand and gave it a ceremonious kiss. In answer, Gran looked closely into Chen's eyes, then nodded after a moment or two and smiled:

"Welcome, Mr. Chen," she said. Then she turned towards the house, gesturing for the others to follow her.

"Come on, boys, those two can catch up when they're ready."

Gran strode away towards the main house, her stride brisk enough to make Mike and Chen hustle to keep up with her. Behind her, the late sun sparkled on the whitecaps in the Bay while the *Straight Up* bobbed cheerfully at her moorings and Becky and Liam continued to hold each other, motionless and lost in wordless communication. Finally, as if at a signal, they broke apart and started walking towards the house holding hands.

"I know what's important now, and none of that other stuff matters," Liam said, "the old stuff—all that stuff we thought was so important, the people we used to be. From now on it's just you and me and we start fresh from right here."

Becky gave him a little Mona Lisa smile: "I couldn't have said it better myself."

Chapter Nine

ran, Mike and Chen were seated comfortably in white-painted wicker armchairs which had been set out in front of the main house. A croquet course had been laid out on the grass in front of them, and a game must have been interrupted by the announcement of the meeting inside, as the mallets and balls were scattered here and there where the players had dropped them.

What was absorbing the attention of Gran and her companions, however, was a display taking place around one of the wickets just in front of them where an outlandishly-dressed little man no bigger than a chipmunk was doing fancy gymnastic spins around the top of the wicket while an equally tiny woman in spangled tights was standing on the grass waiting to catch him.

Gran was watching with a wide grin, absolutely fascinated, while Mike scratched his head abstractedly and looked disapproving.

"My hat's off to ye, Ambrose," Gran said, "we've plenty of Little People in the ould country, but they're real folk, citizens of the Land of Faërie. As near as I could make out, ye made those two out of a couple of pill bugs."

Chen was obviously pleased with Gran's praise and he gestured expansively. "It's just a bit of elementary alchemy,

Mrs. McCool—they're not human at all, of course, but merely pill bugs in altered forms. I know that the Swiss alchemist Paracelsus made all sorts of extravagant claims about creating actual human homunculi in his book *De Natura Rerum*, but I'm quite sure he was, ah, *inspired* by the manuscripts of Marco Polo, who would have seen little creatures like these two on his travels in China."

"There's Liam and Becky," Mike announced with obvious relief. "Hey," he called out, "over here!"

Becky and Liam had been heading straight for the front door, but at Mike's hail they veered over towards the croquet pitch.

"Good Lord!" Becky said, "What's *that*?"

Her attention riveted on the tiny acrobats, she tugged Liam after her and bent closer to examine them.

"Are they real?" she said in a slightly tremulous voice.

"One might say so," Chen answered a little evasively.

"He made them out of a couple of pill bugs," Mike said, with a reproachful sniff.

Liam burst out laughing. "That's just Ambrose putting on the swank, showing Gran what a big uptown magician he is." He pulled his Gran to her feet and gave her a bear hug. "He did save our lives on the way here," he told her, "but he had to wait all the way up to the third act curtain so he'd look extra good when he did it."

"Hmph!" snorted Chen. He clapped his hands lightly and the little figures vanished in a puff of smoke, leaving a couple of thoroughly terrified pill bugs curled up into balls.

"Where is everybody?" Liam asked. "Are they still having that meeting? We need to get moving if we don't want Cap'n Billy getting all in a lather, and I have to talk to President Lincoln before we leave."

Becky tugged on his arm, heading for the front door: "Come on, we'll just interrupt them if we have to."

Inside the main meeting room of the Goodyear mansion, the members of the Freedom Party were seated in rows in front of a cleared space with their leaders sitting in a semicircle facing them. President Lincoln sat in the center, the effect of his shiny, oversized automaton body softened somewhat by a suit of the clothes people were used to seeing Abe Lincoln wear, plain black broadcloth with fresh white linen; while to Lincoln's right, simply dressed and coiffed, sat Countess Lovelace or Augusta Ada Byron or just plain Ada as the down-to-earth mathematical genius and Party technical adviser insisted. On Lincoln's left was the shrewd and cheerful Party Chairman Sam Clemens (never Mr. Twain once you'd shaken his hand) in his perennial white suit, and on Clemens' left the Party's grand old man and Communications Director Frederick Douglass, looking on with courtly dignity and a look of acute distress as a well-dressed woman harangued the audience.

"I'm sorry," she said in a patently un-sorry tone, "but I simply cannot fathom how a Party representing some of our country's finest traditions and best people can *possibly* lend its imprimatur to a common thief, and an Irish one at that! Surely there's a *reason* why establishments throughout New York City display signs saying "No Irish Need Apply"—it's a well-known fact that the average Irish person is a drunken layabout whose morals are no better than they ought to be!"

Liam and the others had entered at the back of the room as the woman launched into her diatribe, and by its end Clemens was on his feet looking anguished and waving his hand as if to clear the air:

"Now, Mrs. Redingote, I expect we all set great store by plain speaking, but even so that's going beyond the . . ."

Liam spoke up from the back of the room: "Don't fret yourself, Mr. Clemens."

Everyone turned around in their seats to see who had spoken and Liam grinned at their obvious discomfiture.

"Really, folks," Liam continued with a hint of a grin, "the life of your average Irish thug is one long round of blood-letting and debauchery, so I like to spend a little quiet time every year in solitary confinement—just so I can get in some prayer and meditation. Seeing as how my incarceration was nothing more than simple self-indulgence I couldn't possibly accept your commendation, though I *do* want to correct the lady speaker on one point: it hurts my feelings to have people call me a common thief when the fact is I'm an absolute crack-erjack, none better if I say so myself."

"Well, really!" cried the scandalized Mrs. Redingote, and a wave of sotto voce comment and laughter ran through the crowd.

Twain was grinning and shaking his head: "Welcome back, Mr. McCool—I'm glad to see that the report of your hanging was an exaggeration."

"You and me both," Liam said emphatically. "Now, if you'll pardon me for interrupting, I'm pushed for time as we've got to race the storm back to the city and I'd like to ask for a private audience with you folks and President Lincoln, no other Party members please."

Twain gave President Lincoln an inquiring look and Lincoln got to his feet, holding up one massive steel hand to quiet the crowd's protesting murmurs.

"Of course," he said with the soulful thrum of his artificial vocal cords. "Ladies and gentlemen, I'll declare the meeting adjourned if I may and I'll see you all again at dinner time."

Liam and his friends made their way through the departing crowd towards the front of the room, and Lincoln held out both hands in welcome:

"I can't tell you how happy I am to see you safe and sound, Liam. It's been a pure misery to me thinking that my request got you into such awful troubles."

Liam shook the President's enormous metal hand and smiled: "Believe me, sir, it wasn't your request that got me into trouble, but I'd rather we were in some more private place when I explain."

Lincoln opened a door in the wall behind them and beckoned to the others to follow:

"Come on, folks. Let's get ourselves comfortable in the library."

The library was a spacious room with thick maroon velvet drapes, green-shaded lamps and floor-to-ceiling shelves lined with enough books to keep Liam reading for a lifetime. *Someday,* he was thinking, *when everything's back to normal, I'm going to come back out here in the middle of the night with a steam van and a couple of the boys and load up—I'll bet nobody but the maids who dust the books will even miss . . .*

"Liam?" Lincoln's tone was politely inquiring.

"Sorry, sir." said Liam, snapping back to the moment. "It's been a long day. But before I head back to the city I want to tell you a couple of important things I've learned while I was away. First—and I heard this from a couple of Spanish lads who are close to Fat Willie Pilkington—Stanton has decided that he isn't going to be comfortable until you're gone for good. But he wants to milk your going for every drop of propaganda he can squeeze out of it, so before he has you executed he means to stage a huge treason trial where he can put you in the stand and paint you as the worst scoundrel in America's history."

Lincoln shook his head slowly, the uncanny swiveling of the great steel head making Liam feel a bit queasy. "Eddie Stanton is the perfect type of the old-fashioned machine politico, eaten up by vanity and greed till, as the Good Book says, there's nothing left but sounding brass and the tinkle of cymbals."

"Yes, sir. But please don't think he's all talk—his gang beats anything I've ever seen for numbers and organization, and it's not going to be long before they come down on you like a hammer on an anvil. And that's the second thing I wanted to tell you: you're running out of time fast, because you've got a traitor in your midst."

For a moment the Freedom Party leaders were stunned into silence, and then they all started talking at once until Frederick Douglass stood up and bowed to Liam:

"Thank you, young man," he said with deep feeling, "I have some experience of what you've been through and I know how much it cost for you to come here to warn us instead of just thanking your stars for your freedom and going to ground somewhere." He crossed to Liam and shook his hand warmly. "Bless you, Mr. McCool. Please tell us how you learned this terrible thing."

"Well, sir," Liam said, "I expect you'll remember that the meeting where my plan was discussed broke up late in the afternoon and that I set off immediately for the city in Cap'n Grogan's boat. He was able to put me ashore not far from the warehouse district where my target was located, and as it was already dark I was able to make my way there without any delay. It couldn't have been more than four hours after I left Shelter Island when I approached the door of the warehouse and started to jimmy it open, but the minute I touched the door a good dozen carbon-arc searchlights blazed down from the rooftops around the warehouse and a horde of bluecoats poured out of every doorway and alley and beat me to the ground. As fuddled as I was, it was plain as a pikestaff what had happened—someone who had been at that meeting of ours tipped off Willie Pilkington in time for him to set the trap just as nice as you please."

This time the Party leaders sat in stunned silence till Liam got to his feet. "That's everything I wanted to tell you, and I'm afraid we'll have to get going right away if we're going to beat the storm. I surely can't tell you how to find out who the rotten egg is. All I *can* say is you need to do it fast. And if you have an emergency hideout you can go to, start getting ready right away, because this place just isn't safe now. I don't know why Stanton hasn't hit you already, but it can't be long till he does."

Slowly and almost grudgingly Lincoln got to his feet, followed by the others as they crowded around to embrace Liam and shake his hand. Ada Lovelace gave Liam a warm embrace:

"It's too bad of you to come and go so quickly, Mr. McCool, I was hoping we'd have time to argue about poetry, especially since I finally read Pushkin's *Eugene Onegin* and now I can answer your comparison of *Onegin* and my father's *Don Juan.*"

Liam gave her a courtly bow and kissed her hand with a flourish: "Nothing would please me more, my lady, but I'm afraid the hurricane won't wait."

"I hope you won't be taking our Becky away with you," she continued, trying to cover real concern with a playful tone.

Becky gave her a hug: "I have to go before long, Ada dear, I must get back to real reporting and I want to work with Liam on his plans for strengthening the opposition. But I'm going to stay long enough to help President Lincoln find a new editor for *Freedom.*"

Before anybody else could comment, Ambrose stepped forward, kissed Ada's hand with operatic panache and murmured in his best continental style: "Ambrose Chen, my lady, your servant. I wanted to compliment you on your *Notes* to Von Reichenbach's *Researches on Magnetism*, which I found far more illuminating than the work itself." And then, before Ada could recover from her astonishment, Ambrose plucked a perfect, long-stemmed rose out of the air and handed it to her.

Liam burst out laughing: "Ambrose, if you start pulling coins out of Countess Lovelace's ear I *am* going to punch your head for you. Come on, folks, time to go!"

With that he opened the door back into the meeting room and disappeared through it.

Outside, the weather had clearly taken a turn for the worse, with dark clouds scudding across what was left of the blue sky and the winds bringing a steamy, sea-weedy smell from somewhere a long way south of Long Island.

Liam looked up at the sky with a worried frown and started towards the pier, but before he could take another step Gran grabbed him by the arm:

"Not quite yet, Liam me darlin'!"

Liam frowned and opened his mouth to protest, but Gran just started dragging him after her as she headed towards the woods.

"Hey!" Liam protested, "Darn it, Gran, hang *on* a minute!"

"Save yer breath to cool yer porridge," she snapped over her shoulder, and Liam made a face and surrendered as Gran led the way into the trees.

Now that the sunny skies were darkening, the forest canopy filtered the remaining light into a faintly green, glowing murk that was eerie enough to reduce even Ambrose to wary silence. But when they reached the circle of white, stately birches and Gran picked up a carpetbag she had stowed behind a bush, Liam finally had to speak.

"For the luvva mercy," he hissed in an uneasy whisper, "what's all this hoopla about?"

"You hush yer worritin', Liam McCool," she said curtly, "and sit over there." She reached behind the bush again and pulled out a highly-polished ebony walking stick, smiling as she saw Liam's face light up at the sight of it. "There," she said, "I kept your stick for you, that ought to cheer you up.

Gram turned to the others and pointed to a cleared spot just outside the circle of trees: "Right, then, everybody, all together over there now!"

Herding them along with peremptory shooing motions until everyone was seated in a tight group, Gran then took a cardboard box of salt out of her bag and slowly emptied it in a circle completely surrounding the five of them.

"There," she said, dusting her hands off, "that's to protect us, so don't be steppin' outside the salt."

"Jeez, Gran," Mike said, "protect us from *what*? You're giving me the willies!" The others agreed vehemently, but Gran just grinned and pointed to the circle of birches:

"In case ye've forgotten what I taught ye along with yer English, Misha me lad, today is Samhain. And that over there's a fairy circle. It's true we'd do better waitin' till midnight, but I know ye've got to be getting' along, so just bear with me and we'll do our best."

"Fairy circle?" Liam said with a touch of uneasiness, "Do we really need to be doing this, Gran?"

"Be quiet for pity's sake, McCool," Chen said in clipped tones, "and let your grandmother get on with it—I've never seen an Irish witch at work, and I wouldn't miss it for the world."

"Thank you, Ambrose," Gran said. "And the answer is yes, Liam darlin'. The Birch Fairy is the one our people call The Lady of the Woods, and when ye need a clear head for some grand new venture and ye need to leave behind all yer bad baggage she's the one we call on. I mean to stay here on the Island with Becky till she's ready to join you and I don't know when I'll be seein' ye next, so this is something we *do* need to do now."

As she spoke, the first roll of thunder came to them across the ocean, accompanied by a distant shimmer of lightning. Gran picked up her bag and hurried into the birch circle, where she took a bowl out of the bag and set it in the middle of

97

the clearing. Then she took a bottle of milk and a jar of honey out of the bag and mixed their contents in the bowl, which she held up in the air as she intoned:

"House of McCool . . ."

Before she could finish Liam gave a sudden roar of pain and fell forward onto his knees, clasping his arms around himself as if he'd been stabbed to the heart. Becky jumped up with an anxious cry and knelt down next to Liam, but for once he barely registered her presence, his brain and his body overwhelmed by the most excruciating agony he'd ever felt—as if the blood had suddenly been sucked out of him and replaced with molten metal while his head rang with a terrifying clamor of voices, some strident and threatening and some low and hoarse and insinuating and speaking languages he couldn't recognize.

Finally, after what seemed like hours, the pain flooded back out of him like the water from a breaking wave and he took a deep, shuddering breath.

"Liam! Liam, are you all *right*?"

"Sweet Mother of God!" he muttered, his eyes shut tightly. "It was like I swallowed a bucketful of blazing coals on top of a lake of whiskey! What *was* that?"

Granny joined them, kneeling next to Liam and laying her hand on his forehead. "Ye're burnin' up," she said worriedly. "I should never have started before midnight . . ."

Liam's eyes opened and he gave her a forced smile, determined not to give in to some superstitious fairy nonsense:

"Come on, Gran," he said hoarsely, "let's get on with it." He straightened the quirks out of his smile with an effort and nodded towards the circle, not quite managing a hearty chuckle: "Really. God knows I've enough bad baggage to be getting rid of."

Gran studied him for a moment, her face full of concern (plus a touch of impatience with his trying to laugh it all off), then she got back to her feet and returned slowly to the circle, where she picked up the bowl of milk and honey and resumed her invocation, her voice a little strained:

"House of McCool has come to bring a gift. If the gift is accepted, please show yourself . . ."

Before she could finish, everything went totally black for a terrifyingly long moment, broken at last by a blinding flash of lightning and a thunderclap so loud it shook the trees and left everyone momentarily deaf.

Gran had dropped the offering bowl to cover her eyes with her hands, and as she lowered them and opened her eyes again she leapt back, crossing herself in terror:

"Aw, Jasus," she cried, "Lord have mercy!"

In front of her in the center of the circle was an enormous great horned owl, easily as tall as she was, staggering a bit as it tried to walk. Suddenly it spread its wings to their full, gigantic length and screeched so hideously that everyone had to clap their hands over their ears. Then the owl folded its wings again and started ruffling its feathers, so energetically that after a moment the bird seemed to blur before resolving itself with stomach-flipping abruptness into a stocky young man with a deeply bronzed complexion, broad cheekbones and an aquiline nose, his long black hair hanging behind him in a single braid. Bizarrely out of place in a faultless morning coat, waistcoat and striped trousers, he looked around dazedly at the trees and the equally dazed little group of people staring back at him, shaking his head as if he were trying to make it all go away.

"*Akh!*" he cried desperately in Russian, "*Bozhe ty moi, kuda zh ya propal?*"

Suddenly Liam leapt to his feet and ran towards the newcomer, grinning like a madman:

"Crazy Horse!" he yelled. "Zhenya! It's me!"

The other man was shaking his head, terrified. "Why I am dead?" he muttered in Russian-accented English. "You!" he shouted at Liam, crossing his fingers over his head to ward off evil. "Spirit! Is *Hell* here, or is some other?"

Liam broke out laughing: "*Slushai, durak!*" Then, pointing at himself, "*eto ya*, Lev Frentsisovich !"

The man's jaw dropped and Liam ran forward and embraced him, still laughing as he kissed him on both cheeks, Russian-style.

"Lev Frentsisovich?"

"That's what I'm trying to tell you! We're on Shelter Island." Then, as the newcomer shook his head in bafflement, "That's a hundred miles from New York City, and we were just getting ready to go back there by boat. What I want to know is where *you* came from?"

Before he could answer Becky ran towards them and threw her arms around the newcomer with a happy laugh:

"Crazy Horse! It *is* you! It must have been Gran's fairy circle!"

"*Akh!*" he said, looking around with sudden comprehension. "*Vot ono chto!* Thank you, Miss Becky! Fairy circle!" He turned to Gran as she approached and bowed deeply: "And you, Madam, are babushka of Lev Frentsisovich, all is comprehend!" He took her hands and kissed them both before straightening suddenly and giving her a shrewd look. "Only he does not tell you are powerful colleague. Please accept heartfelt compliments from humble Lakota shaman."

Liam broke in, eaten up with curiosity: "So, Zhenya, where *were* you, what's with the fancy duds—are you getting *married?*"

Crazy Horse's face darkened: "Not such much fun. A moment ago I am in Santa Monica, wait to see Governor for beg mercy to our friend Georgie. Then your babushka's fairy circle must have opened up ley line . . ." he waved his hand frustratedly, looking for English words ". . . like magic *highway* from this place to Bear Flag Republic."

"Bear Flag *Republic?*" Chen's attention was absolutely riveted.

"In *guberniia* of California," said Crazy Horse with a somber nod. "Our friend Georgie is in irons on orders from this *svoloch'* Lukas, now sits in Catalina Island dungeon."

"Georgie?" Becky cried. "You mean Laughing Wolf? General *Custer?*"

"The same," Crazy Horse said in a heavy voice, "our dear friend and comrade-in-arms. And in only three days he will be taken out and shot!"

Chapter Ten

ow it was Liam's turn to shake his head in denial: "No, Zhenya. Not *Custer.*" He and the onetime cavalry general had fought side by side against the Little Russian Secret Police and soldiers of the Little Russian Aerial Navy, and Liam could see the famous face, with its laughing blue eyes, its frame of curly blonde hair and its prominent nose and slightly receding chin as vividly as he could see Crazy Horse standing in front of him.

Crazy Horse shook his head gloomily. "Stanton has make deal with Mexico to give American soldiers *laissez-passer* from Sonora into Apacheria in Arizona *guberniia,* for seize calorium mines. Georgie was there leading army of the People—Blackfoot, Cheyenne, Comanche, Lakota Sioux and many others—against both enemies, Little Russians *and* Americans." He spat on the ground with an angry growl: "Apache traitor gives Georgie up to Little Russians and now he sits in hole in prison deep under the ground on Island of Catalina."

Becky took hold of Liam's arm and gave him a little shake: "You've got to go, Liam. He risked his life to help us steal Stanton's aerial battleship and escape from Little Russia, you can't do less."

Liam frowned and raised his arms in frustration, knowing she was right but thinking of the work that lay ahead of him organizing the gangs to fight against Stanton, but before he could speak Gran blew up at him, wagging her finger right under his nose and giving her voice an edge he remembered from his school days:

"Liam McCool, don't you *dare* drag your feet just because your precious plans'll be upset! Why do you think this man was snatched here across three thousand miles? He was brought to you by the *Lady of the Woods*, eejit! That means helpin' him and General Custer is *exactly* what your next great venture is supposed to be. Deny that mission and you'll be in a peck of trouble!"

Liam grinned and shook his head. He didn't know about the Birch Fairy, but he knew for sure he'd be in *two* pecks of trouble with Gran and Becky if he said no.

"Fine," he said, "but it's going to be a neat trick getting to California from here in three days."

Mike waved his hand dismissively: "*Nichevo, bratets!* While you were saying your prayers in the cooler, Stanton's people built an Aerial Navy depot in the North Meadow, up by 97th Street. They have a whole fleet of those new attack fliers up there, one of those things will get you to Los Angeles so fast it'll make your head spin."

Liam laughed and turned to Crazy Horse: "*Nu, nu, Zhenya, poekhali!* Let's get going!"

○—╥

The whole group was hurrying across the lawn towards the pier, where Captain Billy was standing with his arms folded on his chest, fuming. Liam had hung back a little to get a few last words in with Becky:

"Promise me you won't hang around here any longer than you have to. I meant every word of what I said to President Lincoln—it's not going to be long before there'll be squads of Johnnies out here doing pack drill on the lawn."

"I promise," she said, giving Liam's arm a squeeze. "You know Mike's going to start organizing the gangs the minute he gets back, and I'll use your headquarters as my clearing house while I get my old information networks running again. I really don't like to see you going to help Custer without me, he was my comrade too. But it's as if Stanton's making time move faster—he wants to bring everything under his hand before anyone has a chance to fight back and we've all got to work twice as fast to stop him."

"Right as always," said Liam with a smile. They were almost to the *Straight Up* now, and Liam folded Becky into a final embrace which continued until they heard Captain Billy's aggravated bellow in the background:

"*Avast there, McCool, ye blasted lollygagger!*"

Grudgingly, Liam let go of Becky and turned to go, but before he could quite make it she had pulled him back and given him one more passionate kiss. Then she whispered in his ear:

"You be very careful, Liam McCool, and come back to me in one piece because I do believe I've fallen in love with you."

With that she gave him a shove and pulled back to join Gran as Liam stood there for a moment with his mouth hanging open.

"Go on wit' yez," called Gran, laughing, "and close yer mouth before a seagull flies in there and builds a nest!"

For another moment Liam stood there in a state of total distraction until Captain Billy sang out again:

"*MCCOOL! NOW!!!*"

Finally getting a grip on himself, Liam turned and ran for the boat, barely making it aboard before Captain Billy swung the *Straight Up* around in a wide arc and tore off across the Bay for the open sea, full steam ahead.

○—⚏

Gran and Becky stood and watched them go for several minutes, each lost in her own thoughts until the boat rounded the headland that led to the Atlantic and disappeared. Then Gran blew out an enormous sigh and put her arm through Becky's:

"Come on now, lass, we'd best be getting back."

As they walked, Becky had to bite her lip to keep back the tears, and Gran—who was keeping a weather eye on Becky—talked to keep her distracted:

"D'ye think ye can find a new editor soon, then, love?"

Becky nodded and swallowed hard: "Mr. Clemens promised that he'd take it over himself until I could find someone willing to do the job, so all I really have to do is get together with him and plan out the next two or three issues and then I'll be free to go."

"Thank goodness!" Gran exclaimed. Then, a little guiltily, "I surely don't want to sound ungrateful, darlin', but I'm that tired of all the jabberin' I can't wait to go. Mind you, I've been underground before, with the Fenian Brotherhood. But that was back in the ould country and there was plenty of action to season the talk."

They had reached the white wicker armchairs in front of the main house and Becky sat down abruptly and heaved an enormous sigh: "I really . . ."

"There now, Becky love," Gran said, bending over and kissing her on the forehead, "you just rest easy a bit while I go in and see what's happening with dinner."

Becky nodded and smiled, grateful for a moment to sit alone and gather her thoughts. But almost as soon as Gran had gone, Becky heard a call from behind her:

"Ah, Miss Fox, thank heavens I've found you!"

Turning in her seat, Becky saw Capt. Ubaldo hurrying towards her, his cheeks flushed and his expression anxious:

"I was just doing an instrument check in the battleship Delta when a message came in for you on the Tesla Vox . . ."

Becky jumped to her feet, her hand instinctively flying to her throat. There weren't even a handful of people who had the Tesla Vox number that belonged to the unique airship that she and Liam had stolen from the Little Russian Aerial Navy and landed on Shelter Island. It could only mean that something *awful* had . . . Suddenly she realized that Capt. Ubaldo's lips were moving and she forced herself to focus on what he was saying:

"... *terribly* sorry to break it to you this way, but I was told that the Secret Service has arrested your father and that he ..."

But Becky was already running towards the field behind the main house, where the captured Delta was hidden in plain sight under an enormous blanket of netting and leafy twigs . . .

○—⌐

Becky hadn't been near the enormous black hulk of the Delta since she and Liam had landed it and turned its resources over to the Party, and she had forgotten the sheer size of the thing. As she approached the little flight of metal stairs that ascended into the belly of the ship, she felt its bulk blotting out the late afternoon sun and halted for a moment as she felt a twinge of uneasiness. Then, scolding herself for being a baby, she shrugged off her disquiet and marched boldly up the stairs.

The inside of the giant airship was breathtaking, like the illustrations of Jules Verne's *Twenty Thousand Leagues Under the Sea* brought improbably to life. The interior of Captain Nemo's submarine *Nautilus* was no more luxuriously paneled in oak nor ornately trimmed with curlicues of brass or impressively packed with mysterious machinery than this experimental behemoth of Stanton's, softly lit by rows of tiny electric bulbs concealed within frosted glass globes.

On the far side of the main cabin, spread in a semicircle beneath a sort of bay window with three thick panes of glass, was a curved panel studded with dials and switches beneath which a hanging jungle growth of wires and cables could be seen—the control panel in front of which Becky and Liam had spent some suspenseful hours trying to avoid crashing or blowing themselves up before they figured out how to run the ship.

What she was looking for wasn't in the main control panel, however, but in what looked like a double-length roll top desk on the wall opposite, and Becky headed for it with unswerving purpose, pulling the cover up and back to reveal a bank of exotic gadgets: a Bausch & Lomb ShurShot Bombing Sight, a TransLux Night Viewer, and finally—the TeslaVox Transmitter and Receiver, a prototype unit that adapted Tesla's new electric-power transmission techniques to the task of making the voicewire work without a wire

Using it was no great challenge: below the brass-and-rosewood handset that did the receiving and transmitting was a simple red knob with a brass arrow at its edge and the unambiguous legend: "ON—OFF." Becky flicked it on, and instantly a green light glowed and Becky picked up the handset to begin the call to her home.

But just as she heard the first thin jabber of voices from the little brass bowl of the receiver, she heard Ubaldo's steps approaching from behind her and turned to look as he said:

"Dear Becky! *Thank* you, I see you've got the TeslaVox all ready for my call."

He gave her a slightly crooked little grin as he approached, and Becky suddenly felt a clutch of apprehension as she took in his odd expression and the strange, sweetish-medicinal odor he was giving off. Had he been drinking?

"You really don't have to help, Capt. Ubaldo," she said uncertainly, "I remember quite clearly how to use the apparatus . . ."

107

"Oh, but you must let me help," he said with a falsely unctuous note as he bent forward over her, and a shiver ran up Becky's spine and jarred her into rising, but too late. Ubaldo had already pulled a folded cloth out his pocket and the sickly smell suddenly got much stronger as he clapped it over her face. For a couple of seconds she struggled with all the force of a born fighter, but the drug was too strong for her and after another moment or two she slumped to the floor. Ubaldo picked her up gently and laid her down on a buttoned-leather sofa, then bent over to kiss her on the lips:

"Rest peacefully, darling, I have some business I must take care of first."

And, sitting down in the chair Becky had just vacated, he jiggled the hooked handset holder up and down until a thin voice came from the handset:

"*Hello? Voicewire operator #81. Hello!*"

"Hello, Operator," Ubaldo said into the transmitter in his most commanding tone, "please connect me with Secretary Stanton."

Chapter Eleven

Stanton and his two satellites were standing at the window of Detective McPherson's Union Square office staring down at the deserted gallows, which were being painted with alternating swaths of sunshine and shadow as the storm clouds broke up.

"I'm sorry the storm has passed us by," Stanton said in an irritable tone, "there's something maddeningly impudent about the sun actually *shining* on the scene where that scum McCool escaped justice!"

"Never ye mind, sorr," McPherson piped up with a reassuring grin. "we'll have that spalpeen back on the scaffold before ye can say Jack Robinson. And wearing a rope cravat into the bargain, I warrant ye!"

"You may be a Great Detective," Stanton said sourly, "but if I made book on your promises I'd end up in debtors' prison." He pulled out his pocket watch and brightened a little as he noticed the time. "There is, however, one advisor so far whose word I've been able to depend on and I believe he's about to call on the voicewire."

Almost as if in answer, there was a timid knock at the door and a secretary opened it just a crack to say:

"There's a gentleman for you on the voicewire Mr. Secretary, sir, and he says he has an appointment to speak with you."

Stanton rubbed his hands gleefully and turned to the others:

"You see? *Dependable!*" And, to the secretary: "Please have him switched over to the receiver in this office, Miss Wilkes."

As the voicewire receiver on McPherson's desk rang, Stanton snatched it up eagerly:

"This is Edwin Stanton—to whom am I speaking?"

A reedy voice came through the earpiece of the receiver: "*My apologies, sir, but I'd rather not identify myself until I'm quite sure we'll be doing business with each other.*"

Stanton's face darkened like a thundercloud: "Business? You speak of doing *business*, sir? This is a matter of doing your patriotic duty!"

"*Inarguably, Secretary Stanton, but at the same time I think it's only fair to ask some recompense for the risks . . .*"

At this point Willie Pilkington stopped eavesdropping and pressed one ear tightly against the window.

"D'you hear that?" he asked McPherson.

McPherson pressed his own ear against the window, listening intently.

"Sure, your honor, and I was by way of thinkin' it was the wind in the eaves, but this is more like . . ."

". . . a swarm of *bees.*" said Pilkington.

McPherson turned and pressed his nose against the window, staring back and forth into the sky as if he were trying to see beyond the limits of the glass.

"Great ugly bees, they sound like," McPherson answered with a quaver in his voice . . .

$\diagup\!\!\!\!-\!\!\!\tau$

On the *Straight Up*, Liam and his friends were also staring into the sky, but in a markedly more upbeat mood as they watched the setting sun tinting the scattered clouds with brilliant streaks of dark rose and orange:

"Red sky at night," said Captain Billy with a chuckle, "sure, 'tis *this* sailor's delight—I was afraid we'd be scalin' ten-foot waves by now. But instead the *Straight Up's* steering itself on a governor and I'm out here takin' the air like a gentleman!"

Mike was peering narrowly at Chen and Crazy Horse: "Five'll get you ten the storm's turning east is on you two birds, am I right?"

Chen returned Mike's scrutiny with an irritable snort: "What on earth are you nattering on about, Vysotsky?"

"I know just what he means, Ambrose," said Liam, "and I was wondering that same thing. Tell me you two didn't cook up some kind of magic trick to send the hurricane off to Bermuda instead of the city!"

Chen and Crazy Horse exchanged an incredulous glance.

"Mr. McCool," the Chinese said sarcastically, "I cannot imagine why you insist on continuing your pretense of man-in-the-street idiocy, but I must say I find it *deeply* tiresome!"

"Wait!" said Crazy Horse, holding up his hand to interrupt Chen. "You are speak Russian, yes?"

"Of course," Chen answered with an impatient shrug.

"Splendid," said Crazy Horse, whose stepfather—Commander of the Little Russian Secret Police—had sent the young Sioux warrior to the Imperial University in St. Petersburg "to acquire culture." "In that case, let us speak Russian for a moment—trying to express myself in English is like running a race on one leg."

"Let's pretend, my dear Lev Frentsisovich," he said to Liam, "that you really don't know how magic works—though Georgie did try to explain it to you back in New Petersburg, remember? In any event, adepts like Ambrose and myself, and . . ." he peered at Liam with an emphasis that Liam found irritatingly mysterious, ". . . some *others* as well, have been born with enough magical talent to do small things that seem huge and frightening to those who don't understand them. Ambrose might be able to make one of those waves become twenty feet tall, for instance, or I might be able to turn Captain Billy into a dung beetle. But move a hurricane?" He smiled and shook his head. "That is for the Great Spirit (whatever anyone may call Him) and Him alone. When hundreds of the People gather together and make a Sun Dance to ask the Great Spirit to change the weather, then it may happen. For one person to try such a thing by himself . . ." he shrugged, ". . . is just stupid and arrogant."

"*Zhenya! Bozhe!*" Liam held up both hands as if to ward off more words. "Do all the magic tricks you like, just don't try to turn *me* into a dung beetle, or I'll run up your leg and bite you on the . . ."

"HEY!" shouted Mike, waving his hands for attention, "Shut up a minute and listen!"

He cocked his head with one hand up to his ear and turned back and forth, staring into the sky with such intensity that the others followed suit. This slightly comical search continued for another minute or two, until Captain Billy, who had been looking further out to sea than the others, broke the silence:

"Aw, Jasus, Mary and Joseph! What's that, then?"

Manhattan lay directly ahead of them, but Captain Billy was pointing away from it to the northeast and as the others turned to look, first one, then another, then with increasing rapidity an entire fleet of airships began to fill the sky, descending from higher altitudes to no more than a couple of thousand feet. As they drew closer their origin became all too obvious: striped in horizontal bands of white, red and blue, they were patently war craft of the Imperial Russian

112

Aerial Navy, though the design was one none of the men on the *Straight Up* had ever seen—torpedo-shaped, with stubby triangular wings and tail, ending in two gigantic air-screws, mounted side by side in graceful nacelles.

Crazy Horse was shaking his head worriedly: "I had heard that Lukas' Japanese advisors were working on radical new airship designs, but I never saw them before. What do you suppose they mean to do?"

"Sure and it's nothin' good!" said Captain Billy. "You boys best hang onto your hats—I'm about to switch from the main engines to the turbines and that means blockade-runnin' speed!"

With that he took off towards the engine compartment, and Liam turned back to Crazy Horse: "Zhenya, old pal. I appreciate your little lecture and all, but do you really mean to tell me you two big shot magicians can't do anything about that?" He pointed into the sky expectantly.

At that moment the *Straight Up* surged forward with enormous acceleration, its bow lifting into the air as its turbines kicked up a rooster tail of water ten feet high. Everyone was thrown to the deck, Chen rolling towards the railing so sharply that he had to stop himself by plunging both hands into the scuppers to keep from going over the side. A moment later he was up on his knees, laughing a bit dementedly as he scooped up big handfuls of seawater and poured them over himself:

"I certainly can't make a skyful of airships go away," he cried, "but I *can* ask the ocean to cloak us from them!" Closing his eyes and muttering feverishly in Chinese he held a cupped handful of water over his head, and then threw it so that the wind spattered the drops across the ship. An instant later the *Straight Up* vanished, leaving the sea as empty as if the vessel had never existed . . .

○━┳

In the Director's Office of the Pilkington Agency's Union Square headquarters, Stanton was deep into his negotiations with the anonymous caller, and McPherson's and Pilkington's moronic antics at the window were starting to wear mightily on his nerves.

"What are you fools playing at?" he bellowed across the room. "Stop it at once!" On top of their distracting contortions, it sounded as though the workmen had finally begun cleaning up the Square outside, and the thudding noise of their steam equipment was almost more than he could bear, a kind of awful whirring thrum like a gargantuan sewing machine. Stanton swiveled sharply around in the desk chair, turning his back on his henchmen and Union Square alike, readying himself to come down hard on the informer at the other end of the line and cut off all this shilly-shallying.

"My dear sir," Stanton said with dripping sarcasm, "I assure you I am no less punctilious than Pontius Pilate—you shall have your thirty pieces of silver in any currency you may desire, whether it be Government employment, a pardon or a mattress full of banknotes. But first you *must* tell me your name, and then where it is that the members of the Freedom Party, including the blackguard Lincoln, have their hiding place!"

There was a long silence at the other end of the wire while the wary traitor chewed on Stanton's words and the sound of steam engines outside built to an excruciating pitch. Finally Stanton could stand it no more:

"Well, dammit?" he barked into the transmitter.

There was an exasperated sigh and the voice at the other end said: "Very well, then, I am a former Captain of the U.S. Aerial . . ."

But before Stanton could hear the rest of it, there was a terrified screech from Pilkington:

114

"Oh dear God! It's the end!"

At which Stanton spun around in the swivel chair to see Pilkington groveling on the floor with a sofa pillow clutched over his head and McPherson kneeling to one side of the window and peering out from behind the curtain as the sky filled inexorably with one Little Russian airship after another.

"Lukas!" groaned Stanton. "That filthy Russian swine, I *knew* he was up to some underhanded trick!"

He leapt up from behind the desk, his phone call forgotten as he sprinted to the window for a better view. But before he even reached it, the building shook repeatedly with the sounds of thunderous explosions and a moment later Stanton saw an oddly stately progression of explosions moving west across Union Square, the giant holes in the ground appearing successively like the footprints of some angry giant until at last they walked into the almost-rebuilt Department of National Security Headquarters and flattened it like a shoebox.

"NOOOOOOO!" roared Stanton dementedly, shaking his fist at the Little Russian airships. "You devious, backstabbing sons of bitches, I will see every *one* of you hanging from St. Patrick's steeple by your bollocks!"

To which another Little Russian ship riposted by beginning a second "walk" of gigantic explosions across Union Square in the opposite direction, ending with a strike so close to the Pilkington Agency's headquarters that the room shook like a baby's rattle and Stanton threw himself to the floor with the others. After what seemed like several centuries, the appalling thunderclaps and seismic shocks of the falling bombs began moving northwards up the spine of Manhattan Island and as they receded, Stanton and his satraps stirred cautiously and sat up. The electric lights were no longer working, but the room was luridly lit by the flames of burning buildings in the Square, and one by one the three men pulled themselves to their feet and crossed to the window to inspect the damage.

115

"Well," Pilkington said in a quavery voice, "at least the gallows got cleared away—they didn't leave so much as a stick of it."

"We'll have our revenge on that Roosian sneak, bedad!" McPherson cried melodramatically. "Mark me words, yer Honor, if I have to lay me life down upon the . . ."

But Stanton was nodding and smiling to himself, not hearing a word of the Great Detective's oration: "Clearly Lukas, or Prince Yurevskii, or whatever he calls himself now maintains his own spies here in our midst, and some simpleton like you two dropped an unguarded word about our preparations for an invasion. But if he thinks he's beaten us just by blowing up a few buildings in this cesspool of a city, he'll have to think twice! We are about to *sue for peace*, gentlemen!"

If Stanton had just delivered a homily in Tibetan, Pilkington and McPherson couldn't have been more dumbstruck. As they stood staring at him with their jaws hanging open, Stanton grinned even more maliciously:

"I take my cue from the learned Sun Tzu, who says in *The Art of War* that while we must keep our friends close, we must keep our enemies even closer. I am going to offer Prince Yurevskii an alliance, a pact which will make us equal partners in peace and war!"

McPherson was shaking his head with dismay: "But sorr, he's a *Roosian*!"

"Tell me, McPherson," Stanton answered, "if you were planning to cut a man's heart out, would it be better to have him standing across the room, or by your side with your arm around him?"

An appreciative smile spread across McPherson's face: "I take yer point, sorr, and a nice *sharp* one it is!"

"Right, then," said Stanton, rubbing his hands cheerfully, "I want you two to get busy finding out how soon the electric will be up again, and how long it will take to re-establish communication with my informer. We need to be free of the

Freedom Party and McCool and all the rest of that seditious rabble, and then we need to get in touch with the illustrious Prince Yurevskii and tell him that despite this little misunderstanding we want to be the very best of friends."

Liam was standing in the pilot house next to Captain Billy, almost deafened by the scream of the steam turbines belowdecks and the constant explosion of bombs not much more than a mile away.

"That was a good call, Billy," shouted Liam, "if we'd sailed up the East River instead of the Hudson we would probably have gone up with the Manhattan Gas Light Company, you can see it burning all the way over here."

The Captain grinned and tugged at his beard self-consciously: "Billy Grogan wasn't born yesterday, Liam me lad, nor yet the day before! We'll be as far as Bloomingdale in a few minutes, and that means there's docks at 92nd Street where I can put yez ashore. I'd bet me bottom dollar the Roosians won't be bombing anywhere near that far uptown, there's nothin' up there but the Park and shanties full of freed slaves and poor Micks like us. So if ye hoof it lively like, ye can get to where our Aerial Navy has their depot in ten minutes easy."

"Thanks, Billy. And don't forget now—Becky and Gran will be calling for Mike in the next couple of days to get them off Shelter Island and into the tunnels."

"Aye," the Captain said with a somber nod, "and that'll be the best place to be for the next little while, it looks like."

Liam looked out the window at the burning city and nodded back with equal somberness, crossing his fingers for Gran and Becky and all the rest of his people. There were going to be a lot of accounts to settle before they were through and everybody he cared about would be a hostage to fortune until they were done . . .

Mike and Chen and Crazy Horse were standing in the lee of the deckhouse, raising their voices over the bedlam of sounds as they argued:

"*Chort evo voz'mi!*" Mike cursed in Russian, "You want me to believe my oldest pal in the world is some kind of witch? You two got bats in your belfry, Liam's a magician when it comes to cracking cribs, but that's *it*."

"*Misha, dorogoi moi,*" said Crazy Horse, "what did you think that was back at the fairy circle, when Liam bellowed like a bull and fell on the ground with his arms around his stomach? His grandmother *is* a witch, and a powerful one even if she's a little out of practice."

"Quite," Chen affirmed. "And when she spoke the name of McCool, the spirits of your old friend's ancestors flowed out of their world and into him."

Mike was shaking his head dubiously: "And I'm here to bet that if you try that palaver on Lev Frentsisovich you're gonna end up with a thick ear for your pains." He grinned as the door of the pilot house and Liam came out to join them: "Here he comes now, and don't say I didn't tell you."

"OK, boys," Liam shouted as he approached, "all ashore that's going ashore!"

The whine of the turbines dropped a moment later as Captain Billy slowed and turned the *Straight Up* in a gentle curve towards the docks, and a scattering of lights from the shanties of Bloomingdale's settlers. From this far uptown, the sound of the bombs was a series of muffled crumps and the burning buildings an orange glow along the horizon.

"According to Billy we shouldn't be more than ten minutes from where the Aerial Navy depot is, but we don't know what we'll run into on the way. Billy gave me the shotgun and a Peacemaker if you're interested, I've already got my sword stick and a Peacemaker Becky gave me . . ."

Both Chen and Crazy Horse shook their heads, but Mike held out his hands: "*Dai mne,*" he said, "this time of night you can never have too many guns!"

Liam handed them over and clapped Mike on the shoulder. "I don't know how long it's going to be before we can get in touch with you, but just remember—get Becky and Gran out of there as soon as you can. And make sure to get in touch with the two Dannys and the Whyos tonight, with them and the Butcher Boys pushing our plan, the rest of the gangs will fall into line fast."

Mike grinned and gave Liam a Russian embrace, kissing him on both cheeks. "Relax, *golubchik*, it's as good as done!"

A low whistle came to them from the pilot house and a moment later the *Straight Up's* fenders kissed the pilings of the dock and Liam, Chen and Crazy Horse hopped ashore and melted into the darkness.

⚊⚿

The three men moved rapidly up Eleventh Avenue, keeping a sharp eye peeled for Johnnies, bluecoats and patrolling Acmes—fortunately for Liam and his companions the middle class hadn't made it this far north yet, which meant that the streets were dark and regular patrols were few and far between.

"How far from here to the depot?" Crazy Horse whispered.

"As soon as we get to Eighth Avenue we'll head up to 97th Street and turn into the Park—there's a road there that crosses between the Reservoir and North Meadow, and once we're that far we'll just have to play it by ear. There are bound to be patrols if there's an airship depot."

The reminder was enough to keep them all silent as they trotted along the empty streets, occasionally startling

119

an owl into flight or a foraging raccoon into paroxysms of angry chattering. As they neared Eighth Avenue they finally saw the lights of the widely-separated gas lamps that served to announce Central Park's northwestern boundary and that slowed them to a fast but stealthy walk, keeping to the shadows of the trees. Then, with heart-stopping abruptness, a loud voice rang out from the Park side of Eighth Avenue:

"*Halt! Who goes there?*"

"Blast!" Liam muttered, sinking into a duck walk and signaling to the others to do likewise as he tried to get close enough to the wall to make out his adversary.

"*I SAID HALT!! STOP WHERE YOU ARE OR I'LL SHOOT!*"

The nervous voice made Liam suspect that their challenger was alone, but he couldn't take a chance, so he flattened out and rolled across the pavement till he was flush with the walls, followed closely by Chen and Crazy Horse. Picking up a piece of broken brick, he pitched it against the wall about ten feet beyond their position and waited while the concealed sentry thought about it, took the bait after a couple of moments and clambered over the wall. In an instant Liam was on him like a mountain lion, and before the man—a young bluecoat—could even grunt, he was lying on the pavement trussed up with his own belt and gagged with the sleeve of his tunic.

"OK," Liam called to the others, "the coast's clear." Unfortunately, the statement was only partly true—it was a fact that for the moment they had no other human adversaries, but the bluecoat must have been patrolling in tandem with an Acme, because at that moment the thing sprang out of the darkness behind the wall and landed in the middle of the pavement with a force that shattered the cement. This one had evidently not been provided with expensive speech machinery but it didn't need it to raise an alarm, as it was equipped with a steam whistle that would put a locomotive to shame and it let loose with a nerve-shattering *HOOOOOOT!* which it followed

120

with a salvo from its Gatling arm that narrowly missed Liam as he somersaulted towards the automaton, unsheathing his sword from its cane-scabbard as he rolled.

The blade was a beautiful old katana that Harry the Jap had turned into a sword cane as a present for Liam, and Liam had cut all sorts of objects with it including a human or two, but never an Acme. Still, there wasn't a lot of choice just now so Liam came out of his somersault into sword-fighting stance with the katana held firmly in a two-handed grip, and as the Acme swiveled towards Liam, lowering the Gatling arm to point at him, Liam sprang into the air and swept the blade downwards with all his might, severing the arm at the shoulder so that it fell to the pavement with a crash. Then, the moment his feet touched the ground, Liam whirled around in one unbroken movement and swept the blade towards the mid-section of the huge automaton, mentally crossing his fingers that he wouldn't end by snapping the blade off at the hilt.

Astonishingly—to Liam, anyway—the blade sliced through the Acme's midsection as if the steel colossus were a tender sapling. For a split second the two halves maintained an illusion of being still one piece, but then, slowly, the top half leaned to one side and crashed down to the pavement, hissing huge gouts of steam from its damaged boiler. Liam had seen something like this before, and he shouted to his two companions:

"Get down! It's going to blow!!"

And sure enough, just as all three men succeeded in flattening themselves on the pavement, the thing blew up with a horrendous *BLAM!*, showering bits and pieces of its innards in every direction. For a moment, the survivors lay there, experiencing an almost overwhelming urge to stay stretched out and rest for a bit, but this fantasy was rudely interrupted by a familiar sound from not too far south of where they lay:

To the unaccustomed ear, it would have been alarming enough: a weird galloping sound coming up Eighth Avenue towards them: *THUMP thump, THUMP thump, THUMP thump*, accompanied by a stentorian, twanging bellow: "*HAHN*, hoo hree, *HAHN*, hoo hree, *HAHN* hoo hree horr hahn hoo hree . . . *HAHR LAYOO!*"

Unfortunately, Liam's ears and the ears of his friends were only too accustomed to the sound and Liam sprang to his feet:

"Time to sling our hooks, boys, it's the Johnnies!"

No more encouragement was needed—the three of them took off like gazelles towards the Transverse Road that cut the Park between the Reservoir and the North Meadow, making the turn just as the first shots began to whistle over their heads. For a moment they ran in silence until Liam saw the airship depot in the distance and beckoned to the others to follow, but Chen shook his head emphatically:

"Forget the airships!"

This was too much for Liam: "What the blazes d'you mean, Chen, are you going to fly us there by flapping your arms?"

In answer, Chen simply grabbed Liam by the arm and pulled him over the low wall into the grassy area around the reservoir.

"Are you crazy?" yelled Liam furiously. "The Johnnies are going to shoot us full of holes!"

But Chen ignored him, kneeling on the turf and rubbing handfuls of soil between his fingers:

"There's a ley line here," he said to Crazy Horse, "and I'm almost certain it's the same one that brought you to Shelter Island from Santa Monica. If we can get McCool to open it up for us we should come out more or less where you started."

"Is there a vortex to draw us in?"

"Mmm hm," Chen muttered. "Right over there where that boulder is."

Liam was listening to them with growing impatience as the sound of the running Johnnies drew nearer. Finally he shouted at Chen: "You listen to me, you medicine-show high-binder, and this is a *promise*! When the Johnnies are through shooting us into Swiss cheese and we finally get to Hell, I am going to pound you to a *pudding*—the Devil's just going to have to wait till I'm through with you!"

"Do shut up," snapped Chen, and grabbing Liam by the collar he half-dragged him to the boulder he had pointed out a moment ago. By now the Johnnies' bullets were starting to fly, and Chen pointed firmly at the boulder:

"Do as I say, or by heaven I will turn you into a *warthog*! Strike that boulder with your sword! Do it *NOW!*"

Liam rolled his eyes. "Sure, why not?" he yelled back furiously. "You want me to kick it, I can do that too! Look out, rock, here it comes!" And, raising his arms in the profound conviction that he was already a dead man, he swung the sword down with all his might just as the Johnnies came pouring over the wall firing their shiny chromed guns and yelling insanely.

In the fraction of a second that it took for Liam's sword to travel through the air it struck him vividly that he would miss all of it, bad parts and good parts alike, but the instant the blade struck the boulder the surrounding earth glowed with unbearable brilliance, swirled like a whirlpool of fiery lava, and in the blink of an eye swallowed up the three companions and winked out again like a blown candle as the Johnnies dropped to their knees in front of the boulder, babbling and weeping hysterically, begging forgiveness for their sins, terrified that it was the Devil who had snatched the seditionists and would be coming after them any minute. Was the boulder about to melt again and suck them down into the fires of Hell?

Listening somewhere, the Devil smiled at the thought that he would ever need to go out of his way to gather fresh sinners. As for the boulder, it just sat there mute and massive as it had for aeons, guarding its gateway to the ley lines . . .

Bear Flag Republic, El Pueblo de
Nuestra Señora de Los Angeles/
Edison City, and Santa Monica
October 31, 1877

Chapter Twelve

ust north of the Santa Monica Pier and a few blocks west of the ley line vortex where Crazy Horse had begun his journey (ley lines, after all, being magical and nothing if not unpredictable), the main plunge at the North Beach Bath house was jammed with bathers, children and grownups alike happily taking advantage of the twenty-five cent admission to dunk their bodies in cold water on a day when the mid-afternoon temperatures had soared into the nineties. The sideline gallery was equally packed with fully-dressed Santa Monica and Edison City folk: watchful mothers, timid spectators considering a plunge and die-hard sex fiends who would have paid a lot more than a quarter for the chance of seeing a naked ankle peeping out from under the dark woolen skirts of a lady's bathing costume.

In fact, by early evening the attendants were already wondering if they ought to tell the Boss to stop selling tickets until some of the bathers went home, especially as the kids had started a splashing game that was soaking the spectators in the gallery and building a level of happy hysteria that might get out of hand any minute if something untoward happened. Like, for instance, an Indian in a monkey suit, a curly-haired Mick and a long, skinny Chinaman suddenly materializing in mid-air ten feet over the most boisterous scrum in the splashing game, hanging there with stunned expressions for what seemed like a half hour but was maybe three long seconds, and then dropping into the water with a cannonball splash accompanied by more screams than anybody had heard since the Chinatown War.

"*Help!*" yelled Ambrose Chen, thrashing around frantically.

"What the blazes do you mean, '*help!*'" Liam snapped irritably as he tried to fend off a screaming nine-year-old. "Swim down to the end and climb out, we have to get out of here before the coppers come!"

"I CAN'T *SWIM*, IDIOT!" bellowed Chen, who was flailing his arms like a pelican caught in a net.

"Big fancy-Dan sorcerer," muttered Liam, grabbing Chen under the arms and dragging him away through the water towards the end of the pool.

Crazy Horse, meanwhile, had been trying to free himself from a hysterical, blimp-shaped bather who had seized hold of his braid with fanatical determination and was tugging on it as if he meant to pull it loose.

"Let go hair, *svoloch!*" Crazy Horse yelled in broken English, giving up at last as he saw Liam and Chen drawing away and punching his captor sharply in the nose.

"*Zhdite menia!*" he yelled to Liam and Chen and took off after them like an otter.

The enormous, vaulted ceiling amplified the bedlam in the baths to a point that made talking a waste of time, so as Crazy Horse pulled himself out of the pool, Liam just pointed towards a sign that said "Gentlemen's Dressing Rooms" and beckoned to the others to follow as he took off at a trot.

"Find something that fits and change fast," Liam said as they closed the door after them, "any bluecoat that sees us the way we look now is going to collar us first and talk later."

Keeping an ear cocked for the sound of police whistles, the trio rummaged through every open locker until they had managed to dress themselves more or less presentably—Chen

128

with his wrists and ankles sticking out of a yellow plaid suit, Crazy Horse swathed in a cowboy's long canvas duster, and Liam spiffy but uneasy in the summer dress uniform of a Navy Commander.

"Well, boys," Liam said with a grin, "I don't expect we'd be welcome at the Opera, but I don't reckon we'll get arrested on the beach either. Come on, let's hook it!"

Jumping up onto a bench under the room's only window, Liam pushed at the wire-mesh screen until the frame came loose and fell out onto the sand. It was twilight, the sky a dark violet overhead and rimmed with orange along the horizon where it met the ocean, and the mob of terrified bathers and spectators was pouring out of the opposite side of the building. Liam beckoned to Chen and Crazy Horse:

"Looks like the coast's clear over here, let's go!"

Suiting the action to the words, he pulled himself up and out, dropping to the sand in a crouch and peering around warily as he fingered the handle of his sword stick and his companions dropped to the sand behind him. There were plenty of people walking on the sand and on a beachfront sidewalk that ran north and south as far as Liam could see, but no sign of the police or of anybody else who seemed the least bit interested in their presence. Liam stood up with a sigh of relief, and then wobbled as a wave of vertigo hit him and reached out to steady himself against the bathhouse wall:

"Whoa!" he muttered. "I'm feeling weak as a kitten!"

"You just did a major feat of magic," Chen said in his most professorial manner. "Whatever religious enthusiasts may claim, magic is *part* of the natural world, not something apart from it, so your weakness is explained simply and elegantly by Newton's Third Law: 'To every action there is always opposed an equal reaction.'"

Liam glared at Chen and Crazy Horse, who were watching him with the eager attentiveness of proud parents witnessing baby's first steps. It was *true*, dammit! It must have been from hitting the rock with his sword, and that meant that all that folderol of Gran's was real and he was *stuck* with this. Whatever "this" was!

Liam shook himself like a wet dog, and then gave his companions a smile of bland innocence:

"Well, I don't know about you fellows," he said, "but I could do with a feed and a night's rest in a decent hotel."

And, without waiting for comment, he turned and set off across the sand. Crazy Horse and Chen gave each other a look and then hurried after Liam.

"You'd better think twice about the hotel," Crazy Horse said in Russian as he caught up. "People in Edison City and Santa Monica aren't too friendly towards anybody that isn't white."

"Neither are most Americans," Chen said, "but I *had* heard that the Bear Flag Republic was supposed to be the sort of wide-open place where they welcomed thieves and smugglers and every other species of lowlife with open arms—surely they have a place for the likes of us."

"The Bear Flag Republic is a sovereign state," said Crazy Horse, "but only because Little Russia tolerates its independence the way Spain and France tolerate Andorra—for the simple reason that you can buy anything from anywhere here if you have the right price, which can be quite useful. However, real behind-the-scenes local power remains in the hands of the old white families who booted the Spaniards out when this was still called California." He spread his hands with a wry smile: "And the good hotels still seem to prefer *white* low-lifes to colored low-lifes."

Chen grunted. "In any event, I'd just as soon stop at a department store first. No doubt large yellow checks are fashionable suiting in Edison City, but I'd rather find something a bit more . . ." he raised an eyebrow.

"Right," Liam teased, "what would they say back at New College?"

Crazy Horse looked intrigued. "You were at Oxford?"

"I read Greats at New College," Chen said with a touch of well-bred smugness.

"I was at the Imperial University in Petersburg," Crazy Horse said, "I used to come over to Oxford every May for Eights Week!"

"Well, I was at Columbia University once," laughed Liam. "Matter of fact, I cracked the Provost's crib while he was up in Saratoga playing the nags and pinched his diamond stickpin and a first edition of *Great Expectations*." He winked at the others: "Let's get a move on, boys. We can talk about school days at *dinner*."

Towering over the beach as far as the eye could see in either direction were palisades at least 100 feet high, and now that night was falling an aurora borealis of multicolored light was streaming into the sky from the city beyond. Liam shook his head wonderingly as they walked, thinking that the light was brighter than anything he'd ever seen in New York, even in the parts that Tesla had wired for electricity. He turned to Crazy Horse and pointed up towards the cliffs:

"You were here before, Zhenya, is it always lit up like a Christmas tree?"

Crazy Horse nodded: "P. T. Barnum came out to Los Angeles a few years ago with his traveling circus and he had Thomas Edison appearing as 'The Wizard of Menlo Park,' showing off his talking machine and light bulbs and all his other tricks. People out here had never seen anything like 'The Greatest Show on Earth,' and Barnum was already dreaming of sugar plums when a *pistolero* named Tiburcio Vasquez showed up and told him he couldn't set up his tent unless he paid $10,000 in gold for a 'license.'"

Liam grinned appreciatively: "I bet Phineas T. was thrilled to hear that one after sailing around Cape Horn with a bunch of seasick elephants."

"Actually, the way I heard the story, it was a for-real Mexican standoff till Edison finally managed to electrocute

131

Vasquez in his bath. Maybe true, maybe not, but one thing's for sure: Edison City barely had gas-lights when it was still what the old-timers called '*Los Anga-leece*,' but nowadays Barnum is Governor of the Bear Flag Republic, Edison was elected Mayor of L.A., and everything in the city runs on electricity. They don't even bother with steam power, except for the generators that make the electricity."

Liam looked intrigued. "You mean to tell me they don't have Acmes out here?"

"Not a one," Crazy Horse answered with a laugh. "The old families that ran Los Angeles and Santa Monica turned their noses up at everything modern from Back East: too dirty and noisy. But when Edison started boosting electricity over coal all the ordinary folks went for it in a big way because it was clean and quiet, and they ended up voting to re-name the town Edison City. Still—the handful of old white families that call the town *Los Anga-leece* are the people who really call the tune out here, and that's probably why Barnum put the government headquarters right here in Santa Monica. Even though Edison City runs right up to the Santa Monica city limits on every side but the ocean, Santa Monica always had its own government and its own police force, and that gives Barnum a little bit of an edge on the 'Old Los Anga-leece' boys."

Not far ahead of them, the Santa Monica Pier jutted out into the Bay, its brilliantly lit deck fitted out like a circus midway with rides and sideshow attractions and swarming with merrymakers. Liam stopped walking for a moment to enjoy the sight and listen to the cheerful piping of a merry-go-round's calliope before he nudged Chen with his elbow:

"Look at that, will you? That beats Coney Island all hollow, and it's all thanks to Edison's electricity. Now *that's* magic for you!"

Chen gave Liam a long-suffering look. "Mr. Edison is a brilliant engineer," he said, "with a genius for taking bits of mechanical rubbish and turning them into machines that let *everyone* do things that seem magical, like lighting a room or recording their voices. But like it or not, a talent for magic is something quite different—an inborn power that works on the natural world in a way quite unlike Edison's. No one without that natural gift can do magic no matter how many spells they recite. But if you do have it, the only real question is: how *much* power do you have? And what are its limits?"

Liam growled something under his breath, thinking that all that talk about power was a laugh. Instead of making him feel powerful, magic made him feel vulnerable, like he was a little kid again and had to keep asking the grownups what the rules were. He wasn't some dumb greenhorn, he was the King of the Cracksmen, a veteran of the Battle of Gettysburg *and* the New York Tombs, and by God there were no flies on him!

With an eloquent snort, Liam turned and started up the long flight of wooden stairs that climbed to the pier from the beach, stomping on the boards with unnecessary vehemence.

Crazy Horse and Chen followed, Crazy Horse chuckling as he watched his friend's petulant display. "Don't be so silly, Lyovushka," he said to Liam's back. "You're just upset because your sword strike opened the gate to the ley lines and you don't understand it. It's really very simple, your family has a heritage of magic and your grandmother's fairy circle sparked it to life. It's in your blood. You might as well get cross about your hair being curly!"

Liam stopped as they reached a platform half-way to the top, spreading his hands with a look of total exasperation: "Dammit, Zhenya, I'm the King of the Silk-Stocking Cracksmen—the best burglar since Little Adam, and *he* said so himself. On top of that, I'm co-chairman of the most successful gang in New York City and a crack shot and the best jiu-jitsu fighter in New York after Harry the Jap. I don't *need* to be a sorcerer, any more than I need to have an udder like a cow!"

Crazy Horse laughed. "And I'm a Sioux war chief and Ambrose is an Oxford classics scholar, but none of us can change our basic natures any more than we can change the color of our skin. Relax! Learn to enjoy it!"

Chen took up the thread, speaking more gently than he had before. "Magic is nothing more nor less than the energy of the universe, McCool. You may call it God instead, if you like, or the Great Spirit, or gravity or electricity—it really doesn't matter. Humans connect with that energy in different ways, and you won't have any idea of the nature or the limits of your abilities for a long time."

"How am I supposed to know what I can *do* with them?" muttered Liam with genuine anguish.

"You'll know it when you do it," laughed Crazy Horse. "Come on, let's go buy new clothes and get some dinner!"

Liam answered with a noncommittal grunt and resumed his climb, speeding up as he neared the top and the lights and the music and the sound of people having fun (not to mention his curiosity) grew more intense with every step. But nothing he heard could have prepared him for the wonderland at the top of the stairs . . .

The first shock was the sheer explosion of light, from batteries of enormous carbon-arc searchlights sweeping back and forth across the night sky to what seemed like a Milky Way of tiny, brilliant light bulbs strung in ropes and garlands on stanchions above the pier and around the front of every establishment and dangling from every possible framework that could hold a few more lights.

And a moment later, the impact of the sounds: music blaring from every side; polka bands, strolling accordion players, a Mexican trumpet and guitar band in mirror-decked costumes, a cigar-chomping black man banging away at ragtime tunes on a baby grand with rubber wheels pulled by a team of donkeys in top hats and dark glasses, an impossibly-contorted India-rubber man playing hymns on a kazoo clutched between his toes . . .

. . . and the *languages*—Liam had an ear for them and had learned Russian and French and German on the streets of New York, but he was hearing sounds now that were so unfamiliar they might as well have been from some other planet. Human languages nonetheless, being spoken energetically by a crowd more varied than any he had ever seen in one place before: impossibly tall Africans swathed in brilliantly colored wraps, bearded Asians in what looked like white nightshirts with hats made of swirls of white bed sheet, their womenfolk walking behind them in black draperies that covered everything but a slit for their eyes, a troop of surly-looking black pygmies in American children's clothes, gnawing hungrily at deliciously brown whole roasted chickens . . .

. . . and oh, *yes*, the *smells* of food: more kinds of food than Liam had ever seen at any street fair in Five Points: Italian sausages and onions sizzling on a grill, barbecued beef and lamb, hot knishes and cold ice cream, roasted peanuts, an unrecognizable animal being turned on a spit, wreaths of bread, mysterious Chinese concoctions being stirred furiously over a fire in concave steel pans . . .

. . . which were finally the straw that broke Ambrose's resolve, pulling him irresistibly towards the booth as Liam and Crazy Horse followed hungrily. The proprietor grinned and flipped his pan's contents into the air, catching them on the fly as Ambrose patted his suit absentmindedly for money.

"I thought you said you weren't eating till you got out of those yellow checks," Liam jibed.

Chen growled inarticulately and Crazy Horse chimed in: "Careful, Lyovushka, if you push him too hard he may strip off right here."

"Insufferable yahoos!" Chen snapped, turning on his heel and striding away through the teeming crowd towards the shore end of the pier as Liam and Crazy Horse followed, laughing.

Ahead of them, beyond an ornamental-iron arch festooned with still more lights, rose an assortment of tidy brick buildings, themselves illuminated by arched street lamps and signs bordered by colored lights wired to create the illusion of an endless rainbow stream. Ambrose and Liam slowed down as they took in this implausibly neat, clean and glowing urban panorama, gawking like a couple of rubes as they took it all in. Crazy Horse, who had seen it before, took off northwards on a street which a signpost declared to be Ocean Avenue, gesturing to the others to follow.

"Come on, fellows," he called, "let's get out of our borrowed finery and into something presentable."

⚷

Here on the primly clean and quiet streets of Santa Monica, the character of the crowd changed sharply from the hurly-burly of the merrymakers on the pier. Now, the pedestrians seemed to be almost exclusively white, with a sprinkling of light-brown Latins, all of them respectably attired in suits or dresses, all of them speaking quietly, their rare gestures well within the bounds of Anglo-Saxon seemliness, their laughter polite and hushed enough to be acceptable in church.

Liam looked around uneasily and turned to Crazy Horse: "Did somebody die?"

Crazy Horse laughed: "Santa Monica is the stronghold of the old California aristocracy and that's them out for their evening promenade, showing the foreign scum how to behave like white men."

"What do you know?" muttered Liam as they turned the corner onto Santa Monica Boulevard, which stretched straight and glittering into the remote distance. On a corner a couple of streets away stood a four-story brick building topped by a sign whose colored light bulb lettering proclaimed it to be "Henshey's."

"There it is," Crazy Horse said with a chuckle, "the best department store in town, and they have readymade suits almost good enough to let us pass for civilized folk."

But before the others could comment, a loud, commanding voice thundered behind them:

"YOU THREE! HALT!"

Liam and his companions froze where they stood, their hearts sinking.

"HANDS UP! DON'T MOVE!"

"What the hell?" Liam murmured in Russian.

"Don't say anything," Crazy Horse murmured back, "just let them do the talking."

An odd, high-pitched whine approached from behind them and a moment later a small, electric-powered vehicle, lacquered in white and blue and bearing the shield of the Santa Monica Police Department, circled around them and came to a stop as two officers in sparkling white uniforms stepped out and approached them cautiously. One of them was holding a long scroll of paper, looking back and forth from it to the three strangers with their hands up.

"By God, Horace," said the one with the paper excitedly, "it's them, the ones in the bulletin."

"Sure enough, Jimmy," said the other policeman, approaching Liam with a sardonic grin. "We really ought to thank you boys, you've made our fortunes—the Commissioner's office just got a telegram from Stanton's HQ in New York telling us to be on the lookout for two fugitives from justice, a tall, skinny Chinaman and a curly-haired Mick with a beat-up mug. Looks like you birds fill the bill to a T." He turned to Crazy Horse with mock politeness: "And if you don't mind, I think we might as well arrest you too, I expect we'll get a bulletin on you before long."

Chen was grinding his teeth with pent-up frustration. "Now see here, my man," he began, but before he could go any further, the one named Horace pulled a Colt Peacemaker out of his holster and shoved the muzzle against the side of Chen's head with a jarring *thunk!*

"Uh, uh, Chink, *you* see *here!* We just plain don't *like* your kind in Los Anga-leece, and I haven't shot me a Chinaman since the riots. So unless you want to spring a couple of leaks before we haul you in, you'd better shut your yap *now.* Savvy?"

He turned to the other officer: "Jimmy, why don't you use the voicewire in Henshey's and tell the Chief we've got guests. And if Secretary Stanton don't want 'em back, why, maybe we can have a necktie party for them right here in Palisades Park!"

In the Air
October 31, 1877

Chapter Thirteen

he room Ada Lovelace had chosen for them was on the second floor, and as airy and spacious as any Becky had ever slept in. With its tall, multi-paned windows facing west across Little Peconic Bay, she and Liam could let the sun be their alarm clock, celebrating the dawn with happy lovemaking and then dozing off again as the sun rose behind the house and moved steadily across the sky until it was shining directly into the room and cooking their bare legs till it woke them for good.

But today she really wanted to drowse on for a bit. Her eyes were heavy, and her thoughts were sluggish with the winy languor that goes with dining too well the night before . . . *the night before?* Before what? She could feel the sunlight heating the skin of her face until it began to feel uncomfortable, but when she tried to open her eyes, tried really *hard*, she could barely make the lids twitch. In fact, it felt like something was pressing against them, preventing the lids from raising altogether.

Becky groaned. *Liam!* Where was Liam? She groaned again, then tried to open her mouth to call for him and discovered that she couldn't speak—some kind of awful, sodden rag was pulled back between her teeth, preventing her from moving her tongue freely or bringing her teeth together. What in God's name was going on?

She tried to speak again, her thoughts struggling desperately to shake off their deep-sea heaviness and push their way to the surface. She groaned again, louder, until the only thing that was keeping back a full-throated scream was the horrid gag in her mouth . . .

"Aha!" said a cheery, familiar voice from somewhere in the darkness beyond her blindfold. "There she is, awake at last! Here, let's get that blindfold off . . ."

And a moment later she felt fingers at the back of her head, untying the blindfold and pulling it away . . . *Dear God!* A bank of powerful electric lights almost directly overhead was pouring its illumination down on her and its impact after the darkness of her blindfold was like having a spike driven through her skull!

She jammed her eyes shut again to gain a moment's respite, then opened them warily to a narrow slit, letting memory flood back along with the glaring light. She should have guessed from the muted but constant vibration and the sonorous hum of the engines under her feet that she was aboard the battleship Delta where—just minutes after Liam and the others had left with Captain Billy—Capt. Ubaldo had lured her with the cruelest imaginable lie . . .

"*I was just doing an instrument check in the battleship Delta when a message came in for you on the Tesla Vex . . . I'm* terribly *sorry to break it to you this way, but I was told that the Secret Service has arrested your father!*"

How *could* he have said such a thing? She had regarded Ubaldo as a friend ever since he had piloted the flyer that took her and Liam to Little Russia. She had *told* him more than once what a razor's edge Papa had to walk between Willie Pilkington's Secret Service and the group of fellow New York jurists with whom he risked everything by reminding the Stanton government of its duty to the rule of law. There wasn't a day

144

when she didn't half expect to receive a real message just like the false one that Ubaldo had given her. It was hard to imagine what had been in that treacherous pig's mind when he did it, but she promised herself that he would be *very* sorry he had. She opened her eyes, ready now for anything.

There was Capt. Ubaldo in the flesh, dressed to the nines in his sky-blue Aerial Navy uniform, smiling solicitously, his familiar trim little moustache and neatly brushed black hair suddenly hateful to Becky's eyes.

"*Dear* Becky," he murmured with obvious sincerity, "I do hope you're feeling better now."

Becky groaned and tried to grind her teeth despite the gag that kept them apart. *Better?* Better than she had been before her captor stifled her with chloroform and trussed her up like a Thanksgiving turkey? What in the name of all that's holy was this fool *talking* about?

Ubaldo answered her groans with a jocular little chuckle: "I know, dearest, the gag is uncomfortable and irksome, but believe me you'll be grateful in the long run that I kept you from saying something you'd regret before I had a chance to share my thoughts about our future together."

Becky closed her eyes so he couldn't see her rolling them. Had he actually lost his mind? It occurred to her with sudden vividness that she had better tread carefully.

"My darling," she heard him say, "I know your expressions so well, believe me it's easy to tell that you're getting impatient with me. But do hang on for just a little bit longer, and I'm sure you'll be glad you did."

She opened her eyes again, keeping her expression carefully neutral.

"There," he said eagerly, "that's better!"

There was a muted chime from the control panel behind him and Ubaldo moved briskly to see what it was about.

"Hah!" he exclaimed, rubbing his hands cheerfully. "Almost there! Before long we'll be close enough to New

145

Petersburg that we can expect to run up against pickets of the Little Russian Aerial Navy. Then, my dear, you will see just what metal your suitor Arturo Ubaldo is made of!"

Becky uttered a strangled gasp, her eyebrows shooting upwards with incredulous emphasis as Ubaldo turned, drawing himself up with military dignity: "That is the lesson I learned from my forebears, dear Becky, the legacy of Rome's imperial glory: man is a creature perpetually at war, and only those who meet the challenge bravely can achieve true nobility!"

Becky stifled an urge to laugh as an unwelcome touch of hysteria crept into her thoughts, no doubt thanks to the unfamiliar sensation of complete helplessness in the face of danger. What made this wretched loony think that the Regent of Little Russia, Prince Yurevskii, who had actually *designed* many of the battleship Delta's improvements in the days when he had been an advisor to Secretary Stanton under the pseudonym Dr. Lukas, wouldn't simply order his aerial gunners to blow the ship out of the sky the moment it was spotted? She hoped very much that she and Ubaldo would both end up in the same part of Hell so that she could pitchfork him till he squealed bloody murder.

Capt. Ubaldo stroked his little moustache with a look of intolerable self-satisfaction.

"Since I know how clever you are, my dear, I know you must be wondering how I expect to escape the cordon of aerial defenses which Prince Yurevskii has erected around his capital." He grinned.

"The answer is simplicity itself—Before we left I simply spoke with the Prince on this vessel's voicewire and requested a *laissez-passer* and a senior command position in Little Russia's Aerial Navy in return for the return of the battleship Delta in whose theft McCool had forced you to be an accessory."

Unable to restrain herself, Becky growled deep in her throat, struggling against her bonds like a chained mastiff.

Ubaldo, however, was so deep into his internal drama that he didn't notice her at all; instead, his face darkening with resentment, he continued his monologue:

"Damn Stanton and his infernal arrogance! I had actually begun to speak to him on the voicewire, ready to offer him McCool *and* the Freedom Party, tied up in a neat little bow and ready for collection, when he had the gall to hang up on me! So what if the Little Russian Aerial Navy *had* just begun a surprise attack on the City? It was unforgivably rude!"

Becky turned pale as parchment: *what* attack on the City? This time, fortunately, Ubaldo noticed:

"Forgive me, darling," he added hastily, "of course you couldn't have known, you were already resting, here on the ship. Fortunately Yurevskii's pilots dropped their bombs exclusively in the poorer areas of the city, along the waterfront—clearly he meant the attack primarily as a warning of what he could do if Stanton didn't sue for peace. I'm sure your father is quite well."

Becky closed her eyes, dizzy with relief and equally dizzy with the urge to do immediate harm to Ubaldo.

Oblivious to everything but his personal saga, Ubaldo continued excitedly: "What a man is Prince Yurevskii, what a genius! I tell you, Becky darling, life as I understand it means duty, conquest, the surmounting of all obstacles, and here is the very man in whose service I can achieve these things—not just for myself, but for you, for *us*!"

He held out his arms in a gesture of entreaty: "For together, darling, once we are married, we shall have everything a man and a woman could dream of: love, children, a chance for you to *fulfill* yourself as a woman and I as a man."

He knelt down beside her, his voice quivering with emotion: "You shall manage our domestic world, cooking and cleaning and entertaining our friends, caring for the children when they get sick, getting them ready for school and church when they're well. During the winter you shall make cakes and

147

pies for the church socials and check the children's lessons, and since I know how clever you are I know how careful you will be not to offend my opinions or those of our neighbors, to be prudent in all your conduct so that I may be easy about you in my mind."

"And I, in turn, promise I shall always be kind to you, I shall never swear in your presence, and I shall always be sure to clean my boots when I enter the house and be true to my marital vows!"

Fortunately for Becky's sanity, at that moment a klaxon went off with a shockingly harsh screech and Ubaldo leapt to his feet and ran to the enormous view port that ran above the Delta's control panels. There in the distance, illuminated by the Delta's brilliant carbon-arc spotlights, they could see a flight of Little Russian attack flyers approaching with the inexorable swiftness of a swarm of wasps and Ubaldo began waving his arms back and forth above his head to make sure they would see him. Slamming a knob that stopped the klaxon in mid-screech, Ubaldo turned back towards Becky, his arms spread exuberantly, his face wreathed in smiles:

"At last, my beloved Becky! At *last* our new life begins!"

Santa Monica
October 31, 1877

Chapter Fourteen

he little tableau on the lower end of Santa Monica Boulevard was starting to acquire spectators; so far, just a fussy old lady walking her dog and asking questions that nobody paid any attention to, but Liam was afraid that if too many more bystanders showed up the copper would feel compelled to show everybody what a big man he was and he was already getting much too big a kick out of Chen's distress at having a loaded pistol pressed against his head:

"What do you think, Jimmy," the copper chortled, tapping Chen's head playfully with the .45's muzzle like a cat batting a captive mouse, "should I just save everybody a lot of fuss and feathers and blow this Chinaman's head off now?"

The officer named Jimmy looked around worriedly: "Come on, Horace, first thing you know we'll have a crowd of rubbernecks getting underfoot. Let's just take 'em to the station and hand 'em over to the Chief."

Horace leaned closer to Chen and sneered at him as Chen glared back coldly. "Too bad you weren't here for the riots, Chinaman! We went from one end of Nigger Alley to the other till we had eighteen of you ginks hanging from the lamp posts. 'Course, that was back in the days when the city was run by white men instead of carny barkers and flim-flam artists!"

Just as Liam was about to gamble on a jiu jitsu foot sweep to knock Horace away from Chen, the old lady's dog snapped at Jimmy's pants leg and the copper made the mistake of trying to shoo him away:

"Scram, you!" he hissed, taking a swipe at the dog with his uniform cap. Immediately the dog—a big mutt with a torn ear—bared its teeth and growled. The threatening sound seemed to spook Horace, who looked alarmed and cocked the Colt, the snick-*clack!* of its hammer sending a sudden chill down Liam's spine.

Liam glared helplessly at the pistol, his anger and frustration focusing on it with no specific intent, but enough intensity to melt steel. Despite his brave words to Crazy Horse, he knew he would always have to bite his tongue whenever he ran into some dumb copper that thought a badge and a six-gun made him God. Ever since he'd been a little nipper running around the sidewalks of Five Points he'd had to kowtow to these morons and by jingo it was enough to give a *rhinoceros* the pip! Liam felt a shooting pain behind his eyes and in spite of himself he pictured Horace's Colt turning to molten metal in his hand. *MELT!* he thought as the pain in his head tightened, *MELT, YOU PIECE OF SHITE!*

Which, a moment later, was precisely what happened: to Liam's total stupefaction the pistol abruptly softened and ran over the copper's hand like candle wax overflowing a sconce:

"*EEEAAARRGGGHHH!*"

With a bellow of agony, Horace threw the distorted glob of metal to the sidewalk and shook his hand frantically, frightening the dog into attacking Jimmy's leg again, this time with more success. As the frightened mutt lunged free of his mistress and sank his teeth into the copper's leg, Crazy Horse simultaneously reached out and dug his fingers into Jimmy's shoulder, speaking softly and rapidly in Sioux.

"HELP!" screamed the terrified copper, trying simultaneously to shake the dog free from his leg and the Indian free

154

from his shoulder, but before he could succeed with either, his eyes suddenly widened with shock and he pulled sharply away from Crazy Horse, turning towards Horace and reaching out with an expression of stunned entreaty:

"*Rrrrrrr . . .!*" he whined. Horace's jaw dropped as he watched Jimmy's face changing, bristling with fur, his nose and jaw lengthening into a snout. The old lady and Horace both emitted screams of panic as Jimmy reached out with both paws and tried to grab his partner's arm. Unfortunately for Horace, as he tried to push Jimmy away the contact seemed to transmit some strange force that caused the second lawman to begin his own transformation, progressing in seconds from a bulbous, jowly beagle head to big, clumsy paws, one of which seemed to be badly burned. Horace sank to the ground with a defeated groan, turned his muzzle up towards the sky and howled mournfully:

"*AROOOOOOOOOOOO!*"

"*Sweet Jesus and Mary and all the Saints preserve us!*" screamed the old lady, spinning on her heel and taking off up Santa Monica Boulevard at a clip that was almost too much for her dog, which was barely able to keep up behind her, trailing its leash and barking frantically.

For a moment or two Liam and Chen and Crazy Horse stood and surveyed their totally confounded and demoralized enemies with deep, ungenerous pleasure. Then Liam forced himself to shake the moment off:

"OK, boys," he said, "we don't want to be around when the reporters start getting here. Let's buzz along to Henshey's and get ourselves some new duds."

"Right," sighed Chen.

"*Absoliutno!*" said Crazy Horse in Russian.

Without any further ado the three companions set off briskly towards the department store, Horace's howls echoing mournfully behind them and Jimmy's frenzied yelping serving as an obbligato.

Half an hour later the trio emerged from Henshey's and stopped for a moment in front of the window display to tug at their jackets and straighten their neckties, surveying themselves with obvious satisfaction. All three had chosen conservatively styled lightweight suits in dark fabrics, with matching vests and white linens; all three were sporting smart new fedora hats.

"That's more like it," Liam said with a touch of smugness.

"I wonder if I should have tried the bowler instead," Chen muttered, tugging at the fedora's brim in a vain attempt to make it look more conservative.

Crazy Horse, who would have been happier in deer-skins, watched them for a moment with a derisive grin and then punched Liam on the shoulder:

"Come on, ladies," he said in Russian, "you can play with your new bonnets after we get some dinner."

As they set off down the street towards the hotels along the ocean front, Liam pointed to the crowd that had gathered around the scene of their recent adventure. Several more of the tidy little white-and-blue police vehicles had pulled up, accompanied by an ambulance and a vehicle with wire-mesh windows that said "Santa Monica Pound" on the side in large gold letters.

"Looks like quite a party," Liam said. "You think they're taking Horace and Jimmy to the Pound?"

As if in answer, a chorus of furious barking arose from the middle of the gathering, which widened abruptly as the spectators backed away from something, chattering excitedly.

Unable to resist the temptation, Liam and his companions hurried down the street to join the other gawkers.

"Why such much barking?" Crazy Horse asked a bystander in his distinctive English.

A tall, rustic-looking type with a prominent Adam's apple, the man shook his head and gave Crazy Horse a slightly queasy look.

"Cain't say as I hold much with sideshows," he said, "them coppers got what looks like a couple geeks escaped from Barnum's Circus. Or leastways a couple great big dogs dressed like coppers, hard to say which." He shook his head and spat on the ground disgustedly:

"I'll tell you this," he said with sudden heat, poking Crazy Horse's shoulder for emphasis, "P. T. should oughter quit that Circus stuff now he's governor of the Republic, it ain't dignified!"

"Good thought," said Liam with a judicious nod. Turning to the others he added: "Maybe we'd better be thinking about business too."

Tipping his fedora to the rustic Liam resumed his stroll towards Ocean Avenue, flanked by Chen and Crazy Horse.

"How do you want to do this tomorrow?" he asked. "We need to locate Ambrose's family and we need to figure out how to get Custer out of Serra Castle. And we should decide how to deal with this bulletin Stanton's office sent to the police. Do you want to split up? Or do we stick together?"

The three of them walked in silence, thinking it over as they approached the corner of Santa Monica Boulevard and Ocean Avenue.

Chen spoke first: "It might be best if we take separate paths to begin with. Crazy Horse and I need to start looking for my family in Chinatown, and people there are far less likely to talk if we have a white man with us. Conversely, McCool, *you* should be the one to pay a call on Governor Barnum tomorrow, under the pretext of bearing a personal message from Custer's family. Tell Barnum the family has asked you to see how he's faring and see if he'll give you a *laissez-passer* to visit the prison. And remember that we're in a *hurry* if we mean to have Custer help us against Stanton's forces in the Apacheria."

Liam started to ask Chen something, then caught himself as he wrestled with some idea, then shrugged and started over again:

"OK, Ambrose, I have to ask you. Can't you do something about springing him with all your sorcery—you know, sit in the hotel bar over a nice stein of beer and say spells so Custer pops up next to us asking for a pickled egg and a shot of rye? Do we have to go through that whole bureaucratic rigmarole instead?"

Chen and Crazy Horse exchanged an amused look.

"You'll learn," Chen said in an almost avuncular tone. "Magic can't be worked at long distance. Or if it can, *we* don't know how. We'll have the best chance of getting Custer out safe and sound if we've been there to do a reconnaissance first. Tiresome though it may be, we need to start with the bureaucracy. And in any event, while you're talking to Barnum you should have a chance to answer your third question, about Stanton's bulletin to the police." He spread his hands: "You're a plausible fellow; perhaps you can convince the Great Showman that it's all a misunderstanding."

Liam gave that thought a small smile. "Maybe. It all depends on how he feels about Secretary Stanton."

As they reached the corner they stopped and looked up and down Ocean Avenue. There were plenty of small guest houses and inns along the Avenue fronting the Palisades. But the hotel that caught Liam's eye was on the other side of the street, a few hundred yards beyond the glittering fantasyland of the Santa Monica Pier. Nearly as long as a football field and several stories tall, facing the city so that its myriad brightly lit windows seemed like a continuation of the Pier next door, it was grand and stately and welcoming all at once, and Liam's mind was made up the moment he saw it:

"That's for us," he said to the others, "let's go!"

Crazy Horse and Chen exchanged a sort of mutual wince, both shaking their heads at once.

"Ah, Lev Frentsisovich . . ." Crazy Horse said in a dubious tone that made Liam look at him curiously.

"What?" Liam said crossly, in no mood for pettifogging arguments.

"That's the Arcadia Hotel, my friend. That's where Old Los Anga-leece and its nearest and dearest hang their hats, it's not for the likes of us."

"Says who?" Liam said.

And with a pugnacious set of his jaw he tugged his fedora to a rakish angle and set off towards the hotel at a rate so brisk that the others had to trot to keep up.

The reception area of the Arcadia seemed to Liam to be as lofty and spacious as Grand Central Station, with a vast staircase rising towards the upper floors and a cathedral-sized stained glass window at each landing. Dimly visible in the distance to his right and left were the dining room, a conservatory and a ballroom, and in the central area opposite the entrance was a comfortable and uncluttered collection of armchairs, settees and occasional tables, with scattered newspapers, books and smoking accessories that gave it a sitting-room feel despite its size.

Liam looked around and expelled a sigh of pure pleasure:

"Now *this* is a class joint! Come on, admit it—this place makes the Fifth Avenue Hotel look like a Greenwich Village fleabag!"

Chen and Crazy Horse followed his gaze with markedly less enthusiasm—especially as they took in the guests strolling towards the dining room in full evening wear.

Chen spoke first: "Don't you think we might be . . . ah . . . just a trifle under-dressed?"

159

Liam spread his hands indignantly: "Are you serious? We look like we just stepped out of one of those fashion-plates in *Harper's Magazine*! Come on, let's go sign in."

He set off towards the desk with total self assurance, followed uneasily by Chen and Crazy Horse.

"Yes, sir?" the desk clerk said with a faintly disapproving inflection. He was tall and thin, dressed like an expensive undertaker and a little too perfectly groomed, his long face and slender fingers fishbelly white and his carefully plucked eyebrows arched with disdain.

"How may I ... ah ... *help* you?" he added with obvious insincerity, looking around at the same time as if he were hoping to catch sight of a hotel detective.

Liam's expression was darkening steadily as he read between the lines.

"Easy," he said in a flat tone that would have frozen any New York hard guy, "just sign us in and give us our room keys."

"Ah ... I'm afraid that won't be possible, sir," the clerk said with patently bogus regret, "at the moment the hotel is completely occupied and I don't believe we'll have a vacancy in the near future."

"No kidding?" Liam said between his teeth. "Everybody's in town for Halloween, huh?"

The clerk's lips drew together in a prim little rosebud: "I'm afraid I don't quite take your meaning, sir."

"You don't have to take it," Liam said in a tone that could split granite, "I'll give it to you for free. If you don't sign us in right now my friends and I will be very upset."

Confident in his unassailability, the clerk heaved a long-suffering sigh. "Very well, *sir*, since you force me to make my meaning clearer, it is a policy of the Arcadia that guests may only be of the ... ah ... *white* persuasion."

"'*Persuasion*'"? Unable to restrain himself, Liam burst out laughing at the ridiculous euphemism. Then he leaned

160

closer and took the clerk by the knot of his cravat. "Why don't you let me persuade *you* a little?"

Chen was rolling his eyes and Crazy Horse reached out and laid his hand on Liam's shoulder: "Lev Frentsisovich," he began, but Liam held up his hand to silence him:

"Shush!" he said emphatically. Turning back to the clerk he continued: "My Indian friend here is a famous Sioux war chief, and my Chinese friend is the Jade Emperor's closest pal. Are you persuaded yet?"

"Really!" snorted the clerk in a disgusted tone. "I'm afraid if you won't leave on your own I'll have to call for assistance!"

With that, he took hold of the earpiece of the voicewire apparatus and started to lift it to his ear, but before he could complete the motion his arm froze in mid-air and he stared at the earpiece with a horrified expression as Liam peered intently at his hand, smiling. It had struck him the moment the clerk lifted the earpiece that there was something amazingly *sinuous* about the wire, something that he wanted to share with Chen and Crazy Horse if he could just get a handle on it . . .

Liam laughed gleefully, *staring* at the wire as he pictured a terrarium he'd seen at the Central Park Zoo, and in the next moment the wire from the earpiece to the apparatus gave a disturbing *wriggle.* "That's it," Liam murmured, "come on, now," and before the clerk could open his mouth both wire and earpiece had turned into a thick, rosy snake with a rattle at one end and a small, triangular head at the other, the snake wrapped around the clerk's arm with its head at the end where the earpiece had been. As the totally petrified clerk stared at it in horror, the snake *rattled* and its tongue flickered out and brushed his chin delicately, evoking a choked little groan.

"What do you know about that?" Liam asked jovially. "*Crotalus ruber,* the red rattlesnake. Very rare, not many people get a chance to see them that close up. Don't make any sudden moves, now, will you? They're touchy little fellas."

A tiny whine of pure misery escaped from the clerk's nose.

"What's that?" Liam asked, bending closer and cocking his ear.

"Please, sir," the clerk gasped in a transport of terror, "*please* don't let it hurt me! You and your friends may stay in the Presidential Suite for as long as you like compliments of the Arcadia, just make it *go away!*"

"Oh, well, in that case," Liam said in a magnanimous tone, and flicked the ends of his fingers as if he were brushing away a fly. Immediately the snake vanished, leaving the clerk grasping the earpiece of the voicewire apparatus and trembling like a sapling in a gale wind.

"You were saying . . .?" Liam said with mild encouragement

"Oh, yes, sir! Oh, yes, oh yes, oh, *yes*, right *away*, sir!"

The clerk slammed the earpiece back onto its cradle and started scribbling furiously in the registration ledger. Liam turned to the others and gave them an innocent smile. After a moment, Chen spoke, a faint grin turning up the corners of his mouth:

"Nice snake," he said to Liam.

"Yeah," said Liam with an answering grin, "it was, wasn't it?"

In the Air/On the Ground
in Little Russia
October 31, 1877

Chapter Fifteen

s Capt. Ubaldo stood gesticulating wildly towards the viewport that ran above the battleship Delta's control panels, the sky outside filled inexorably with lethal-looking Little Russian attack flyers, their stubby wings and fore-and-aft Gatling gun emplacements filling Becky with dread. If she were going to be blown out of the sky by some anonymous Little Russian aeronaut, she certainly didn't want to go to the next world bound and gagged.

"*Nnngg!*" she moaned. Then, more emphatically, "*Rrrrrrrr!*"

Startled, Capt. Ubaldo turned away from the viewport and gave Becky a contrite look.

"Forgive me, Becky dearest," he cried, hurrying over to join her. "I was so excited by the thought of meeting my future colleagues that I completely forgot your predicament!"

He dropped to his knees next to her and fixed his moist brown eyes on her with a look of supplication that made Becky long passionately to mash a custard pie into his face.

"*Rrrrrrrr!*" she groaned with a rising inflection, the underlying threat in her tone sending a little chill of uneasiness along Ubaldo's spine.

"Let us reach an agreement, then, darling," he said with false brightness. "If you'll promise to think twice before you take issue with my opinions and to remind yourself of the importance of a certain modesty and deference towards my new colleagues when we meet together in social situations, then I can set my mind at ease about removing the gag. Do you think you might agree to that?"

Becky furrowed her brow into an absolute washboard of earnest wrinkles and nodded up and down in heartfelt pantomime: *Oh, yes. Oh, absolutely!*

Ubaldo heaved a sigh of relief and undid the knots on the gag, stepping back out of the way as Becky spat it out in a fury of revulsion.

"*Water!*" she croaked, and Ubaldo scurried away and returned a moment later with a carafe, which he held to her lips as she gulped it down thirstily. Once she had drunk her fill she gestured the carafe away with her head and then looked her captor directly in the eyes.

"Now, my dear Captain Ubaldo," she said with decisive crispness. "Unless you actually mean to introduce me to your 'new colleagues' in chains, I think it might be useful to remove my bonds as well."

Ubaldo hesitated for a moment, and Becky picked up on it instantly: "For mercy's sake," she said soothingly, "relax!" And opening her blue eyes wide with all the guileless candor she could summon, she added: "Honestly, what harm could a mere girl do to a big, intrepid warrior like you?"

Blushing with embarrassment, Ubaldo bent over and rapidly undid Becky's bonds, waiting to speak again until she had finished chafing her wrists and ankles and risen a little unsteadily to her feet.

"Is there anything I can . . ." Ubaldo began in his most solicitous tone.

"As a matter of fact, I absolutely *must* withdraw to the W. C." She looked around to remind herself where the Officers'

Quarters were, as Ubaldo blushed again, twice as furiously, at this indelicacy. She patted him gently on the arm:

"There, there, Captain," she said, "I'm sure you'd rather I didn't have a disgraceful accident right here in front of you. We can have a nice talk when I get back." Hastily, clenching her fists less to control her bladder than to keep herself from turning back and punching Ubaldo squarely in the nose, she took off and trotted up a couple of steps to the passage that led to the Officers' Quarters.

○━┰

The Officers' water-closet was just as Becky remembered it from her aerial journey with Liam—a surprisingly commodious room, paneled throughout with walnut and rosewood, lit with electric lights and highlighted with brightly polished brass fixtures. But the memory that was uppermost in Becky's mind just now was of a recessed cabinet located over the marble washbasin; surely if she just rummaged a bit she would find something there she could make use of . . .

"Ahhh!" she exhaled with a joyous grin. Incredible, even better than she had dared hope. Humming cheerfully to herself she removed the brown glass flask with the pharmacist's label and set it on the counter next to the washbasin, then continued searching in the room's other cabinets until she had the rest of what she needed. She chuckled gleefully. Whoever said that revenge is a dish best served cold must have been some dilettante with too much free time on his hands— for a busy girl the best revenge was one served piping hot and fresh from the oven!

○━┰

As Becky returned to the main deck, she found Ubaldo seated in front of the TeslaVox transmitter/receiver unit, talking animatedly into the handset; in the background, she could see that the Little Russian attack flyers had ranged themselves in squadrons on either side of the battleship Delta, clearly intending to escort it to its landing area.

As he spoke to his unseen listener, Ubaldo gestured with his free hand as if he were painting castles in the air, smiling broadly and oozing a sort of unctuous toadyism:

"Of *course*, Your Highness," he was saying, "both I and the battleship Delta itself are at your service, and any small experience I may have acquired in my fifteen years as a U. S. Aeronaut is yours to make use of as well."

Whatever His Highness might have been saying in reply, it was obviously more than satisfactory, as Ubaldo started nodding like a bobble-head doll while his grin spread till it looked like the corners of his mouth were about to meet at the back of his head. After another moment or two, Ubaldo hung the handset back on its hook, breathed out a vast sigh of satisfaction and turned his head to smile at Becky, who had approached him from behind.

"Imagine that!" Ubaldo began in a euphoric tone . . .

"No," Becky replied, "*you* imagine *this*!" And before Ubaldo could utter a word, Becky whipped a sodden washcloth out of the pocket of her gown and slapped it squarely over her persecutor's nose and mouth.

"*Eeeemmmmph!*" Ubaldo wailed, his eyes wild and incredulous. He was trying to rise and extricate himself from Becky's grip, but without much success.

"Yes, you deranged, egomaniacal pervert," Becky hissed, "it's chloroform, from the very same bottle you used on me, or I miss my bet!"

At that, Ubaldo redoubled his efforts, struggling madly to free himself, but Becky was filled with an emotional energy that could have subdued a mountain gorilla.

"Give it up, Captain," Becky said with a cheerful grin. "I may be nothing but a girl, but I once wrestled one of the Sultan's *Bashi-Bazouks* to the ground for a bottle of arak!"

Either this bit of news or the chloroform finally proved too much for Ubaldo, who suddenly slumped in his seat and started snoring loudly, his chin sunk on his chest. Resuming her happy hum, Becky picked up the knotted sheets and ropes that had been used to bind her and put them to work trussing up Ubaldo. After a couple of minutes she finished with the last knot, dusted off her hands and curtsied to the totally immobilized and dead-to-the-world Ubaldo:

"I must say, Captain dear, that this seems the perfect instance for testing the old chestnut about sauce for the goose and sauce for the gander. I only regret that I won't be here to hear you explain your bonds to your 'new colleagues.'"

Turning briskly back to the airship's controls, Becky took a moment to peer out the view screen to check on their whereabouts.

"Oh, dear!" she murmured, catching sight of the rapidly approaching sky-line of New Petersburg, the onion domes of its innumerable churches silhouetted against the setting sun. Clearly Ubaldo had been bound for the giant military compound of the Little Russian Aerial Navy from which she and Liam had originally stolen the battleship Delta, and at this speed it wouldn't be long until they reached it.

Considering the fact that she should have been on her way to New York with Captain Billy and Liam's Gran just about now, Ubaldo had already turned her life totally upside down simply by abducting her. But if she actually allowed herself to be taken prisoner by the Little Russians, things would become too complicated to bear thinking about. Fortunately, on this side of New Petersburg there seemed to be an abundance of meadows and fields, some cultivated and some not—possible landing sites whose number was diminishing rapidly as they approached the outskirts.

That didn't leave much choice. In the center of the control area two very comfortable kidney-buttoned chairs of dark-green leather were set on shiny brass pedestals that let them swivel in any direction they pleased—probably, she and Liam had decided, meant for the vessel's captain and an assistant. Seating herself in the chair nearest the central controls, Becky rapidly located a large brass wheel with a rosewood handle affixed to it at right angles. At the left side of the wheel, where the handle was stopped against a peg, was a sign with two-inch letters and a curved arrow pointing clockwise declaring: "DESCEND," and Becky firmly gripped the handle and spun the wheel all the way around to the right.

Instantly, there was a change in the sound of the engines and the regular chiming of a bell declaring that a descent was in progress. Becky looked out the view screen again and let go of a pent-up breath that she had been holding without realizing it. They were already low enough that she could tell they'd land in what looked like an alfalfa field, just beyond which began the first ramshackle buildings of the city's outskirts. Overhead, the Little Russian attack fliers were flitting back and forth in unmilitary disorder, suggesting nothing so much as a hive of giant wasps that had just been kicked. No doubt they had been expecting Ubaldo to fly the Delta directly to the base, and now they were buzzing around in a panic trying to get new orders. That meant there wasn't much time—Becky jumped up and ran for the Officers' Quarters again, hoping against hope that no one had moved the things she'd left behind a few months ago.

On the ground, the battleship Delta seemed far larger than it had in the air, its dark bulk looming menacingly against a luminous orange sunset, and the detachment of Little Russian aeronauts approached the huge craft warily.

"Are you sure it isn't a trap, sir?" one of the enlisted men quavered, gripping his carbine so tightly that his knuckles were white.

"Don't be such a moron, Vasia," the officer scoffed, though the knuckles gripping his Nagant service revolver were equally white. "Why would the American turncoat set a trap for us? He expects us to take him to Prince Yurevskii for tea and cakes and hearty backslapping!"

As the little group drew closer to the edge of the vessel, they slowed down more and more, and it was with a disproportionate sense of relief that the officer in charge welcomed the distraction of a bystander watching curiously from the shadows of the dilapidated buildings.

"You there, boy!" he called gruffly, pointing to the buildings. "Do you live in that slum?"

"Yes, your Honor," the boy said timidly, "I was just watching the big airship as it landed so I thought I'd get a closer look."

"Well, then," the officer continued, "have you seen anybody leave that vessel since it landed there?"

"Oh, no, your Honor, the boy said vehemently, "I thought there would be someone when those little stairs came out of the thing's belly, but from where I was standing I couldn't see another soul."

"Hmm!" the officer grunted with an uneasy frown. "Well, you can't stand here all night, so be off with you before you start getting in the way."

The boy nodded and bowed humbly, backing away from the officer as if he were a great personage. "Yes, your Honor, of course, your Honor, thank you, your Honor!"

And with that the boy spun around and took off towards the dark buildings as if the Devil himself were on his heels.

The officer, however, was nowhere near as formidable as the boy had seemed to think. In fact, as he and his little party drew nearer to the set of metal stairs which descended to the field from the battleship's belly, he slowed more and more until he came to a halt a dozen feet away from it. He turned to his men:

"You, Vasia," he said brusquely, gesturing towards the stairs with his pistol, "and you, Ippolit! Get up those stairs at once! And don't come back till you have a full report on what's happening in there!"

The two men exchanged the mute "can you believe this clown?" look of enlisted men everywhere and began their grudging ascent, jumping at every unexpected sound and cursing their chicken-hearted commander. Not to mention the American himself, who obviously thought himself too high and mighty to come out and say hello to a handful of lowly Russians.

Vasia, who'd had the misfortune to be deputed first, stopped warily at the very last stair-step between himself and the ugly necessity of sticking his head up into the interior, cocking his rifle as he did so just to make himself feel better. No two ways about it . . . whoever this mysterious American was, he had better turn out to be worth all this fuss!

Chapter Sixteen

he boy, meanwhile, was trotting briskly through the shadowy neighborhoods at the very edge of town towards a dim halo of illumination that rose from a quarter not far ahead of him.

"Thank goodness," the boy said cheerfully, "that wretch Ubaldo didn't throw out any of my working costumes."

Becky—for the boy was indeed Becky in one of her favorite disguises, her "newsboy" getup—felt totally secure in her incognito. Between the tweed cap that covered her curls, the shapeless brown suit that covered the rest of her, the fluent Russian she'd picked up while reporting on the Russo-Turkish war and the Hopkins & Allen pocket revolver she'd pinched from Ubaldo she felt ready for any adventures that might arise. After all, she mused, why not use the opportunity to put together a nice little article for Harpers along the lines of "Undercover in New Petersburg"?

Exiting from a narrow alleyway onto the fully electric-lit main street of New Petersburg's business district, Becky basked gratefully for a moment in the piquant sense of total anonymity that any busy downtown street gives a born city-dweller. The sidewalks were crowded with *Peterburzhtsy* of every class, the well-to-do suited and cloaked against the early autumn chill and the lower classes dressed in layers and warmed by vodka. Somewhere nearby buskers were playing Russian folk songs on a balalaika and a squeezebox called a *garmoshka*, everyone cheerfully (if a bit doggedly) ignoring the taciturn presence of Secret Police watchers pretending to study storefront windows while keeping an eye on the reflected crowds.

Suddenly, a real newsboy (dressed pretty much like Becky, she thought with a touch of self-satisfaction) stepped out into the street ahead and started waving a handful of freshly printed evening papers:

"*ПОСЛЕДНИЕ НОВОСТИ!!!*" he bellowed. "*ДОГОВОР СО ШТАТАМИ!!!*"

Becky hurried towards the newsboy: *A treaty with the States?* she marveled to herself. *Now what?*

Giving the delighted newsboy a handful of U.S. silver, she grabbed a paper and stood aside to read it: incredible! Apparently, after the bombing of New York, Stanton had actually flown to New Petersburg on a U. S. Aerial Navy battle cruiser to meet with the Little Russian Regent, Prince Yurevskii, (whom she remembered with an ironic grin as the mad scientist and totally bent schemer Dr. Lukas), as a result of which the two leaders, effusively protesting eternal friendship, had just concluded a mutual non-aggression pact.

"*Surely,*" she muttered to herself in English, "*we are about to see pigs flying!*"

"My dear Becky . . ." a familiar voice murmured into her ear in Russian.

Starting so sharply that she almost dropped the paper, Becky turned to see a slender, dapper gentleman wearing a dark overcoat and hat, a neat little Vandyke beard and an amused expression. Standing next to him was an absolutely enormous man muffled up in a heavy overcoat, a fur *shapka* pulled down over his head and a woolen scarf wound around his face.

"Georgii Valentinich!" she exclaimed in astonishment, but the moment she said it he was holding a finger to his lips and saying: "*Shh!!*"

"Arkady Antonich Veresayev, at your service," he said with quiet but unmistakable emphasis. "And this," he said, gesturing to the heavily-muffled giant, "is my colleague Grisha Dva."

"Grisha *Two?*" she queried in baffled English, as the giant bowed solemnly.

"It's rather a long story," said her mysterious acquaintance with a smile. "Perhaps we should go someplace where we can get a glass of beer and chat without worrying about being overheard."

"Excellent idea," Becky said. Then, dropping her voice and whispering right into the man's ear: "As long as you promise to tell me just what Georgii Valentinich Plekhanov, notorious revolutionary and leading light of the Land and Freedom party, is doing skulking around New Petersburg pretending to be someone named Veresayev."

Plekhanov grinned broadly: "Perhaps I shall, Becky dear, let's see." And with a little bow and a gesture towards the next side street, he set off down the sidewalk accompanied by Becky and the hulking Grisha Two.

Pivnaia Leinenkugel, Plekhanov's favorite tavern, turned out to be a cellar dive another three or four side streets away from the bright lights and even farther down the social scale, since it reminded Becky of nothing so much as the dismal hangouts—fogged with tobacco smoke and funky with beer—described in Mr. Dostoevsky's novels. On the far side of the room from the steps by which the trio entered was a wooden counter twenty feet long, fronted by a series of tall, dilapidated stools and backed by a series of enormous kegs with taps set into the bung-holes, from which the proprietor—a bald man in shirt sleeves, nearly as big as Grisha Dva and twice as thick around the middle, poured endless steins of beer for his shouting customers.

The place seemed to Becky to be a total Bedlam in which it would be impossible for her to hold a conversation without shouting every word, but at an imperceptible signal from Plekhanov a harried-looking waiter in a dirty apron appeared like a genie and led them to a nook in one of the far corners of the room where they were magically seated at a table, equipped with steins and a huge pitcher of beer, and walled off by a thick curtain of green felt almost before Becky could draw a breath.

Plekhanov poured beer for Becky and himself and then raised his glass for a toast: "*Za vashe zdorov'e*," he said, adding with a grin: "and while we're at it, to the Dictatorship of the Proletariat."

"I'll drink to that," Becky answered with a smile, adding as she turned to Grisha Two: "Have you taken the pledge, Mr. Dva, or do you just not like beer?"

Despite the stifling heat of the *pivnaia*, the giant was still heavily swathed from head to foot, and he answered Becky without unwrapping his face in a peculiarly deep and hollow voice that Becky found familiar without quite being able to say why:

"Ah, dear lady, that may be an even longer story than why Mr. Plekhanov is *pro tempore* Mr. Veresayev."

Becky turned back to Plekhanov and raised her eyebrows. "All right, Georgii Valentinich, I can only stand so much mystification. What's going on here? And why don't you begin your story with how a dyed-in-the-wool devotee of land and liberty for the peasantry is suddenly drinking instead to the industrial proletariat?"

"As for the peasantry," Plekhanov answered in a tone of urbane amusement, "I'm sure you remember that my attempts to improve their lot ended with my being thrown in jail. Twice.

In truth, the *muzhiki* are quite hopeless politically. They *love* the Tsar. If you tell them that he means to rob them forever, until they haven't two *kopeks* to rub together, they'll say you lie—it's all the fault of their crooked landlords."

He shrugged and spread his hands: "After I escaped to England, I fell in with Karl Marx and it was he who convinced me that factory workers are much better revolutionary material—for one thing, they're simply smarter than peasants. Unfortunately in Russia there aren't yet many factories, so I decided to move here and see what might turn up."

Becky frowned and shook her head, baffled. "I heard that Yurevskii was building more factories to make airships and automatons, but who are the proletarians supposed to be? The Little Russian peasants are just as ignorant as the *muzhiki* back in the Motherland, and I can't see Apaches or Cheyennes settling down to operate lathes."

Grisha Dva chuckled resonantly, a sound at once sardonic and melancholy. "Who are Yurevskii's factory workers? I can answer that one easily . . ."

Taking off his fur hat, the giant slowly unwound the scarf that had been covering his face . . .

"Dear Heaven!" murmured Becky. Grisha Dva didn't even have to finish the unwinding process before she realized that the reason he had sounded familiar was that he was speaking with vocal machinery designed by the same man who had supplied President Lincoln's metal body with a voice box: Grisha Dva was one of Yurevskii's (or Dr. Lukas', as she couldn't help thinking) automatons!

Deeply moved, she reached across the table and took one of Grisha's giant, gloved hands between hers.

"You poor man," she said. "Who were you before Yurevskii got you on the operating table?"

Grisha turned his head to look questioningly at Plekhanov, who gave him an affirmative nod. The automaton turned back to Becky:

"Do you remember the explosion in the New Petersburg Regent's Palace this past spring?"

"Indelibly," Becky said with a wry smile. "I was in the process of escaping from New Petersburg on that very day."

The automaton chuckled: an unnervingly dry, rasping sound.

"As it happens, that was my work." He bowed slightly from the waist: "Lev Alexandrich Tikhomirov, at your service."

Becky was genuinely taken aback: "Tikhomirov, the terrorist mastermind of Land and Liberty and the People's Will? The . . . ah, the . . ."

"Don't be embarrassed," he said, "yes, the assassin of Alexander III, the Regent and Tsarevich. Believe me, I have paid dearly for that dubious distinction."

"Can you bear to tell me about it?" Becky asked.

"Why not? My squeamishness has gone the way of my old body. I was the one who set the dynamite charge and the explosion was premature—I hadn't quite escaped from the palace and the blast blew me through a window. When I awoke, I was deep in the bowels of the local Okhrana HQ, and a couple of weeks later Yurevskii showed up to take over as Regent for his deceased half brother. His idea of a fitting punishment was to remove my brain and put it in one of his automatons."

Becky shook her head, speechless. Plekhanov gave her an ironic smile: "It scarcely seems fair, does it? Here my friend Lev Alexandrich had just blown up the only obstacle between Yurevskii and his eventual coronation as Tsar of All the Russias, and the ingrate rewarded his benefactor by sawing open his head and installing his brain in an airship-factory automaton."

Tikhomirov leaned forward again and fixed his glowing red eyes on Becky: "But the key thing to note here, Miss Fox, is the fact that Yurevskii's process for supplanting my earlier, human will with *his* will, as broadcast by the Wireless Automaton Control Center, *failed* in my case. And, as I discovered later, the process has failed far more often than Yurevskii realizes. Our beloved Regent suffers from the delusion that he has exclusive control of a single, common automaton brain that makes every individual automaton revere and obey him as the "Father" of them all. In reality . . ." again Tikhomirov produced that awful rasping chuckle.

"In reality," Plekhanov continued, "this mechanized 'proletariat' has produced a substantial revolutionary underground, and if you'd care to keep us company for another few days you will be privileged to witness Lev Alexandrovich's finest moment: the destruction by dynamite of Prince Yurevskii's Wireless Automaton Control Center . . ."

Here Tikhomirov chimed in, his voice trembling with emotion: ". . . *and* the launching of the Little Russian Revolution, which will crush Prince Yurevskii and every trace of Tsarism's ugly works!"

Chapter Seventeen

iots?" shouted Stanton. "*Bread* riots in Madison Square *Park*? Where are the Johnnies? Where's the militia?"

Secretary Stanton and Willie Pilkington, both of them looking overstuffed and uncomfortable in the elaborate morning dress required for diplomatic occasions, were taking a break from Prince Yurevskii's court and talking to New York via the TeslaVox receiver/transmitter on the U.S. Aerial Navy battle cruiser that had flown them to Little Russia.

Both Stanton and Pilkington had individual handsets connected to the TeslaVox, but Stanton was doing all the talking, while Willie watched him with the anxious wariness of a much-beaten dog.

On the New York end, Seamus McPherson was striving madly to defend himself while Stanton glared and fumed, his rage checked by the merest hair trigger:

"*Sure, yer Honor,*" cried McPherson's tinny voice, "*we're stretched that thin, what with all the homeless folk that was bombed out by the Little Roosians sleeping in the parks and on the streets, and them with nothing to eat and the weather turning cold! There's Johnnies and bluecoats and soldiers scattered all over the city now, trying to protect the big stores and the markets and just this morning some anarchist set off a dynamite bomb at City Hall!*"

"*What?*" Stanton screeched. "Do you mean to say some swine blew up *City Hall?*"

Barely suppressing a groan, Willie Pilkington covered his eyes with his free hand, peeking out surreptitiously between his fingers in case his master decided to throw something.

"*Begorrah, sorr,*" McPherson whined out of the handset like an imprisoned leprechaun, "*would I not have called you meself if there had been a real disaster? It was them dirty Whyos as done it, though some says it was the Butcher Boys, but all they done was bring down a few of them big marble pillars on the front of the building, Cicatelli over to Public Works swears it'll be fixed in a jiffy!*"

Stanton tugged at his starched cravat as if he felt it strangling him, his face growing redder and redder until Willie found himself wondering uneasily if it were really possible for a man's head to blow up.

"Tell me at least, McPherson," Stanton said in a voice choked with anger, "that you *finally* have Liam McCool and that arch-bitch Becky Fox under lock and key!"

"*Ah, well now, sorr,*" McPherson began in his most wheedling tone, "*while 'tis true that we'd almost laid that spalpeen by the heels, we had a bit of a setback and he . . .*"

"AND THAT VILE TRAITOR ABRAHAM LINCOLN?" Stanton bellowed. "AND HIS FILTHY FREEDOM PARTY?"

"*Ah, there now, yer Honor,*" McPherson said brightly, "*we've finally had some definite good news, as 'tis said by them that's in the know that the entire kit and caboodle of dirty villains from Lincoln on down to the cooks and bottle washers has thrown in the towel and hauled themselves off to Canada . . .*"

Stanton took the handset away from his ear and sat staring at it for several long moments as Willie tensed, waiting for the explosion.

"CANADA!" Stanton shrieked. Grasping the handset by one end he smashed it repeatedly against the table in front of him until finally it broke in half. That seemed to ease the Secretary's feelings a bit, and he pulled himself effortfully to his feet, breathing in heavy, rasping gasps.

"Are you quite well, sir?" asked Willie timidly.

"Shut up," Stanton said in a flat tone as he struggled to get himself under control. Finally he let out a deep breath and pulled himself up straight, his eyes glittering with angry purpose:

"I'm afraid it's time to go suck up to Yurevskii and sign the treaty." He grinned without mirth, like a wolf baring its fangs. "But that's all right, Willie my boy, I have a long memory—it won't be anytime soon I'll be forgetting it was *Yurevskii* who ordered the sneak attack that's forced us to pretend America's knuckling under. And believe you me: as soon as Professor Lee's experiment is completed back home and we have a bottomless supply of calorium to fuel our Acmes and our airships it'll be Edwin M. Stanton that blows *Yurevskii's* brains all over the wall."

0—ᴇ

Standing before an ornately filigreed pier glass running a tiny silver comb through his beard, brushing non-existent specks from the lapels of his morning coat and making microscopic adjustments to his starched cravat, Grand Prince Nikolai Aleksandrovich Yurevskii, Regent of Little Russia and Heir Apparent to the throne of the Russian Empire, otherwise known as "Prof. Lukas," brilliantly gifted neurosurgeon, inventor, bare-knuckle boxer, and criminal mastermind, regarded his immaculate person in the mirror and glowed with deep and well-earned self-satisfaction.

"Though I tempt fate by saying it out loud, my dear Boylan, it seems that my gambles have succeeded beyond all our expectations!"

184

"Aye, 'tis the Gospel truth, Boss! And once we've seized the Arizona calorium mines and the ones up in Saskatchewan there'll be nothing to stop us taking whatever we like wherever we want to!"

Daniel Xavier Boylan, or "Boyo" if you dared call him that to his face, onetime Bowery leg-breaker and terror of the Pennsylvania coal fields, grinned like a baby with a new rattle, his big shiny red face with its glittering black plastered-down hair and glossy black handlebar moustache almost shimmering with pleasure as he basked in his role as aide-de-camp to Prince Yurevskii, a villain twice as bad and immeasurably more powerful than any he'd met in a life rich with villains.

"'Twill be a treat beyond compare to watch you wiping your feet on that pumped-up mouse turd Stanton, let alone his bum-boy Willie Pilkington!"

Stealing a glance at the pier glass over his master's shoulder, Boylan nodded approvingly at the way the court tailor's endless fittings had camouflaged his six-foot-seven-inch, 300-plus pounds of muscle and hard fat with morning dress every bit as fashionable and flattering at the Prince's. Yurevskii chuckled:

"You look very smart, my boy, you must give me the name of your tailor."

"Sure now, your Highness," Boylan said with a grin, "me dear departed mither would have gave her eye teeth to see her little Danny dressed up like the headwaiter at Delmonico's."

Prince Yurevskii tugged at a Petrine silver ruble he used as a watch fob and drew a luxuriantly enameled Fabergé watch out of his waistcoat pocket, grinning sardonically as he noted the time.

"What do you think?" he asked. "Have we let Stanton simmer long enough?"

"Sure, your Highness," Boylan said, echoing the grin, "I'd reckon he must be about parboiled by now."

"Well, then," Yurevskii said, "let's go stick a fork in him and see."

○━

In the royal audience chamber, Secretary Stanton was pacing back and forth with grim determination, the increasing redness of his face sending up a flag that was starting to worry Willie Pilkington more by the second. The one hope anytime soon for an improvement in his master's mood was for the Chinaman—Stanton's tame metallurgist Professor Lee—to wire them that the experimental process for producing calorium from molten lead had finally succeeded, an event he had been promising every day for the past week. But Willie knew better than to say anything to his irascible boss, so instead he did his best to escape from his worries by losing himself in the mystifying scene depicted on the ceiling . . .

At least 100 feet long and fifty feet wide, the mural was framed in richly gilded plaster grapes and vine leaves and showed the reclining figure of a colossal, muscular young man wearing little but a crown of laurel leaves and a strategically-draped bit of upholstery while a dozen or so plump young women wearing nothing at all plied him with plates of food and goblets of wine and a centaur stood nearby strumming a lyre and looking cynical.

Hungry as ever, Willie found himself wondering what the redhead at the end of the line had on her plate. It looked like éclairs, or maybe some kind of grilled sausages; whatever it was it looked like it was killing her to have to stand in line behind the woman with the suckling pig, fretting at the delay till she could stuff whatever it was down that conceited pansy's gullet. Really, it was galling to think of all the food being lavished on the idle wastrels of the world while he, Willie Pilkington, head of the U.S. Department of National Security's Secret Police, and heir to the world's most successful detective agency, was forced to sit here thinking of the absolute aeons it had been since breakfast and all the while his stomach grumbling and gurgling at the thought of a dinner still light years away. Where was the *good* in being the all-powerful secret policeman Willie Pilkington when his honors and his baubles couldn't bring him even *one* little éclair, or a couple of paltry sausages, or even . . .

"HIS ROYAL HIGHNESS GRAND PRINCE NIKOLAI ALEKSANDROVICH YUREVSKII!" bellowed a voice at the opposite end of the chamber, so loudly and suddenly that Willie jumped and almost tipped over the chair. As he leapt to his feet a gaggle of flunkies pulled open the enormous, bas-relief-decorated bronze portals that led into the Regent's private chambers and bowed obsequiously as Yurevskii and Boylan entered.

The Prince strode up to Stanton and held out both hands in an almost-convincing gesture of spontaneous welcome as both he and Stanton wreathed themselves in grins of pure delight at the unexpected pleasure of meeting each other *here*, of all places, in the royal audience chamber of the Regent of Little Russia.

"My *dear* Secretary Stanton," enthused Prince Yurevskii, "how good of you it is to come all this way for our chat! I must say you're looking wonderfully fit and unruffled after your journey!" Thinking even as he uttered the obligatory flattery that Stanton had become a veritable tub of lard since they'd last met. Not to mention the broken veins in his nose and the flush on his cheeks—if the man wasn't careful he'd die of a heart attack and cheat Yurevskii of the pleasure of killing him at a genuinely useful moment.

Secretary Stanton, for his part, seized Yurevskii's proffered hands with a cry of delight:

"Ah, Your Highness! How good of you to receive us on such short notice! And as for 'fit,' I can only say that you look as if the effort of ruling half the North American continent were mere child's play!" Stanton thinking meanwhile that the Russian looked uncommonly like a gorilla he'd seen recently at the Central Park Zoo. What a thug! It was said he'd once competed for purses as a barroom brawler in the Bowery, and it was easy to believe!

While this display was taking place, Boylan and Pilkington—free to be themselves—eyed each other narrowly after curt nods while thinking wistfully—each according to his own favorite fantasies—of what fun it would be to skip over the diplomacy part and get right down to some serious mayhem.

"And how is the Mexican expeditionary force faring?" Yurevskii asked Stanton.

Glad to turn to business, Stanton pulled out his watch and made some quick calculations. "I received a telegram from their commander this morning," he answered, "and I would estimate their crossing of the border into the Arizona *Guberniia* within the hour. At that point, as we agreed earlier, they will make camp and await the arrival of your airships and troops—once they join up, the joint command will begin the operation to seize the mines from the Apache brigands who claim to control them."

Yurevskii grinned and rubbed his hands in a moment of genuine pleasure. Of course when the time came his people would turn around and put an end to the American forces, but for the time being it was really most opportune to have their help against the savages.

"Come," the Prince said with an expansive gesture, "let us make our first joint appearance before the inhabitants of my capital."

And—giving his flunkies an imperceptible nod to fling open the doors to the balcony—he beckoned Stanton forward:

"After you, my dear colleague!" he said, and the two of them moved forward to accept the plaudits of the multitude . . .

. . . Which unfortunately seemed to be a bit on the meager side. Across the vast square in front of the Palace, where Stanton had expected to see thousands, perhaps tens of thousands of cheering Little Russians, there were scattered perhaps a thousand or so people, most of them police and soldiers, with a few knots of sullen-looking civilians scattered among them, hugging themselves against the unaccustomed autumn chill.

"Hip, hip, hoorah!" cried a solitary voice from among the palace guards at the front of the crowd, and the meaningful way in which the guards fingered their rifles and glared at the others, called forth a few fitful and patently bogus cheers.

Prince Yurevskii, thoroughly mortified, turned to Boylan and jerked a thumb towards the square. "Get down there at once, find who is supposed to be in charge and have him put in chains. I'll attend to him later, *personally*!"

And, turning back to Stanton, he said: "It's too cold to stand on the balcony anyway. Let's go have a hot grog and talk about more pleasant things." And then, more or less to himself, he added: "These damned people seem not to understand that it's the *government* that knows what's best for them, not their friends or their family or anybody else, and by God I'll make them see it if I have to flay every inch of skin from their worthless bodies and put every last one of them in chains!"

Amen to that, thought Stanton as they moved towards the royal chambers, *for once I can agree with this wretched creature!*

Bear Flag Republic, El Pueblo de
Nuestra Señora de Los Angeles/
Edison City, and Santa Monica
November 1, 1877

Chapter Eighteen

martly togged-out in his brand new finery, luxuriantly bathed, shaved and bay-rummed, his hat tucked tidily under his arm, Liam McCool strode up to the ornately carved mahogany door and rapped on it with the head of his stick.

"*Hello?*" he called in a voice calculated to penetrate the wall, let alone the door. "*Anybody home?*"

"*Criminy!*" a child's voice yelled back. "*Pipe down, willya? Whyn't ya try the doorknob, like a gentleman?*"

Shrugging, Liam turned the knob and pulled the door open, revealing a handsomely furnished antechamber in the center of which stood an extremely big desk behind which sat an extremely small man—so small in fact that at first Liam thought he might be some sort of tiny automaton. A moment later, he recognized him and grinned sheepishly:

"General Thumb?" Liam asked, "General *Tom Thumb?*"

"None other!" the little man said with a piping chuckle, jumping up and coming around the end of the desk with his hand held out for a shake. Roughly three feet tall, fashionably turned out in a dark suit and waistcoat, smoking a cigar and bustling with cheerful energy, he took Liam's hand and gave it a brisk shake.

"And you must be the notorious King of the Cracksmen," he chuckled, at which Liam gave him a little half-bow. "But I'll call you by your real name if you'll call me Charlie Stratton, which is mine. Governor Barnum and Mayor Edison will receive you in half a tick if you don't mind waiting."

"As long as you like," Liam said. "I'm here to ask a favor so I don't want to get pushy about it. But if you don't mind my asking, tell me how *you* came to be here—I thought you had retired."

Stratton grinned a bit sheepishly. "Tell you the truth, McCool, I was starting to get a little tired of the whole bourgeois householder thing, and then Phin drops by for a drink and tells me he's thinking of putting together a new show for the Big Top and taking it out to California just for fun. Well, I mean!" He spread his arms in a gesture of surrender: "How could I say no?" He grinned with delight: "Now Phin's Governor of the Bear Flag Republic and I'm his Cerberus!"

"*CHARLIE!*" a ringmaster's bellow sounded out from the office behind Stratton and he gestured for Liam to follow him.

Santa Monica's Government Building was the only ten-story structure in town, and from the Governor's office on the top floor Liam could see out across Santa Monica Bay towards the Pacific, which today was a sun-sparkled blue with a dusting of whitecaps, dotted here and there with sailing ships and steamships riding at anchor while their owners did business ashore.

Standing behind a desk which gave him a panorama of the Bay and the long, curving white beach which embraced it as far as the eye could see, was America's Greatest Showman himself, Phineas T. Barnum, tall, broad, heavy-faced, with black, curly hair over a high forehead, a big smile and a

194

pugnacious chin. Next to him stood a slightly shorter man in his thirties in a rumpled white suit. He had a shock of brown hair over his forehead and his serious expression belied the smile lines at the corners of his mouth. Barnum strode towards Liam holding out his hand and smiling widely:

"By Jingo!" he cried. "Here's someone from back in Civilization, come to visit us *vaqueros!*"

Liam grinned back and pumped Barnum's hand: "Glad to meet you, sir! But if where I just came from is Civilization I'm for Darkest Africa any day."

The man in the white suit held out his hand and greeted Liam warmly. "Tom Edison," he said. "Glad to meet you, but sorry to hear the dear old States have sunk so low." He smiled slyly: "I mean to say, I'm not surprised to hear that of New *York*, after all they've let that bohunk putz Tesla string up his toy lights on every street corner. But New *Jersey?* Surely Jersey stands a step or two above the Congo."

"Maybe it does now, sir," Liam said with a smile, "but it won't stand there long if Secretary Stanton has his way."

Barnum and Edison exchanged a cryptic look.

"Why don't you have a seat, Mr. McCool?" Barnum gestured to a couch and some chairs arranged around a low table and turned to Stratton:

"Charlie, would you bring everybody a nice cold Anchor Steam?"

The little man grinned and crossed to a piece of furniture Liam had taken to be a wardrobe, but which now turned out to be some sort of ice box with an electric light in it. As Stratton took out four bottles of beer and set them on a tray, Liam peered at the lighted interior curiously,

"I'm calling it a 'refrigerator,'" said Edison with a smile. "It's not quite ready for a patent but it beats hauling blocks of ice up ten floors."

Stratton passed the beer around and Barnum held his up for a toast: "Here's confusion to Eddie Stanton and all his thugs and success to Liam McCool and his boys when they kick the invaders out of the Arizona territory!"

Liam threw him a startled look: "Say, how do you know . . ."

Barnum held up a hand to calm him: "In a place as remote as the Bear Flag Republic, Mr. McCool, information is the most valuable of all commodities. We may seem pretty far from the mainstream, and it's true that it'll be a while yet before the telegraph reaches us, but we do get a fast airship every day with all the latest news along with the passengers and cargo and we have a special information bureau down-stairs that sorts out everything from vague rumors to the latest editorial in *Freedom*. So we have a shrewd idea about your plans for freeing Custer as well, and we're more favorable to them than you might think. But we have to get some rules clear first."

A bit bemused, Liam spread his hands: "Fire away!"

"I have to admit we weren't that serious about staying on here when we first got to California. Charlie and I are pure showmen, and Tom's got a powerful showman side to go along with all those brains, and for a while we were just having fun packing the rubes into the big tent. But after a while we began to realize there was something special about this place—you could dream as big as you liked and still make your dreams come true. But we're very vulnerable—this little corner of the world is devoted to building things while the rest of the world seems to be devoted to destruction."

Liam nodded, remembering a bit wistfully the dreams he'd shared with his sweetheart Maggie when he was an invol-untary undercover in the Pennsylvania coal fields—they were going to go to San Francisco and Maggie would start a great restaurant while he would start a bookstore to rival Brentano's in New York . . .

"I don't suppose you have a really good bookstore here, do you?"

Barnum—who had the showman's intuition for other people's dreams—smiled and pointed to a large oil painting showing the troupe of one of his side-shows including Charlie Stratton in a circus getup—full Highland regalia including kilt and sporran:

"Let me tell you a story about big dreams. Those folks in that picture were our most popular side-show ever, and the Fat Lady—see her?" Liam nodded and Barnum continued: "That was Billy Mae Sweetwater, the finest Fat Lady that ever worked with a circus."

Stratton piped up: "She was something special, like an auntie to everybody under the Big Top."

"That she was," smiled Barnum reminiscently, "and I'd sooner have lost my eye teeth than Billie Mae. But after we'd all been out here in the Republic doing our show for a few months, she came to me one day looking upset and told me she hoped I wouldn't think she was crazy, but she had always dreamed of being a veterinarian. The long and short of it was we enrolled Billy Mae in the Los Angeles Normal School's Veterinary College, and she's going to become *Doctor* Billy Mae Sweetwater next spring."

He grinned at Liam while he let the story sink in and then held out his hand:

"So here's a promise: you help us end the threat of Yurevskii and Stanton and I'll help you build that bookstore myself, brick by brick!"

Liam smiled slowly and then shook Barnum's hand: "All right, Governor, it's a deal."

"You can count on me, McCool. But there's a proviso: we can't come out in the open to help you, there are too damned many spies in this city, and we can't afford to bring those evil thugs in Washington and New Petersburg down on our heads lusting for revenge. But we won't *oppose* you either, and we'll make it as easy for you as possible, starting with springing Custer."

Liam looked a little dubious. "I appreciate that, Governor Barnum, but if that's the case I hope you can tell me something about Serra Castle first."

Barnum shrugged and spread his hands, giving Liam an uneasy flash of memory: a thimblerigger insisting he had no idea which shell the pea was under. "Tell you the truth," Barnum said unconvincingly, "it sounds a lot worse than it is. Back when the Spanish were in charge they say it got pretty bad, especially when the Indians started resisting the padres and the Missions. But Custer's the first actual prisoner they've had in years, and the fact is they've just been holding him till Stanton sends someone to take him back East."

"How about the guards. Are they Army? Police?"

Barnum hesitated and looked uneasy. "Well now . . . that's the one place there might be bit of a problem. Before the war there was only a skeleton staff at Serra, but from '65 on, there got to be more and more hard-case types hanging their hats there. People say they're mostly Confederate fugitives, men with prices on their heads."

Liam shook his head incredulously: "You're telling me there are Confederate fugitives guarding the man they knew in the War as *Union* General George Armstrong Custer?"

For the first time Barnum's showmanly veneer showed a crack or two. "I admit it may sound a bit iffy," he said with an abashed little grin, "but from everything I've heard about the King of the Cracksmen, if there's anybody that can get him out, it's you. And to be *completely* candid . . ." He stopped and gave Liam an appraising look, which the Irishman returned with an ironic lift of the eyebrow . . .

"Crackerjack idea, Governor."

"Well, then. If something were to happen that rendered Serra Castle totally uninhabitable and drove that congeries of lowlifes out for good, I would be eternally grateful."

"Hmm," said Liam with a speculative glint in his eye. "Anything is possible."

Barnum grinned widely. "Delighted to hear it. And in case you need official bona fides . . ."

He took a sealed letter out of his jacket pocket and handed it over to Liam.

". . . that's a *laissez-passer* for you and Mr. Chen and Chief Crazy Horse to visit Custer at Serra Castle—the rest will have to be up to you."

Liam weighed the envelope in his hand, smiling thoughtfully. "Forgive me for saying so, Governor Barnum, but I'm surprised you've included my friends. The atmosphere here didn't seem that welcoming for people of color."

Barnum shook his head and groaned: "The old-guard *'Los Anga-leece'* whites, I might have known. Sorry for that, my boy, I think that deep down they all feel guilty about helping the good padres in the Missions destroy California's Indians. But if you want to know where P. T. Barnum stands, a human soul that God has created and Christ died for is not to be trifled with. It may tenant the body of a Chinaman, a Turk, an Arab or a Hottentot, but it is still an immortal spirit!"

Liam smiled and got to his feet: "That's good enough for me!"

Before he could head for the door, Mayor Edison laid a hand on his arm: "Promise me you'll do everything you can to keep Yurevskii and Stanton out of the calorium mines. I've experimented with the stuff just enough to know it's incredibly dangerous, which both of those animals probably think is a wonderful thing. And I just heard something from a colleague on the latest airship that makes my blood run cold: the whisper in scientific circles back East is that Stanton has a Chinese metallurgist named Lee working day and night on a process to convert molten lead into calorium. I hate to sound like the Book of Revelations, but I feel in my bones that Lee's foolishness could be the end of us all unless he's stopped."

Liam nodded somberly. "We'll stop him, that's a promise."

199

The Los Angeles business district's Calle de Los Negros was only a dozen or so miles from Santa Monica, but it might as well have been in Calcutta. Or maybe, Liam thought, back in Five Points, the boisterous New York slum district where he'd grown up. There were plenty of side streets there as rough as this one, though maybe without so many exotic languages and so much action crammed into such a small space.

The Calle de Los Negros was only about forty feet wide and a block long, but he'd never seen so many people rushing along and crowding into so many saloons, gambling joints, dance halls and cribs. And every single one of these dives seemed to have some kind of band tootling and sawing and plucking away at every kind of music you could imagine, creating a bedlam that made the sober listener long for deafness. Maybe, Liam thought, the plan was they'd shut up if you paid them enough.

Liam strolled along trying to look relaxed while expecting to need his sword stick at any moment and wondering where Chen and Crazy Horse could have strayed off to. None of these hangouts seemed to have a sign, so looking for Chinese writing was a waste of time. And every one of them had to be looked over carefully, because the crowds were so motley that a tall Chinese and a stocky Sioux Indian would blend right in. In fact, Liam was about ready to give up and stand on a box shouting *"Ambrose Chen!"* over and over again when he spotted a Chinese grocery store about four feet wide crammed in between a dance hall and a shooting gallery full of drunken British sailors.

Liam veered off the street and approached the store crossing his fingers, finally letting go a huge sigh of relief when he spotted Ambrose in the back of the store holding forth and gesticulating at another Chinese—probably the grocer—while Crazy Horse stood closer to the door with his arms folded on his chest, staring up at the ceiling. Liam came right up to the window and waved madly, shouting:

"*Ei! Zhenia!*"

Crazy Horse turned and caught sight of Liam, heaving his own heartfelt sigh of relief as he extricated himself from the tiny store. Once outside he threw his arms around Liam, giving him the whole enthusiastic Russian embrace including a kiss on both cheeks.

"*Bozhe moi!*" he groaned. "I thought listening to a band of Arapaho fur trappers argue about muskrat pelts was the most exquisitely boring thing I've ever had to endure, but *this*!" He gestured towards Chen and the grocer, at a loss for words. "This is the absolute nadir . . ."

"Wait a minute," Liam exclaimed. Chen was bowing to the grocer and backing towards the door, and a moment later he was outside on the sidewalk looking around. Liam and Crazy Horse waved to him, since catching anybody's attention was no joke in the midst of the rushing, jostling Bedlam.

"*Hey, Ambrose!*" bellowed Liam.

"*Siuda, durak!*" yelled Crazy Horse.

Chen stopped abruptly, looked towards his companions' voices, and then pushed his way towards them through the crowd wearing a look so grim that Liam immediately feared for the worst.

"Are they OK?" he asked Chen.

Chen shook his head. "They're prisoners," he said in a voice cracking with anxiety. "Evidently that blackguard Stanton circularized every port on the continent, warning them to look out for members of a family trying to secure passage back to China and to arrest them immediately and hold them. They were to notify Stanton at once, and upon physical receipt of the Chen family Stanton's representatives would pay a reward of $50,000 in gold." He cursed bitterly in Chinese, then went back to Russian: "Naturally every criminal gang from the California *Guberniia* to northern Maine joined the

201

search as well, with the result that my family are presently in the custody of a local gangster named McCluskey!"

Liam frowned and shook his head. "I knew Fergus McCluskey back in New York after the War," he said, "and he was as poisonous a snake as Stanton. He killed one of the baby Whyos for picking his pocket—beat him to death with a blackjack—and he had to light out for California when the two Dannys put a price on his head. Did the guy in the grocery tell you how to find him?"

Chen nodded heavily, unable to speak.

"Relax," Crazy Horse said to Chen in a kindly tone, "we'll have them back for you by dinnertime. Right, Lev Frentsisovich?"

Liam grinned wryly. "In time for a midnight snack, anyway. Come on, let's go!"

He gestured to Chen to lead the way, and a moment later Liam and Crazy Horse were struggling to keep up as Chen shoved his way through the crowds like a battering ram, heading back the way they had come.

Chapter Nineteen

ollowing Chen at a semi-trot, they had rapidly moved out of the stinking rookeries of the Calle de los Negros into a series of increasingly pleasant middle-class streets and finally into a classy district that reminded Liam of Shore Road in Brooklyn: big houses set well back from the road amid enough greenery for an arboretum or two. Liam hoped they would be reaching their destination soon, since the only thing that was keeping him from getting tetchy about the pace Chen was setting was the thought that Chen had, after all, been tortured a lot worse than he had and it had barely been two days since they had escaped from Stanton's clutches.

The trouble was, Chen was so obsessed with freeing his family that he hadn't uttered a word throughout their crazy half-sprint, so Liam had no idea when they were supposed to be reaching their goal. If it wasn't going to be a whole lot longer, he could stay mum. But if this was going to be some kind of cross-country race, like maybe to those mountains over there in the background, he was going to have to put his foot down. And not pick it up again until they hired a carriage! For the luvva Mike! He wasn't an athlete, he lived a nice quiet life cracking cribs, and what's more he'd just finished three months in *solitary*, it's not like you could get a lot of exercise organizing *cockroach* races!

And he was starting to *pant*, which was embarrassing. If only he could think of something that would catch Chen's attention, something that long-legged madman might think was really gripping, maybe he'd have to slow down a little while he thought it over. Something about Oxford? Something about alchemy? Something . . . after a moment or two of deep thought, inspiration struck:

"Oh, right, Ambrose!" Liam called out. "I forgot, Tom Edison told me something really big that he wanted me to pass on to you!"

Chen threw him an irritable look, like: "Don't bother me with petty stuff," but Liam ploughed on doggedly:

"Yeah, it was about that guy Lee that you told us about, you know, the alchemist?"

Without missing a beat, Chen turned and snapped at him crossly: "The man is *not* an alchemist, he is the paltriest sort of dabbler, and furthermore he has betrayed my trust over and over again! What on earth would Thomas Alva Edison, the Wizard of Menlo Park, know or care about a self-promoting scoundrel like Lee?"

Liam smiled to himself: the hook was setting, he just had to play it right and maybe they'd get to draw a breath or two:

"I don't know about the alchemist part, but Edison said he was just talking to a colleague from back East who arrived in Los Angeles yesterday by fast airship. It seems Lee is billing himself as a metallurgist now, and . . ."

"A WHAT??" roared Chen, coming to a halt so abrupt that the three of them almost ran into each other. "That insufferable simpleton doesn't know any more about metallurgy than I do about the fine points of Azerbaijani cuisine!"

Liam shrugged. "It's just a word, Ambrose. Lee probably figured out that calling himself an alchemist would make an old mossback like Stanton nervous, so he picked himself a nice, modern, businesslike title like metallurgist . . ."

Chen interrupted him with an impatient wave of the hand: "The difference between the world of magic and the world of business is too fundamental to be tut-tutted away by talk of 'mere semantics.' You can't standardize magic or package it or market it in carefully measured units. Above all, magic stands in a totally different relationship to the natural world. Magic depends on a deep *empathy* with the natural world, on acceptance of the basic identity of the magician and the world around him.

"Business, on the other hand, strives to *manipulate* the world, to chop it up into easily handled pieces whose characteristics can be reproduced over and over again. The antimagical science and technology that have developed out of the business world's need for dependable processes of manipulation have led to a basically *bullying* relationship towards the natural world—that's why people of that sort are always speaking of *'conquering'* nature. That's how a metallurgist relates to metals—they must be made to bow to his purposes so that the results can be measured and marketed."

Chen ground his teeth frustratedly and glared at Liam as if he might bite him just to relieve his feelings. Liam held up his hands in a placating gesture:

"Hey, do I look like a businessman? I *rob* businessmen, OK? I'm just passing along what Edison told me. He said he's extremely worried about the dangers of calorium in general, and he was even *more* worried now that he'd heard that Stanton had Lee working on making calorium out of molten lead."

Chen swayed as if he'd been struck, his face turning that horrible parchment color that Liam had seen on him only once before, back on the *Straight Up.* "Oh, dear God in Heaven!" Chen said in a strangled voice. "If we can't get back to Washington in time to stop him . . ."

His voice trailed away and he stood there lost in thought for a moment before he visibly forced himself to push his thoughts aside. "We have no time to waste," he said to Liam and Crazy Horse, "literally *no* time to waste. There are a few things I can do at long distance, but they will only be palliative. We must get to Washington as rapidly as possible and make sure that Lee is stopped or there will be a terrible accident!"

With that he took off down the street at a flat run, leaving his companions to stay with him as best they could and Liam to give himself a talking-to about keeping his brilliant ideas to himself. And also to wonder about McCluskey, who seemed to have come up in the world amazingly since Liam had known him back in Five Points.

Liam looked around curiously as they jogged along, automatically casing the big houses as possible jobs and wondering: how had a two-bit house sneak and swindler like Fergus McCluskey managed to buy a home in a swell neighborhood like this—a wide, tree-lined street of walled estates any one of which Liam would have loved to visit in the middle of the night with his little black bag. And which Chen sailed by one after another like they were only mirages until he came to a second abrupt halt outside an eight-foot wrought-iron gate with a giant, gilded "McC" worked into a shield in its middle.

"This is it," Chen said in a grim voice. "McCluskey's lair."

The others caught up, panting, and moved in to look over his shoulder at a long, curving gravel driveway lined by gnarled old live oaks and—a hundred yards or so from the gate—a sprawling three-story red-brick house in the ugliest and most forbidding Victorian Gothic style surrounded by smaller red-brick outbuildings like military barracks.

"Well, look at this!" Liam said with a big grin. "They must have known I was coming." Underneath the gilded "McC" was a steel plate a foot square with a dial lock in its center, strongly reminiscent of the lock on a bank safe.

"Stand back, boys!" he said, and rubbing his fingertips briskly on the brick wall he took hold of the lock's knob and with his ear against the metal plate spun the dial slowly to the left until he'd turned it a couple of times, then repeated the operation in the other direction.

"Pooh!" Liam muttered, making a face. "Too easy, that's no fun!"

And quickly turning the dial again, this time right, left and then right, he opened the lock and gave the gate a push so that it swung back towards the house with a protesting squeak.

"After you, gentlemen," he said, bowing low and gesturing them in.

As they walked up the drive towards the house even Chen slowed down, feeling a kind of oppressive heaviness in the twilight shade of the massive live oaks and the eerie silence of the grounds. Squatting down next to the lawn, he picked up a clump of sod and knocked the earth out into his hand; then he inspected it, nodding as if some guess had been confirmed, and transferred the dirt to his coat pocket.

"There's something wrong with this place," Chen said, "and I don't just mean McCluskey. Do you feel it?"

Crazy Horse and Liam nodded wordlessly, Crazy Horse wearing a queasy look as if he were on the verge of throwing up.

"Many deaths," he said in Lakota Sioux; then, as the others looked at him curiously he held up his hand and shook his head, unable to say more.

As they reached the front door it swung open even before Chen reached for the knocker, revealing a huge, ape-like bruiser with a jaw like a gorilla and a sneering smile of purely human meanness:

"Well, well," he said in a heavy brogue, "if it isn't Liam McCool and a couple of his pansy pals. Give us a kiss, then, will you Liam me darlin'?"

Liam made a disgusted face. "Mikey Finnerty," he said, "still beating the odds after all these years. I was sure somebody would have rid the world of you long ago, but maybe Fergus taking you under his wing has changed your luck."

Finnerty's face set hard as he felt the sting of Liam's contempt. "I reckon me luck's just lovely," he said in a flat tone. "How's yours?"

Without any further warning he threw a looping punch at Liam, who moved under it so fast that his companions could barely follow it, pushing his shoulder hard into Finnerty's gut and grabbing his legs behind the knees at the same time that he went into a squat, pivoting under the big man and standing up again abruptly as he let go of his burden so that Finnerty was launched through the air like a boulder from a ballista. Screaming with terror as he flew across a spacious vestibule tiled in alternating squares of black and white, Finnerty careened into a huge stuffed horse clad in battle armor, bearing an equally huge armored knight holding a battle axe in one hand and a broadsword in the other. The impact was spectacular: Finnerty, pieces of armor, knight and horse flying in every direction and crashing to the tiled floor with a din that resounded through the building like a train wreck.

The three companions surveyed the wreckage with the judicious half-smiles of connoisseurs contemplating a great painting:

"Well done." Chen said.

"*Molodets, ty!*" Crazy Horse said.

Liam smiled appreciatively as he picked up his stick and his hat. "Jiu jitsu," he said modestly, "sometimes you just don't have time to fool around with all that magic stuff."

At that, a door across the hall was flung open with a resounding bang and a fat, red-faced man with a fringe of grizzled red hair burst into the vestibule yelling . . .

"What in the bloody hell . . . ?"

. . . and came to a sharp stop as he took in his trio of visitors.

"Well, well, well!" he said with oily mock pleasure. "What a treat! Liam McCool, as I live and breathe. And I expect you must be Mr. Chen," he said to Ambrose, "come to ask after your nearest and dearest. And you've brought along a redskin to round out the menagerie!"

A groan issued from the wreckage where the display of armor had stood and a series of clanks and clatters arose as Finnerty struggled to regain consciousness. In spite of himself, McCluskey darted a look at the pile of junk and frowned. Liam grinned:

"It's a cryin' shame you can't find better help, Fergie," he said. "I'm thinking Finnerty must have tripped over his own shoelaces."

McCluskey returned the grin with clenched teeth: "Is that so? Well normally Mikey would be my butler but under the circumstances maybe you won't mind if I show you into the study meself." He gestured towards the open door: "After you, boys."

"Maybe not," Liam said. "Backshooters make me nervous."

"Suit yourself," said McCluskey with an edge, heading into the study without looking back.

"I'll go first," Liam murmured to the others, reaching around under his jacket and pulling his Colt Peacemaker out of the back of his pants. Clicking back the hammer he entered the study and found McCluskey seated at an elaborately carved mahogany desk. Radiating hostility and a kind of sneering self-confidence, he waved dismissively at Liam's pistol:

"You can put away the blunderbuss, McCool, if I decide you need shooting, I'll have one of my boys do it."

"Maybe I'll just keep it handy," Liam said, dropping it into his jacket pocket. "Anyway, we're not planning to stay long, so just have one of your boys bring us Mr. Chen's family and we'll be on our way."

"Did you know my place is built on an old Indian burial ground?" McCluskey asked with a grin. Crazy Horse cursed in Lakota Sioux and McCluskey's grin turned into an unpleasant laugh. "That's right, redskin, it's packed to the rafters with Gabrielino Indian stiffs, and in fact all of Los Angeles used to be a Gabrielino village called Yang-Na until the good padres from the San Gabriel Mission started civilizing them. So I don't see myself being too put out by digging three new holes out there for the three of you."

"How about that?" Liam said. "You've moved up in the world, Fergie. From being a cheap punk you've turned into a real honest-to-goodness murderer."

"Hey," McCluskey said, "why do you think they call it the Land of Opportunity?"

"Well here's another opportunity for you," Liam said. "Have Chen's people brought here right now and we'll be on our way without doing you any harm. OK?"

McCluskey laughed uproariously. "Say, McCool, you've got some brassbound gall. Why not? I'll kill the three of you right in front of them. That should be good for some fun!" He picked up a voicewire apparatus and spoke into it: "Frankie? Round up those Chinks we got working in the kitchen and bring them to my office. Yeah, right now, whaddyou think, tomorrow?"

"So," Chen said quietly. "You have my family working in your kitchens, do you?"

"That's right," McCluskey said, "what did you expect, I'll feed them for free? Tell you the truth, I don't even like having Chinks around, you people give me the willies. I'd kill your family right along with you if I weren't expecting to get good money for them from Stanton's boys. As for 'murder,'

McCool, obviously you don't get how politics work way out here in the Bear Flag Republic. Sure, Holy Joe Barnum wants law and order, and Mayor Tommy backs him, but the real law around here is the police, and I own them. Get it?"

Before Liam could answer, there was a knock at the study door and a moment later it swung open as a half-dozen terrified-looking Chinese were herded into the room by a man dressed in a cook's uniform.

"Here they are, Boss," the man said.

"OK, Frankie," McCluskey said, "now get out of here."

Frankie gave him an uneasy little half bow and left in a hurry. McCluskey turned and watched Chen, grinning as the tall Chinese exchanged eye language with his family.

"Some reunion, huh?" McCluskey sneered. "Any last words before I have you scragged?"

"Yes, actually," Chen said in an even tone. "I hope you are aware that this whole enterprise of yours is founded on quicksand."

"Ooooh!" McCluskey laughed, pretending to be impressed. "You're going to be poetical, huh?"

"No," Chen said, "it's simply a fact." He reached into his pocket, took out a handful of the dirt he'd put there earlier and then rubbed it between his fingers, letting it dribble to the floor as he murmured something in Chinese. Then he smiled politely at McCluskey and continued: "Step to the window, you'll see what I mean."

McCluskey sat and glared at Chen for a moment, but when he heard panicky shouting outside followed by the sound of falling masonry, he jumped to his feet and crossed to the window. As he looked out, his jaw dropped, and his jovial facade fell away. Liam moved to get a better look and what he saw made him grin. One of the barracks-like buildings was located nearly opposite the window, and as Liam watched, the building tipped precariously at one corner and part of its front wall collapsed as it started to slide into what looked like a lake of quicksand, its panicky occupants yelling with terror as they poured out the windows only to end up floundering wildly in the gooey soil.

"You see?" Chen asked McCluskey in a tone of mild reproof. "I would never joke about a thing like that."

"But don't worry," Crazy Horse added. "Even though we're going to have to leave you now, I want to make sure you have some company. There!" he said, pointing to a hole in the baseboard, speaking as he did so, in Lakota Sioux. A moment later, a plump tarantula scuttled out and approached Crazy Horse, who picked it up gently and murmured to it as McCluskey backed away in horror.

"Get that thing out of here," he screamed, "I *hate* spiders!"

"Tch, tch!" Crazy Horse said. "You need to learn to overcome your fears like a man!" He bent closer to the tarantula and whispered something to it, pointing to McCluskey with his free hand. Then he set the fuzzy creature down gently, and it immediately scurried across the carpet and took up station directly in front of McCluskey, simultaneously doubling in size and then doubling again till it was about the size of a snapping turtle. McCluskey started emitting a series of crazed little shrieks as the spider doubled in size again to about the size of a footstool.

Chen spoke to his family quietly in Chinese and as they all started moving towards the door the walls of the room creaked and groaned ominously and then cracked from ceiling to floor as plaster spilled into the air.

"Try to meditate," Crazy Horse said to the terrified gangster, "it's really the only thing to do in a situation like this." He waved and turned for the door, as the spider doubled in size again to something about the size of a champion hog. McCluskey's yelps started climbing the scale into the soprano range as Liam moved after Crazy Horse.

"See you around, Fergie," he said with a cheery grin. "Or maybe not. Anyway, thanks for your hospitality!"

As he headed towards the door the tarantula doubled in size again to the size of the kidney-buttoned love seat and McCluskey started screaming rhythmically and insanely.

"Some people just can't take a joke," Liam said with a shrug, stepping out into the vestibule and closing the door after him with a soft click.

Chapter Twenty

ow long do you think we've got before Stanton's people get here?" Crazy Horse was shivering constantly, despite the hotel blanket he had wrapped around his shoulders.

Liam shook his head and pulled the mouton collar of his overcoat up around his neck—at six a.m. the sea fogs around Santa Catalina island were bone-chilling, and an unseasonable cold snap wasn't helping.

"All Governor Barnum said in the message he left at the desk was that he had just gotten a telegram from Prince Yurevskii's HQ saying an airship would arrive from New Petersburg sometime this morning with a special emissary and a detachment of Little Russian aeronauts they were sending to collect me, you two birds, General Custer and everybody in Ambrose's family, and that Yurevskii expected local authorities to give them every assistance in rounding us up. That was it. Period. Like Barnum said before, figuring out what to do about it is up to us."

Chen snorted irritably, doing his best not to shiver—he had decided that 40° Fahrenheit wasn't cold and that carrying on about it was simply childish.

"Then perhaps we'd better get busy and *do* something before they do arrive! We could study the place from a distance for another week and I doubt it would make the least bit of difference."

"All right, all right," Liam said irritably, "I was just hoping we'd see something that would give us an idea of how people go and come—I've never done any kind of job where I hadn't already picked out at least two escape routes, but that heap over there is buttoned up like an ironclad."

He made a frustrated gesture towards a colossal fortified keep whose spires and battlements were reminiscent of Mad King Ludwig's Bavarian castles. Like Ludwig's Neuschwanstein, Serra Castle was built on a commanding height, in this case Mt. Orizaba, at 2,097 feet the highest point on Catalina Island.

"Barnum didn't tell me it was built on top of a mountain, for Pete's sake!" Liam grumbled. "What do we do once we find Custer, grow wings and flap away like a herd of damned buzzards?"

"I believe," said Chen mildly, "that the proper collective noun for a group of buzzards is a 'wake.'"

Liam flushed with annoyance: "I'll wake you, you New College teetotum! How about a pop on the snoot, will that do it?"

Crazy Horse laid a soothing hand on Liam's shoulder: "Lyovushka. Ambrose is trying to restrain himself from reminding you that you don't have to count on jiu-jitsu to get Georgie out of there, you can use your really quite substantial powers as a sorcerer if you need them."

Liam glared at nothing in particular for a moment or two, then heaved a sigh and gestured to the others to follow as he set out across a sloping meadow that led to the main gate of Serra Castle:

"OK, boys," he said, "let's go!"

⚬━⟂

Hugging himself to stay warm despite the clinging fog, Capt. Ubaldo tromped back and forth in front of the aerial battleship, crossing his fingers that his dimwit Russians would return soon with some prisoners and glaring dyspeptically down the street towards the palm trees that lined the edge of the palisades. Very pretty, no doubt, but not enough to keep him from regretting this whole adventure—not just flying the aerial battleship to Little Russia in the first place, but *everything*: especially his disastrously ill-fated plan to play the Byronic hero and sweep Becky Fox off her feet. There had obviously been some key detail missing from his analysis of how to fan the banked embers of Becky's esteem for Captain Ubaldo the Intrepid Aeronaut into a blaze of swooning passion for Ubaldo the Man. But what?

Where had he gone wrong? He had been sure she would see the beauty of the plans he'd made for their life together, but instead she had met his magnanimity with treachery—drugged him and trussed him up like a hog for the slaughter. Which was very nearly what had happened when the Russian idiots who found him dragged him, still senseless and immobile, to the headquarters of the Secret Police!

Finally, after hours of humiliating pleading with his captors, Ubaldo's request for a royal audience had been granted. But when Prince Yurevskii had arrived at Okhrana HQ it was not to set Ubaldo free but to put him to the test: if he were to fly the aerial battleship to the Bear Flag Republic, place Liam McCool and his gang under arrest and bring them back to New Petersburg in chains, his earlier disgrace would be forgotten and he would be given a command in the Russian Aerial Navy. A simple task, surely! A snap for a veteran aeronaut like Ubaldo!

What choice did he have? Plainly dubious about Ubaldo's chances for success, an Okhrana Lieutenant had briefed him on everything the police had learned about McCool, the magician Chen and his family and the infamous Crazy Horse/General Custer duo. Then he had accompanied Ubaldo to the battleship and shaken his hand with a kind of lugubrious finality before wishing him good luck. It was all too plain that he was convinced the American would need it.

⊶

Capt. Ubaldo sighed and pulled the collar of his overcoat further up around his neck. Here in "sunny" Santa Monica it was six-thirty in the morning, he'd had nothing for breakfast except some Navy-issue hardtack and a mug of cold coffee, and the weather in the supposedly balmy and benign Bear Flag Republic promised to go on being raw and wet and every bit as cold as New York. *Madonna mia!*

He kicked an empty baked bean tin viciously, sending it flying towards the aerial battleship, which he had landed and moored in a vacant lot not far from the Santa Monica Government Building. This was the third time he had walked over to Barnum's headquarters in the hope of finding Fergus McCluskey, the elusive Irish gangster with whom he'd agreed by voicewire to exchange the six members of Ambrose Chen's family for $50,000 in gold. It didn't make sense—what gangster would pass up that kind of money?

Ubaldo had finally sent his detachment of Little Russian aeronauts into Los Angeles under orders to investigate the home address he had for McCluskey and find out what was going on. But there was still no word from any direction and he was going to have to speak to Prince Yurevskii soon, a thought that filled him with dread.

"*Sir! Sir! Hang on a minute!*"

Ubaldo turned to see a Santa Monica policeman running towards him from the direction of the Government Building, waving his hands and shouting:

"*It's about McCluskey!*"

Ubaldo stopped short and walked back to meet the man half-way.

"Well, man, what is it? Speak up!"

217

The policeman came to a halt and bent over with his hands on his knees, panting.

"Sorry, sir. I'm afraid I'm not much of an athlete!"

"For God's sake, man!" Ubaldo was almost jumping up and down with the suspense.

"It's your squad of Rooskies, sir; we've had a voicewire message from the precinct house in Live Oaks Estates saying your lads couldn't find any sign of McCluskey. Seems as how the lot where his house used to stand is just a swamp now and they couldn't find hide or hair of him nor anyone from his gang."

Ubaldo clutched his forehead and groaned. "I hate this place!" he said feelingly, and then turned on his heel and trotted back towards the aerial battleship.

In New Petersburg, Stanton was seated at the desk in his suite, jiggling the receiver of the voicewire instrument and trying to keep from screaming at it:

"Hello?" he barked. "Hellohello*hello*? *Speak* to me, you blithering imbecile!"

An offended female voice piped out of the receiver: "Really, sir!" And then, in an insufferably schoolmarmish tone: "Sticks and stones may break my bones, but names will never hurt me!"

"Madam," hissed Stanton, "either connect me immediately to the number I'm calling in the Bear Flag Republic, or I will move heaven and earth to find out *your* name and *then* we'll see about the sticks and stones!"

"*Hmmph!*" said the voice in the receiver, and a moment later the sound of ringing replaced it.

"Pick it up, Ubaldo, damn you!" Stanton grated. At the same moment, there was an appalling *BOOM!* outside, and all of the windows came smashing into the room. Instinctively flattening himself on the floor, Stanton looked across the room towards the square outside the hotel, where a thick column of oily black smoke was rising towards the sky. Halfway across the room, unconscious on the floor and surrounded by a considerable pool of urine, Willie Pilkington lay sprawled where he had fainted.

"Bah!" muttered Stanton. "Poltroon!"

He got to his feet and scuttled across the room in a crouching run, stopping at the window and peering out at the square from behind the curtain. Below, clanking across the paving stones, came the forces of the anti-Yurevskii rebels: a couple of hundred of his "Brainy Acmes" throwing sticks of dynamite and firing a variety of weapons (one of the metal giants was even carrying an Armstrong rifled cannon with no carriage and firing it as another Acme walked behind and served as loader).

Facing them in the foreground, and in total disarray, was a mixed force of defenders—Little Russian soldiers and Yurevskii's Japanese technical advisers, most of them aeronauts from the Japanese Imperial Navy. For the moment they were firing an ineffectual assortment of small arms, but their resistance was wavering even as Stanton watched.

"Damn it!" Stanton muttered. "And damn that insurrectionist swine Plekhanov!" Once again he scuttled across the room in a half-crouch and snatched the voicewire receiver up off the floor.

"Hello?" he shouted. "*Hellohellohello! Answer me, Ubaldo, you duplicitous dago!*"

0—⚡

At that very moment Ubaldo was starting up the flight of stairs that rose into the aerial battleship's belly, and the moment the ringing began in the main cabin, he leapt up the last stairs and ran across the cabin to the voicewire console.

Snatching up the receiver from the TeslaVox transmitter/receiver Ubaldo babbled breathlessly:

"Yessir, Your Highness, sorry sir, unavoidably detained on the way to . . ."

"SHUT UP!" Dear God! Was that Stanton? Where had *he* come from? The bellow from the tiny receiver was nearly ear-piercing. "WHAT ABOUT THE PRISONERS, DO YOU HAVE THEM IN YOUR BRIG? IN CHAINS?"

Ubaldo's face screwed up in agony. How was he supposed to deal with *this*? "Ah, sir . . ." he said, "I've been assigned to this mission by Prince Yurevskii and I'm afraid I can't discuss it with anyone else."

There was a long silence at the other end, and for a brief moment Ubaldo hoped against hope that perhaps all the screaming had finally brought on an apoplectic seizure, that at this very moment Stanton was lying on the floor frothing at the mouth and clawing at his collar . . . but no such luck. After a moment, he resumed, his tone now simply brisk and businesslike:

"*Listen to me, Ubaldo. As it happens, I overheard Yurevskii telling that clot Boylan about your mission to arrest McCool and the rest of those miscreants, and I was shocked to hear how little he offered you. After all, you came to me first with your offer of service, isn't that so? It's not my fault those damned Russians interrupted with their treacherous aerial attack. So why don't you just forget Yurevskii and consider the mission to be an assignment from me? If you land the prisoners at the Aerial Navy Base in Central Park I will make you an Admiral in the United States Aerial Navy on the spot! And I will give you $100,000 in gold into the bargain!*"

"But sir," Ubaldo began, his voice quavering with stress, "what if Prince Yurevskii . . ."

"*Tut, tut, Ubaldo,*" interrupted Stanton, "*don't you worry about a thing! I'll take care of Prince Yurevskii, never you fear. Just get McCool and his gang of lowlifes back to New*

York and I'll see to the rest. Now, according to what that blow-hard Boylan told his master, he had word from a Santa Monica police informant that McCool and Crazy Horse and the Chinaman have gone to Catalina Island to set Custer free. So all you need to do is fly the aerial battleship to Catalina at once, arrest the lot of them and put them in chains. I'll be back in New York in time to meet you in Central Park and pin your Admiral's stars on your collar myself! Do I make myself clear?"

"Oh, yessir, yessir, totally clear!"

Ubaldo's head was nearly spinning as he tried to re-orient himself, but he did his best to sound like the bold and intrepid Ubaldo he needed to be if he were going to come out of this insanity alive.

"*Good,*" said Stanton. "*Now do it, and be quick about it!*"

There was a sharp *CLICK!* from the receiver and Ubaldo sat there for a long moment, almost paralyzed with terror. Then at last he got to his feet and started frantically flicking switches and entering new settings on the battleship's instruments. Thank God Catalina Island was only ten or fifteen minutes away and the ship had been designed to be flown by one crew member if an emergency dictated. Because this *definitely* qualified as an emergency.

Chapter Twenty-One

pen that damned door *now*!" shouted Liam at the top of his lungs.

He and his companions were standing out-side the main entrance to Serra Castle, a ten-foot-tall oak door bound with iron straps, looking frustrated. The solitary keyhole was a good three inches high, suggesting a key of truly heroic proportions, and after trying to pick the lock for several minutes Liam had to admit defeat.

"They probably don't get up this early," said Crazy Horse. "Why should they?"

"OK then," Liam said, "at least we ought to case the place a little better before we try busting down a door that size. Why don't we go for a little stroll, walk around the thing and see if there are some doors or windows we can use without getting into a lot of magical hijinks."

"May I remind you," Chen said with a touch of asperity, "that time is a luxury we don't have. We need to stop Chiang Lee before he does something we shall all regret."

"How about this," Crazy Horse offered. "Ambrose and I will split up and take a quick walk around the place while you have another go at the lock. We'll meet back here in ten minutes or less and decide what we want to do."

"Let's get started," Liam said. He got out the Swiss folding tool that Harry the Jap had modified for him, flipped out a selection of picks and went to work on the lock, humming distractedly. Just as he was starting to get totally frustrated for the second time, he heard a sharp little bark from behind him and turned with a start.

Sitting on a boulder a few yards behind him was the smallest fox he'd ever seen, a pretty little creature about a foot high at the shoulder and a couple of feet long, its body furred in gray and red with a white throat and belly, and a black stripe along the back of its tail. It cocked its head inquiringly as Liam turned to look at it and growled as if to ask him what he was up to. Liam bowed politely:

"I tried knocking," he said, "but nobody answers. You have a better idea?"

The fox barked again and took off loping across the meadow until it disappeared amongst the tall grass. Irritated with himself for wasting time, Liam turned back to attack the lock again and recoiled in shock as he realized that where the lock had been moments ago there was now literally nothing: no lock plate, no keyhole, nothing but a smooth plank of oak with no hint of a way in.

Liam was just about ready to throw a fit. "That's the damn limit," he said out loud. "Now what?"

"Perhaps I can help you, sir." The voice came from behind him: a woman's voice, sweet and strong and musical, like Becky's, but even more . . . *more* . . . unable to resist, Liam turned to see what the speaker looked like.

Standing behind him was a slender blonde woman with her long hair done up in a braid, carrying a wire basket filled with pint bottles of cream. She was wearing a blue gingham dress, the sort of thing Liam was used to seeing the working women of Five Points wear but not dowdy the way he was used to; instead, the commonplace look of the dress seemed to emphasize an unbelievably intense sensuality, as if the partly unbuttoned collar were inviting him to . . .

The woman had the face of a Madonna, but when she laughed, the white flash of her teeth and the pink plumpness of her lips sent an involuntary shiver up Liam's spine.

"You seem a bit distracted," she said with a merry giggle. "My name is Siobhan," she said with a curtsy, "and if you'll let me, I'm sure I can help you. I bring fresh cream every day for the men in the Castle and they've given me a key so I can take it straight through and put it in the pantry." She took a huge brass key out of a pocket and held it up for Liam to see.

"Siobhan," he murmured stupidly, somehow unable to keep from embarrassing himself further. "That's a beautiful name and you're a beautiful . . ."

She cocked her head expectantly, tapping her plump lower lip with the tip of the key as her smile spread into a grin.

"My, you *are* a flatterer." she said. "You do have a name, don't you?"

"My name?" Liam said, feeling stupider than ever. The thing was, his brain seemed to have gone completely to sleep and instead all he had were sensations—a kind of warm, tingling sensation in his guts that was spreading slowly, making every nerve ending so abnormally aware that he felt as if the touch of a feather might make him jump out of his skin. Even so, he wanted more than anything he could think of to feel the touch of this woman's skin on his, and he raised his hand towards her slowly, as if it weighed a hundred pounds . . .

"My name?" he repeated. "My name is . . ."

"*GET AWAY FROM THAT THING!*"

It was Chen bellowing at him with an unfamiliar note of panic in his voice, and as he turned to look Liam saw Chen and Crazy Horse pelting towards him, Chen waving his hands back and forth over his head in an emphatic signal and Crazy Horse running with his eyes closed and his lips moving rapidly in a chant.

From behind him Liam heard a deep, bloodcurdling *HISS!*, and as he turned back he saw the most horrifying sight he had ever seen: atop the woman's body, instead of the sweet, merry face of the milkmaid Siobhan, there was the head of some colossal insect-like creature whose pincer jaws were clashing together hungrily and whose multiple red eyes were glowing with an absolute fury as it *SCREEEEECHED!* at something overhead and the seductive body abruptly melted away like a coating of wax revealing the hideous, praying mantis-like thing underneath.

Totally unnerved, Liam leapt backwards as if he were levitating, while a colossal shadow swept over both him and the milkmaid thing and a golden eagle the size of a Little Russian attack flyer suddenly swept down and grabbed the creature in its huge talons, covering the giant bug's renewed screech with a tearing, earsplitting eagle's squawk as it beat its wings and vanished upwards.

Sweating like a pig and crossing himself feverishly, Liam muttered: *"Hail Mary, full of grace, the Lord is with thee, blessed art thou amongst women and blessed . . ."* and then broke off as he saw the cockroach thing, far overhead by now but still distinctly visible, turn suddenly into a huge snake, writhing wildly as it tried to strike at the eagle and escape from its grasp.

"Ah, dear Jesus," Liam shouted, "it's going to . . ."

"It isn't going to do anything at all," Chen said as he laid a reassuring hand on Liam's shoulder. "Our friend Crazy Horse is a shape-shifter, and a very powerful one at that—he'll be rejoining us in a moment."

Suddenly, Liam felt himself trembling, sweating even more copiously and shaking like a leaf as his brain began to take charge again. He leaned forward with his hands on his knees, fighting a wave of nausea.

"What *was* that thing?" he asked in a choked voice.

Chen spread his hands and shrugged: "A demon of some sort, probably expelled from some poor wretch back in the days when the good padres ran Serra Castle. No doubt after the churchmen left the demon stayed and became a sort of housekeeper for the Castle. You'll meet many more creatures like it before you decide you've had enough, not to mention ones that are far worse. But," he added in a reassuring tone, "I expect you'll be all right."

"Many more of *those* things?" Liam said incredulously.

"Certainly. The world is changing; we're entering a whole new cycle and none too soon, if men are to escape enslavement by their machines. However, as some American wit has pointed out, *There is No Free Lunch* . . . the obverse of a renewed spirituality is renewed contact with the less presentable denizens of the spirit world. Don't worry," he said with a sudden grin, "sometimes I think you're not terribly bright, but you have a powerful will and that will carry you a long way."

"Golly, thanks, Ambrose," Liam said sourly.

"Don't mention it, my boy. But you must learn the rules, and rule number one when you are dealing with creatures from the Spirit World is: *never* give them your name. Giving them your name will put you instantly in their power and the consequences of that can be quite horrific."

Shuddering at his narrow escape, Liam took Chen's hand and shook it fervently. "Thank you, Ambrose. I think you'll find me paying closer attention in the future."

Chen smiled and nodded. "Good. And now . . ."

With a sudden vast beat of wings the golden eagle swept to the ground next to them and repeated the feather-ruffling and hopping dance the great horned owl had performed back on Shelter Island, finally resolving itself with the same stomach-flipping abruptness into Crazy Horse.

Crazy Horse grinned at Liam: "Sorry I had to interrupt your tête-à-tête with the charming milkmaid." He made an exaggerated kissy-face at Liam: "She said she was sending ums a great big kiss!"

Glaring and red with embarrassment Liam raised a fist: "That's nice, because I'm about to be sending *you* a great big *lip!*"

"All right, children," Chen said crisply, "you can play later, right now we must free General Custer and head for the Apacheria with the least possible waste of time." He turned to Liam and gestured at his stick:

"Mr. McCool, if you would do the honors . . ."

Liam looked at him doubtfully: "What, on the door?"

Ambrose nodded. "The sword is an extension of your will; just picture Miss Siobhan and her charade with the key—think, if you will, of what a simpleton she seems to have taken you for . . ."

Liam's expression darkened for a moment as he contemplated the memory; then he fell into a half-crouch, lifted the sword in a two-handed grip and let go with a mighty stroke and an explosive shout of "*Keeyai!*"

A microsecond later there was a blinding flash followed by a groaning rumbling noise that made them back away instinctively even as they were rubbing their eyes.

"I don't believe it," muttered Liam.

The door had been neatly chopped in two, as had the stout oak doorjambs and the mortared stones that supported them, so that in a moment or two the entire doorway had crumbled to fragments, leaving a gaping hole in the wall. Ahead of them the interior of the Castle revealed a dark, high-ceilinged antechamber barely illuminated by a gaslight on the wall. A furious shout sounded from further on in the shadowy interior:

"*You bastards stand right where you are! Don't you move a muscle, you hear?*"

As the trio peered into the gloom to see who was yelling, the distinctive *click-clack!* of a pump-action Spencer 12-gauge chambering a shell froze them where they stood, and a moment

227

later the guard himself appeared. An ordinary-looking middle-aged man with thinning brown hair and a drooping moustache, he was wearing a patched and faded Confederate captain's uniform and holding the shotgun at port arms.

"Bill Quantrill?" Liam asked incredulously. "The Butcher of Lawrence, Kansas? I thought you got shot in a barn somewhere in Kentucky."

"There's one *damnation* big difference between being *thought* to be shot and being shot for sure and certain and you three are about to learn it if you don't skedaddle right now!"

Chen's answer was quiet, but so weirdly deep and resonant that it sent chills up Liam's spine:

"Sir! You are more than kind, thank you for bringing bread and salt for three weary travelers!"

Quantrill's jaw dropped and he jumped backwards a step; the shotgun had vanished, and in his left hand he held a long, thin loaf of bread while in his right he held a big shaker of salt. He opened his mouth and closed it again two or three times in a row as he looked back and forth between his two hands. Then he knelt abruptly, shaking as if he had a chill and holding the bread and salt out in front of him.

"Welcome, *sifu!*" Quantrill said in a trembling voice. "What is your will?"

Chen took the bread and salt from him and handed them to Crazy Horse.

"Thank you, my son. First, you must tell me where the prisoner Custer is being kept."

Quantrill bent his head: "At the far end of the corridor in front of you, *sifu*, in the cell on the right."

"Excellent, my child. Now as you see, the Castle is beginning to fall apart . . ."

Chen raised his hand and spread the fingers wide towards the gap they had entered by. As if at a prompt, a huge additional chunk of the wall crumbled away and tumbled down the hill with a roar. Quantrill looked towards the hole with wide eyes.

"Oh, *sifu!*" he quavered. "Will we perish?"

"No, my son," Chen answered, "but you must run now and summon all the other people who are in the building apart from Custer and tell them to leave the building at once or they will be doomed, soon there will be nothing here but a heap of rocks!"

Quantrill leapt to his feet and bowed deeply. "It shall be as you say, *sifu!*" he said, and instantly took off down the hall bellowing over and over: "EVERYBODY OUT! FIRE! GET OUT!"

For a moment the trio stood and stared after him.

"Well, Ambrose," Liam said, "I didn't think you could ever top your giant shark turn, but as far as I'm concerned this one absolutely takes the cake, and I don't care who knows it!"

"Come on," said Crazy Horse impatiently, "let's go get Georgie and get out of here while we can!"

He took off running down the corridor with his companions right on his heels. "Georgie!" he shouted in English. "It's us. Time to go!"

Custer's voice sounded weakly in the distance: "*Crazy Horse? Is that* you?" A moment later they were at the cell door, a thick slab of oak with a sliding wooden window (now closed) and a big, old-fashioned iron key stuck in its lock. A moment of over-eager fumbling, and then the door swung open to reveal Custer, wild-haired and long-bearded enough to be Rip Van Winkle himself. Overwhelmed and incredulous, he bear-hugged Crazy Horse, and then Liam and Chen, laughing and talking all at once:

"Crazy Horse! Liam! And . . .?"

"Chen," the Chinese chimed in, "Ambrose Chen, delighted to meet you, General Custer."

"Please, that was another life—I'm Laughing Wolf now, and an honorary Lakota Sioux." He held Chen away at arm's length and surveyed the three of them, looking as if he might start hugging them all over again.

"Come on, Georgie," Crazy Horse said, grabbing hold of Custer's sleeve and dragging him after him: "we can tell stories later, right now we have to get *out* of here!"

Puzzled but cooperative, Custer joined his liberators in a mad run down the corridor towards the gap in the wall, which was continuing to get larger with an accompanying din of creaks, groans and rumbles of falling masonry, mixed with panicky yells and angry shouts as the entire staff of Serra Castle struggled to be first in line to escape the impending collapse. Finally, after a bloody nose for Liam and a split lip for Custer, the foursome was ejected with a wad of struggling humanity that burst out of the side of the Castle with explosive force and rolled part of the way down the hill towards the meadow below before they separated themselves from each other and registered Quantrill, who was standing on a hummock and roaring at them:

"GET UP OFF YOUR DEAD BUTTS AND FALL *IN*! DO YOU HEAR ME, PEOPLE? FALL IN BEFORE I COME OVER THERE AND MAKE YOU FALL *DOWN*!"

Custer was shaking his head incredulously: "Bill *Quantrill*? I thought he was supposed to be . . ."

Liam made a face. "It's a long story and I'm not sure you'd believe me if I told you."

Despite a constant obbligato of curses and complaints the men gradually fell in and stood at a sloppy attention, and finally Quantrill came over to Chen and bowed deeply.

"They're all out, *sifu*. What now?"

As if to accent the question, the pace of the Castle's collapse picked up, an enormous central section sinking in on itself with a thunderous *KRRRRRUMP!*, making the towers lean crazily until they too fell into the rest of the debris with an apocalyptic roar. A great cloud of dust rose from the wreckage and hung above it for a moment or two until the ocean breezes caught it up and dispersed it eastwards, towards the coast.

Chen nodded approvingly and turned back to Quantrill. "You've done well, my son, now tell them to spread out and form a circle, and then to sit down on the grass and join hands."

"It shall be as you say, *sifu*," Quantrill said, and a moment later he was kicking and yelling at the men, chivvying them into obedience like a border collie with a herd of unruly sheep.

Well beyond mere incredulity, Custer watched the men for a moment or two and then turned to Chen:

"*Sifu?*" he queried. "And '*my son*'? Come on, Ambrose, help a simple soldier out here—these people are the absolute lowest scum on the face of the North American Continent! Deserters and bandits and murderers, every one of them."

Chen smiled. "No one ever falls too low to be raised up again, Laughing Wolf. These men are about to build and take up residence in the first Taoist Monastery in North America."

Custer looked a little dazed. "Monastery?"

"And they will become known far and wide for the piety of their prayers and the kindness of their good works."

"Huh!" said the totally befuddled Custer.

The men were all sitting on the grass now, holding hands in a circle fifty or sixty feet in diameter and looking irritated. Quantrill turned towards Chen and spread his hands questioningly.

"Excuse me for a moment," Chen said to his companions and crossed the meadow to join Quantrill, speaking to him slowly and patiently with occasional gestures towards the circle of men.

Custer shook his head. "Well, Liam, you do take up with some odd folks."

"It's a fact," Liam agreed. "There's you and Crazy Horse, for openers." He grinned. "You might as well just take it easy; you've got a bit of catching up to do." At that point Chen came back to rejoin them, while Quantrill started walking around the circle, speaking to the men quietly and earnestly.

"There," Chen said with a satisfied look. "They're going to chant for a while now, and tomorrow, when it's quite safe to venture into the ruins, they'll start sorting the rocks and other materials and cleaning up the mess. They should be able to start building their monastery and studying the *Tao Te Ching* in a month or so."

A deep, thrumming chant arose from the circle of men, repeating over and over again: "*Om mani padme hum . . .*"

Chen looked pleased and nodded. "It's a Buddhist chant," he said, "but that doesn't matter a bit—it's a fine place to begin."

"Well, Ambrose," Liam said, "whatever else, I don't reckon you'll ever be in any danger of having me figure you out."

Chen gave that a minute smile. "Westerners make altogether too much fuss about understanding one another. We are not treatises nor rune stones. We are living creatures. So if there's one simple thing I'd like you to learn today it's this: when you use magic on people, first make quite sure that you will be *adding*, not taking away."

Liam cocked his head, thinking that over, but before he could respond, Crazy Horse cried out: "Look! Up there!"

The others turned to follow his pointing finger, and saw Stanton's aerial battleship coming their way on a rapidly descending path.

"Well, well," Liam said with a bit of an edge. "You boys won't have seen that before but I know it well. As a matter of fact Yurevskii stole it from Stanton and Becky and I stole it from the Little Russians. And somebody else must have stolen it from Freedom Party Headquarters on Shelter Island. I wonder who Stanton decided to send after our friend Laughing Wolf?"

The circle of chanting men seemed to be too involved to notice the airship's approach, but Liam and his companions strolled across the meadow towards a spot that looked like the end of the battleship's trajectory. Settling on a hummock a cautious distance away, they waited as the ship set down gently, fired a series of tethered stakes into the ground to give it a firm anchorage and turned off its engines.

After a few moments, the landing stairs slid down into place and locked with a *clank!*, and then Capt. Ubaldo exited and looked around with a frown.

"Where's the Castle?" he muttered. He'd seen pictures back at the Santa Monica Government Building, and the Castle should have been standing right over *there*, on that rocky promontory.

Waving the others to keep back for a moment, Liam walked up softly behind Ubaldo and then answered him:

"I'll tell you that one if you'll tell me when you started working for Stanton."

Ubaldo jumped, then flushed a deep, angry crimson and spun around to confront Liam.

"You damned criminal swine!" He gave Liam an angry sneer: "I don't know how you came to be here, but even if you decide to shoot me in the back like the cowardly cur you are, I have already triumphed over you!"

"Is that so?" Liam asked in a tone of mild interest. Not mild enough to fool anyone who knew him, though, and Chen promptly moved out of the shadows to referee the encounter.

"Well, well," Ubaldo said with a scornful grimace. "You seem to have found your allies among all the gutter trash of the world. Chinamen! What could be next?"

Disconcertingly for him, Ubaldo's rhetorical question was answered by two more of Liam's allies as Custer and Crazy Horse stepped up to join Chen. "How about a Sioux war chief and his sidekick Laughing Wolf, once known as General George Armstrong Custer?" Custer asked cheerfully.

Ubaldo backed away in spite of himself, trying to cover this cowardly telltale by blustering:

"I'll have you know that I am under direct orders from Secretary of National Security Edwin M. Stanton to arrest you, General Custer, and your accomplices McCool and Chen and Crazy Horse, and bring you back to Washington to face trial."

Liam stepped forward and crowded into Ubaldo's space, a move that made the sweat pop out all over the aeronaut's face. "I tell you what, Arturo, I'll consider coming with you if you answer my question: when did you start working for Stanton?"

Sternly resisting the urge to wipe the sweat off his face, Ubaldo jutted his chin out at Liam and redoubled his sneer:

"I've been onto you from the very beginning, you jumped-up little thief! It was me that gave you up to Stanton in the first place, it made me *that* sick to see you fawning all over that sweet noble creature Becky Fox!"

Something like a black cloud began to sweep over Liam and he started forward with no clear thought in his mind except revenge, but Chen's hand on his shoulder restrained him:

"Mr. McCool," Chen said quietly.

Liam stopped and came slowly back to himself as a thoroughly frightened Ubaldo babbled on, making it worse:

"That's right! And I informed the authorities of the Freedom Party's hiding place and then I left for Little Russia and took Becky with me so that she would not be tarred with the brush of your criminal machinations . . ."

"You what?" shouted Liam, and this time it took both Crazy Horse and Chen to hold him back.

Realizing dimly that he might have just signed his own death warrant, Ubaldo babbled in near hysteria:

"Oh, never fear, she was far too corrupted by the time she had spent in your company to recognize the attractions of an honest, decent, manly sort of man. Instead, she treacherously drugged me and escaped into the slums of New Petersburg!"

Liam clutched his forehead. "New *Petersburg*?" He started towards Ubaldo with such patently clear intent that Ubaldo backed away until the airship's staircase hit him in the back and made him shriek.

"Liam!" said Chen sharply, and the unfamiliar use of his first name made Liam freeze where he was and turn curiously towards Chen.

"*Add*," reminded Chen sternly, "not take away. Consider this your first real test."

Liam closed his eyes and knit his hands together, forcing himself to breathe slowly and evenly despite the crazy speed with which his thoughts were moving. Finally, after what seemed like ages, he blew out a long, slow breath and grinned broadly. He opened his eyes again as Chen watched him like a hawk.

"My criminal machinations, eh?" he murmured.

"That's right," Ubaldo said with all the firmness he could muster, which wasn't quite enough to keep his voice from breaking and squeaking like an adolescent's. "And as I have been deputized to arrest you by the properly constituted authorities of the United States of America, I will take you back in chains or my name's not Arturo Ubaldo!"

"It's not," Liam said.

Ubaldo was sharply taken aback: "Eh?" he said.

"Your name is not Arturo Ubaldo," Liam said, and spreading his hands above his head he closed his eyes for several long moments and then clapped his hands. There was a blinding flash of light, and as everybody's vision slowly returned, they saw—on the spot where Ubaldo had been standing—a dark-haired, cheerful-looking woman of about the same height as Ubaldo but at least three times his weight. She looked around uncertainly, clearly not at all sure where she was.

"Artura?" Liam asked. "Artura Ubaldo?"

"Why . . . why, yes," she answered in a high but quite pleasant voice. "Pardon me for troubling you, but could you possibly tell me where I am?"

"Certainly, madam," Liam said, throwing a pointed look at Chen, "with the greatest pleasure. You are about to board this airship and be flown directly to meet someone who will be *very* pleased to meet you! In fact, I can safely say you are about to become a new source of happiness for a very large, lively family that has been coping for some time with a sad but unavoidable loss."

"I am?" she asked with a puzzled frown. "Are you sure?"

"Never been surer of anything in my life," Liam said with a smile. "Come along, boys, we're heading back to Santa Monica." He held out his hand to Artura: "Allow me, Miss Ubaldo . . ." and with an encouraging smile he led her up the stairs into the ship. For a moment Custer, Crazy Horse and Chen stood at the foot of the stairs, sunk in thought. Finally Custer nudged Chen with his elbow and grinned: "Bet you didn't see *that* one coming, Professor!" Then, chuckling delightedly, he led the way back into the ship.

Chapter Twenty-Two

overnor Barnum, Mayor Edison and Charlie Stratton were standing in the vacant lot next to the
Government Building, Barnum and Edison scanning the sky impatiently, Stratton strutting back
and forth smoking a cigar and enjoying the morning sunshine.
Barnum turned to Stratton looking a little on edge:

"You sure that's all he said, Charlie?"

"Yup," said Stratton, blowing a nice fat smoke ring.
"Just that he had a present for Tom, and someone he wanted
you to meet and they'd be here in about fifteen minutes."
He took a watch out of his waistcoat pocket and looked at it:
"Which, I gotta remind you, Phin, was just about ten minutes
ago."

Barnum pulled out a big calico handkerchief and
mopped his brow. "Sorry, Charlie, I'm afraid McCool has got
me a little on edge. I mean, I just got a call from the Avalon
Chief of Police saying Serra Castle *fell down* this morning, not
one stone left standing on another, and meanwhile all those
hidebound villains Quantrill's been collecting there since '65
were sitting in the meadow nice as pie, holding hands and
having a sing-song like kiddies on a school picnic."

Edison shrugged and smiled: "Something tells me Mr.
McCool is a man of unplumbed depths."

"Hey!" piped Stratton. "There she is!"

They turned to see the aerial battleship coming fast from the direction of Santa Monica Bay, descending as it approached, and in less time than it took for them to back away nervously and make sure they were leaving it enough landing room, it had already settled on the field and fired its mooring bolts into the ground. A moment later Chen and Crazy Horse and Custer came trotting down the steps from the ship's interior and Barnum's party hurried over to greet them.

"By Gad, General," enthused Barnum, "I never thought I'd see you again!" He and Custer exchanged a hearty handshake and then Custer bent over Stratton, sniffing the air with a passion that made the little man grin.

"I don't suppose you could use a see-gar, could you, General?" teased Stratton,

"It's a good thing my dear old sainted mother is already gone to a better world," said Custer, "for if she weren't I would gladly sell her lock, stock and barrel for one of your stogies."

"Always glad to honor a veteran," chuckled Stratton, holding out his cigar case, "help yourself!"

As Custer rapturously went through the ceremony of selecting, rolling, sniffing and snipping his Havana, Edison turned to Crazy Horse and Chen:

"Say, fellows, you didn't leave McCool back on Catalina, did you?"

"No, sir," said Crazy Horse, "but he has a surprise he wants to spring on Governor Barnum and he had a request: would you please blindfold him? As soon as you do he'll come and join you."

Edison and Barnum exchanged a quizzical look and a shrug, and a moment later Barnum had knotted the big calico handkerchief over his eyes.

"Bring 'er on!" he said with a smile, and Crazy Horse put thumb and forefinger into his mouth and gave a shrill whistle. No sooner had he done so than Liam came down the stairs, leading Miss Ubaldo gently by the hand till she was on terra firma.

The minute Edison and Stratton saw her they gasped with astonishment:

"Well, I'll be switched," murmured Stratton.

"Incredible," said Edison.

"Say," complained Barnum, "you fellows are kind of twisting the knife! How about letting me take off this hankie?"

"In a minute, Governor," Liam said, grinning with anticipation as he led a slightly nervous Artura over to a position right in front of Barnum.

"Okay, Governor," Liam said, "just imagine a fanfare from the band and the ringmaster saying '*And now, ladies and gentlemen . . .*' and then you can take off your blindfold."

Overcome with suspense, Barnum whipped off the handkerchief, but the moment he took in the newcomer his jaw dropped and he shook his head in disbelief:

"Young lady," he said, "I don't know where Mr. McCool met you, but you are the absolute spit and image of Billy Mae Sweetwater, and if you would do me the honor of accepting a long-term contract with P. T. Barnum's Greatest Show on Earth, you would make me the happiest man in the Bear Flag Republic!"

"I would?" she asked, more than a little bowled over.

"You certainly would, my dear," said the obviously ecstatic Barnum. "And if you'll come along with me I'll sign you right now! Is there anything else I can do to make you happy?"

Artura gave him a big smile: "Well, I *am* pretty hungry!"

Barnum crooked his arm for her and she put her arm through it: "Dear lady," he said, "before we fuss with contracts and such, I am going to take you over to Bob Burns' steak house on Wilshire and 2nd and treat you to the finest sirloin in Santa Monica!" He turned back to the others. "Boys," he said, "lunch is on me, will you join us?"

"We've got to get going," Liam said, "but thanks anyway."

"I owe you a very big one," Barnum said, putting his hand over his heart.

Liam grinned: "*Bookstore*," he intoned pointedly, "just make sure to save me the best lot on Ocean Avenue, and I'll be here inside six months!"

As Barnum and his new Fat Lady and the quondam General Thumb strolled away towards the ocean, Liam turned to Edison:

"Well, Mr. Mayor, I happen to have a surprise for you as well."

"For heaven's sake, McCool," Edison said, "I'm too old for the suspense—what *is* it?"

Liam smiled and gestured to the aerial battleship:

"It's all yours, sir. I don't know if it will square with your idea of not doing harm to anyone, but it's certainly true that harmful people are likely to think twice about spoiling this paradise if they know it's your first line of defense. Anyhow, there are a lot of interesting toys in there for you to play with, and at the very worst you may decide to beat a bunch of swords into a bunch of plowshares."

Edison took Liam's hand and shook it warmly: "Like I said to Phin, you're a man of unplumbed depths."

"Nah," Liam grinned, "just your garden-variety Mick cracksman looking for a nice place to settle down."

He turned to Crazy Horse: "Now you can show us *your* surprise," he said.

"This way, gentlemen," the Sioux war chief said with a grand gesture: "down past the Government Building to Ocean Avenue, and then left through that little park towards the stairs to the beach."

As the four companions strolled along towards the sparkling waters of Santa Monica Bay, Chen looked around appraisingly.

"This really is a remarkably pleasant place," he said, "are you thinking seriously of returning here to settle?"

"Yup," Liam said cheerfully, "unless somebody kills me along the way. I hope Becky can see setting up shop as a reporter here in California, and I don't see why not if we succeed in getting rid of Stanton and Yurevskii. There'll be railroads and airships going and coming nineteen to the dozen the minute those crooks are out of the way, and I hope you boys," he turned to Custer and Crazy Horse, "have already got some ideas about tossing out the Little Russians and going into business with the U.S."

"You bet we have!" said Custer. "No reason to throw out any Russian that wants to be partners with The People and start something new out here, either!"

"Nor any 'brainy' Acme, as far as that goes," Crazy Horse said, "we can make them all citizens."

"Hmmm," murmured Chen. "I wonder if this might not be a good place to start a North American College of Alchemy and the Magical Arts? After all, I have a baccalaureate from Oxford."

Liam smiled. "Like Governor Barnum said, it's definitely a good place for big dreams."

Each of them happily absorbed in his own dreams, the Four Musketeers strolled westwards towards Ocean Avenue and then turned south through a pleasant, palm tree-lined esplanade that ran along the top of the cliffs fronting the Pacific Ocean. After a block or two, they came at last to a small, slate-roofed brick building entirely without windows which bore a brass-lettered sign reading: "Camera Obscura."

"*Et voilà!*" said Crazy Horse with a grin. "*Nous sommes arrivés.*"

"I don't want to be rude, Zhenya," said Custer, "but this is *it*?"

"I discovered this place the last time I was here," Crazy Horse answered. "You know what a camera obscura is?"

"Ahh...sort of," Custer said, thoroughly baffled, "you have a dark room with a pinhole in the wall, right? And you see things that are outside the room inside the room, but upside down?"

"'Sort of' is good in this case," Crazy Horse said with a mysterious smile. "Come on!" He gestured for the others to follow and as he approached the door he added: "The thing is, this place is a bit like Ambrose's ley lines, only it's what a Sioux medicine man would call 'spirit lines.' I'll show you." And he disappeared through the door, followed—after a moment's hesitation—by Liam, Chen and Custer.

⚷

Inside, the darkness was startling, but after a moment the four friends realized that a ghostly mirror image of the esplanade and the building across Ocean Avenue was being projected upside down on the wall farthest from the street. As a fashionable—and upside down—young woman strolled by twirling her parasol, Custer muttered:

"Tarnation! You'd think her skirt would fall down enough to show us her ankle, wouldn't you?"

"Ever the vulgarian," said Crazy Horse with a grin.

Then he walked over and leaned against the projected image with both palms, chanting something in melodic Lakota Sioux. For a moment or two the others just watched in some puzzlement, until abruptly the projected scene was replaced by another—this one as bright as day and showing a mountain landscape strewn with huge, cracked boulders and occasional sage and greasewood bushes.

"Now wait a minute . . ." Liam said uneasily.

As he spoke a big chuckwalla scuttled across one of the boulders in the foreground and stopped abruptly as it appeared to notice them. Immediately, it started doing pushups and puffing up its chest, an aggression display that said he was warning them away from his territory.

"That's crazy," said Custer flatly.

Crazy Horse turned and grinned at them: "Come on, fellas, we haven't got all day!"

With that, Crazy Horse walked through the wall, frightening away the chuckwalla.

"Well," Liam said, "here goes nothing." With that he crossed himself and followed Crazy Horse, realizing as he did so that the Camera Obscura and Santa Monica itself had disappeared, leaving him standing somewhere in the mountains on a very hot afternoon.

"Come on," shouted Crazy Horse, waving towards something Liam couldn't see, and a moment later Chen and Custer stepped into view, Custer with his jaw hanging and Chen muttering to himself in Chinese. Crazy Horse swept his arm in a grandiloquent gesture, taking in what looked like an endless expanse of tumbled boulders framed by a cloudless sky of brilliant, eye-watering blue.

"Welcome to the Apacheria," he said.

And a moment later a deafening fusillade of rifle and Gatling-gunfire broke out from somewhere altogether too nearby, sending shrieking ricochets and sharp chips of stone flying in every direction.

"Hell's *bells*!" shouted Custer, flattening himself to the ground behind a boulder, where he was instantly followed by the other three.

As they lay there gritting their teeth and grimacing in anticipation of connecting with a bullet or a flying rock chip, Custer shouted:

"You can keep your damned Apacheria, Crazy Horse, it reminds me of *Gettysburg*!"

"Yeah," Liam shouted, "me too! Only *worse*, they didn't have this many rocks—and I was on Little Round Top, so I know from Gettysburg and rocks!"

"Know *from* Gettysburg and rocks?" Chen queried, raising a quizzical eyebrow.

"That's New York talk," Liam said grimly, "and I use it whenever I'm really *terrified*."

"Well," Crazy Horse said, ducking as a ricochet *whannnged* overhead, "you just have to look on the sunny side! We seem to have arrived here in plenty of time to stop Stanton's invasion of the calorium mines."

"That's grand," Liam said as a spent bullet tore past with a stomach-churning *whup-whup-whup* sound. "How about you go first?"

Little Russia—New Petersburg &
Chiricahua Mountains, Arizona
Guberniia
November 2, 1877

Chapter Twenty-Two

rince Yurevskii's pioneering work on mating live human brains with brilliantly engineered metal androids had resulted in a small army of the most sophisticated automatons in the world. So sophisticated, in fact, that his metal men formed the backbone of his infantry's shock troops, the most trusted of his Palace Guards and the most skilled and capable cadres among his factory workmen.

For all of them to function at the peak of efficiency and reliability depended on the most spectacular of all Yurevskii's technical innovations, the crown jewel of his budding empire: the Wireless Automaton Control Center housed in an imposing sandstone building across the Square from the Regent's Palace. Once the administrative offices of Yurevskii's ill-fated predecessor, his half-brother Aleksandr Aleksandrovich (blown up by Plekhanov's revolutionaries), the building now housed guard barracks, offices for the technical staff and a giant, wire-festooned machine that hummed like a steamship's turbine and broadcast commands to all the individual cells of Yurevskii's giant automaton organism: in fact, a sort of huge and powerful central brain.

But if the Control Center itself was a genuine marvel of up-to-date science and technology, the troops who stood guard outside it—men of the 4th Imperial Brigade of Dragoons—were ordinary, government-issue flesh-and-blood. And who could blame a red-blooded Little Russian soldier for being ravenously hungry after hours of standing guard in the numbing winds of an autumn cold snap?

"*Pirozhki*, your Excellency, delicious *pirozhki* stuffed with juicy mushrooms and savory steak and fresh hard-boiled eggs, nice and hot from the oven!"

The grandmotherly old babushka, round as a polar bear with layers of skirts and shawls, stood in front of the Dragoon manning the guardhouse outside the main gate of the Control Center and held up her wares for him to inspect. The mouthwatering smell that wafted up from the basket she was carrying, strong enough to penetrate even the warm towels that covered the pastries themselves, was more than enough to make the sale, and as the soldier mentally crossed his fingers that none of his superiors was watching, he pulled off a glove and fumbled a ten-kopek piece out of his overcoat pocket.

"*Mmmmm!*" he groaned in ecstasy as he ate half the *pirozhok* in one bite. "*Akh, bozhe ty moi!*"

"It wasn't God who made these *pirozhki*, young man," she reminded him tartly, "and if you're going to gobble them like that, you'll need to pay me more for my labors!"

"How much for the lot of them?" he asked as he licked his fingertips hungrily. "My mates would skin me alive if I didn't buy enough for everybody."

"Weeell," she said, pursing her wrinkled old lips thoughtfully, "I suppose I could find it in my heart to offer a discount to men who serve God and the Tsar . . . what do you say to five paper rubles or three silver ones?"

"Done!" he said with a big grin, and handing over the coins he took the basket from the old lady and gave a piercing whistle for someone to come and get the *pirozhki*.

"Thank you, fine sir," the babushka said, "I'm sure you'll all find yourself dreaming of home when you eat those little darlings," and with a grandmotherly curtsy she took off in the direction she'd come from, thinking that her promise was one of those rare cases when advertising and reality agreed.

⊙━ᴇ

"Dear God," Tikhomirov said as he watched the babushka's progress through binoculars from a suite on the third floor of the Hotel Evropeiskaia, "I am so besotted with that woman that my heart would be in splinters if I had one. As it is, my brain is hurting quite enough to do the job."

Plekhanov watched his friend—for it was truly just as much Lev Aleksandrovich Tikhomirov speaking through the rubber vocal cords of that metal monster as it had been when he inhabited the familiar lanky, bearded body back in Russia—and felt his own heart twinge in sympathy. Materialist that he was, he still hoped there was a Hell, and in it, special circles of suffering where someone like Yurevskii could be sent to roast on a spit for his cruelty.

"I don't blame you," he said to Tikhomirov. "We've had some of the most remarkable women in Russian history as comrades in the struggle, and yet Becky Fox is the superior of all but a few. A rare combination of heart and brains," he said, adding with a grin: "and not terrible to look at, either."

"No, not intolerably so, anyway," Tikhomirov said, and his tone let Plekhanov imagine the wry smile that would once have accompanied it.

Setting the binoculars on a table, Tikhomirov turned away from the window and checked the clock that sat in the center of the mantelpiece.

"Almost noon," he said in a worried tone. "According to our informant the automatons who are still responsive to the Control Center should be staging their counterattack in the next hour or so, which means that we don't have a lot of time to disable the Control Center."

Plekhanov picked up the binoculars and peered down at the sentry in his guard box, adjusting the focus until he could see the man's face clearly enough to count his whiskers. Suddenly the man held his hand up to cover his mouth and yawned rackingly. A good sign.

"Becky has the dynamite under that umbrella of skirts," he said, "enough to bring down the whole building. And by now she will be waiting with Frol and Semion Lazarich, who will guard her as she places it. The moment they see the signal they'll be off, and at the same moment we must begin our mobilization."

Behind him, he heard the clanking taps which told him that even after all they had been through, Lev Aleksandrich still crossed himself when the moment of action approached. As if in answer, the guard collapsed slowly in his box, his helmet askew and his mouth wide open in a drugged snore. Moments later, Becky—now wearing her newsboy uniform— and two men in equally nondescript dress started diagonally across the Square towards the Control Center. Plekhanov turned towards Tikhomirov:

"They're on their way. Time to begin!"

With a hasty embrace, the two old friends picked up their valises and left the room.

○—┰

Prince Yurevskii—in full military regalia now, with medal ribbons and a holstered Smith & Wesson Model 3 revolver—was listening to someone on a voicewire receiver as Stanton and Pilkington—sharing the slightly rumpled look of men who have overstayed the fresh changes of clothes in their suitcases—stood by looking impatient and uneasy.

"No opposition at all?" he asked. "What happened to the Apache rebels?"

He listened for a moment and then smiled: "Excellent! If they have the temerity to come out of hiding and show their faces again kill enough of them to set an example, mount their heads on poles around your camp and then put the rest of them back to work in the mines."

He put the handset back in its cradle and turned to the others. "Well, gentlemen, it looks like our assault on the Arizona calorium mines will prove to be a success. Once our joint force has secured the area completely, I propose that we transport them at once to the Saskatchewan calorium mines. As usual, the British think no one would dare bother them, so the diggings are guarded only by a handful of old-age pensioners. If we can strike while the iron is hot it will take but a handful of days to make us lords and masters of all the calorium deposits outside the continent of Africa and we shall thus gain a head start that will make our two nations the leaders of the world."

"By George, I like the sound of that," said Stanton heartily. "What do you think, Willie, should we go for it?"

"Oh, yes sir," Pilkington said earnestly, "oh, absolutely, sir!" Thinking to himself that if he could discover some way to escape from these madmen and go to ground in the south of France, he might be able to lose himself entirely, become a country schoolmaster or a chef or paint watercolors . . .

"Meanwhile," said Yurevskii, rubbing his hands briskly, "we must put down these insurrectionist scum and see them all hanged from the nearest lamp-standards. The leader is said to be that Land and Freedom swine Plekhanov, the one who blew up my brother, but his two Lieutenants are said to be one of my rebel automatons and a *newsboy!*" He snorted contemptuously: "A newsboy! *C'est à rire, n'est-ce-pas?*"

Stanton grimaced, feeling a totally unexpected shiver of . . . what? Guilt? Conscience? Preposterous, he hadn't time for either. And yet he couldn't quite drive away the sharp image of the boy who'd been distributing that rag *Freedom* in Union Square and the intensity with which he'd wished the boy's death, which had arrived moments later at the hands of one of his agents . . .

Yurevskii took out his revolver, inspected it meticulously and spun the cylinder to make sure it was moving freely. Then he slipped it back into its holster and gave Stanton a querying look:

"Would either of you gentlemen care for a revolver? This is the new 'Russian' model from Messrs. Smith & Wesson and it's quite impressive."

Stanton shook his head irritably, thinking that there was no earthly reason to dirty your hands if you could hire people to shoot guns for you. Not that it would be quite polite to say so to Yurevskii. As for Willie, he blenched so sickly a color at the thought of more violence that a verbal reply was unnecessary.

"Very well," said Yurevskii with a grim little smile. Don't say you weren't offered one when the shooting starts. Come along now, I want to show you the little surprise I've prepared for the insurrectionists. According to my informers they will be launching a counterattack in the next hour or so, and you'll have a box seat for the show I mean to put on for them."

⊶

"Where the devil are Yurevskii's troops?"

The anxious thrum of Tikhomirov's rubber vocal chords underlined the disquiet Plekhanov was feeling himself as the two of them stood at their forward observation post in the shopping arcade on the south side of the palace square.

They had expected to see a show of force, with cannons being dragged into strong points and Gatling gun emplacements being erected with sandbag walls. Instead, there was no sign of life except for one of their own men standing in the Control Station sentry box dressed as a dragoon and a stray dog urinating on the palace gate.

Plekhanov shrugged. "We can assume they're getting ready for our next move," he said, "and Yurevskii's too clever to show his hand early. However, he doesn't know that we have already seized the Control Station since Becky and her helpers surprised the technicians and tied them up along with the drugged soldiers—the whole lot are safely under lock and key in the stables behind the main building. The Control Station will continue to operate as Yurevskii expects it to until the very last minute—we even have one man guarding the Station's voicewire terminal in case of a call from the Palace, and he'll stay on his post until he sees our signal rocket. Then he'll light the fuse and get out."

"Hmmm . . ." thrummed Tikhomirov. "And all our forces are in place and well hidden?"

"Don't be such an old woman," teased Plekhanov, "we've all been over this so many times by now that the only real danger is falling asleep from sheer boredom before the signal rocket goes up."

Tikhomirov slowly swiveled his great steel head back and forth: "It sounds as if there's nothing that can go wrong."

Plekhanov laughed with genuine amusement: "Am I speaking with Lev Aleksandrovich Tikhomirov of Land and Freedom and the People's Will, seedbeds of a handful of successful political acts and a thousand failed ones? Something *will* go wrong; we must simply be ready for it."

"It's true," rumbled Tikhomirov in a gloomy pedal tone, "I'm getting too old for this."

"There," said Yurevskii with a proud gesture, "what do you think?"

The Prince and his U.S. guests were standing on a balcony at the north side of the Palace, looking down onto a parade ground which seemed to be absolutely packed with hundreds of android fighters, every last one of them armed with a Gatling gun.

"How do you know that none of these are rebel automatons?" Pilkington asked curiously.

"A good question," Yurevskii said with a grim smile, "and one which you may imagine exercised my thoughts to no small extent. When the dimensions of the problem became clear I quarantined all those which had not yet gone over to the rebel side and discovered that a small error had crept into the manufacturing process making some of the newer models incapable of responding to wireless commands from the Central Control Station. Each of the ones you see here has been vetted thoroughly to make sure that error is either not present, or is fully corrected. Either way, the android troops you see before you will now respond to my commands as if they were a single automaton. Observe!"

"ANDROIDS!" Yurevskii called out in drill-sergeant tones. "ATTENNN . . . *SHUN*!"

Instantly, the ranks of metal giants came to attention with a thunderous, synchronized clang of metal feet.

"Eh?" asked Yurevskii, grinning ecstatically. "Impressed?"

Stanton was almost speechless. "My God," he said in a hollow voice, "nothing will be able to stand up to them!"

Pilkington gripped the balcony railing and nodded wordlessly, wondering where he had gone wrong. Probably, he thought, when he had decided to stop being the drunken wastrel he'd been through four years of Yale, and show his father—the Pilkington Agency's Old Man—that he was as good as any operative in the Agency's stable. Fool! He could have cashed in his bonds and opened a brothel in Montparnasse, by now he would have become a happy and respected member of Paris society!

"And did you take note of their armaments?" Yurevskii asked Stanton.

Stanton peered down towards the androids, squinting and shaking his head. "I can see that each of them has some sort of contraption under his right arm, but I can't quite make out what it is."

Yurevskii chortled and rubbed his hands with glee. "That happens to be my very latest invention. Each of them is carrying a standard Army-issue Gatling gun in .45-70 caliber, adapted for use by an android. On his back, each of them is also carrying a pack containing two thousand rounds of belted ammunition, which will feed into the gun for as long as the android turns the crank. If you multiply that times the 600 androids you see below you, the total firepower of which they are capable is almost beyond imagining!"

Stanton simply shook his head, finally speechless; Willie swayed and considered throwing himself from the balcony.

"ANDROIDS," bellowed Yurevskii again, "FORWARD, *MARCH*!" With a thunderous clank, the metal men moved forward in perfect unison, following the road that led around the back of the Palace towards the Palace Square. Yurevskii turned back to Stanton and Willie with a look of smug satisfaction:

"We could actually sit down and have a cup of tea if we felt like it," he said, "from this point on they will simply follow the orders which I have already issued to the Central Control Station. However, I'm sure you'd hate to miss the fun, I know I certainly should! Come along, then, let's head back to the other side."

And, humming a little tune, he trotted back into the Palace towards the reception area, leaving Stanton and Willie to follow at a much less buoyant pace.

By now, Becky and her two bodyguards had joined Plekhanov and Tikhomirov in the shopping arcade, waiting tensely for the moment to fire the smoke rocket and blow up the Control Station. When the androids started marching around the Palace towards the Square, they all jumped at the noise, even Tikhomirov, whose brain retained memories of moments like this all too vividly.

"My God," he thrummed, "what's *that*?"

"Lots of automatons on the march," said Plekhanov in a grim tone, "fire the rocket!"

Instantly one of the men with them fired a military smoke rocket into the air, and moments later, a man tore out of the inside of the Control Station building and ran across the square towards his comrades with the fake "dragoon" guard right on his heels. Meanwhile, the pounding of metal feet grew louder and louder, enough that the watchers began to feel the vibrations through the soles of their feet.

"Well," said Becky with a slightly strained grin, "now we find out just how good Little Russian Ordnance Corps fuses really are."

Plekhanov grimaced tensely. "This is a bad failing you Anglo-Saxons have," he said. "Is it really necessary to make such a fetish of showing your *sang-froid* in moments of mortal danger?"

Just then the phalanx of giant automatons rounded the corner of the Palace and set forth inexorably on the last two hundred yards of pavement between them and the waiting rebels. The ground was definitely vibrating now.

Becky gave Plekhanov a slightly uneven smile: "If you really prefer, Georgii Valentinich, it would be no trouble at all for me to throw myself on the ground and have a fit of hysterics."

Abruptly, with a thunderous, simultaneous crash of metal feet, the phalanx of Gatling gunners came to a halt and raised their guns at a 45° angle.

"FIRE!" bellowed their leader.

Immediately a deafening storm of heavy-caliber gunfire broke out, followed by the merry tinkle of thousands of brass cartridge cases hitting the pavement.

"CEASE FIRE!" the android bellowed.

Instantly, a deafening silence reigned, broken after a moment by another bellow:

"REBELS! THROW DOWN YOUR ARMS AT ONCE IF YOU WISH TO LIVE!"

"Damn it," said Plekhanov a little tremulously, "the dynamite should have blown by now!"

There was one more beat of silence, and then Becky grabbed the spool of fuse and blasting caps that one of her two bodyguards was holding.

"Save my place," she said with a grin, and took off towards the Control Station at a run.

"Becky!" Plekhanov shouted. "Stop!"

Becky waved her free hand without slowing down, and a moment later disappeared through the front gate before the enemy could respond.

"Dear Heaven," groaned Plekhanov, "she'll never make it!"

"Oh, yes, she will!" rumbled Tikhomirov, and a moment later he was clanking across the pavement at furious speed, right behind Becky. Now the phalanx of loyal automatons woke up, and started firing in earnest, but Tikhomirov had too good a start, and he disappeared through the gate after Becky.

"*Bozhe moi!*" murmured Plekhanov. Without even thinking about it he crossed himself and murmured a prayer.

Chapter Twenty-Three

Is anybody shooting *back* at those people?" Custer asked.

He started to raise himself on his elbows, but a good-sized rock chip whined by almost close enough to part his hair and he dropped to his stomach again, cursing under his breath.

"I thought they taught you soldier boys to save your ammunition," Liam said in an aggrieved tone. "Those birds aren't even slowing down."

As if to emphasize his complaint a second Gatling gun started up from the attackers' position, filling the air above their heads with a hail of rock chips and bullet fragments.

"Why should they slow down?" asked Chen acerbically. "They came here in airships; they probably have enough ammunition to blast this mountain into gravel."

Crazy Horse was feeling bitter, thinking that the other fellows were blaming this whole thing on him, which was manifestly unfair. He thought his discovery of the spirit lines inside the Camera Obscura was a really pretty nifty bit of magical serendipity, and instead of patting him on the back his pals were just moaning and feeling sorry for themselves because of a little gunfire. It was petty, that was what it was, and . . .

"HEY!"

A hand grabbed Crazy Horse by the ankle and he almost disgraced himself by yelling out loud before he caught sight of a familiar and friendly face pressed to the rocks behind him—Apache Chief Victorio's sister Lozen, a renowned warrior in her own right.

"*Lozen!*" he hissed. "How did you . . .?"

"There's a way through the rocks the soldiers can't see. Follow me!"

She backed away without raising herself and Crazy Horse threw a stone at Liam to get his attention:

"The Apaches found us," he yelled over the gunfire, "let's go!"

Crazy Horse slithered around and went after Lozen while Liam shouted to Custer and Chen to follow, thinking as he crawled away from the insane racket that from now on anybody who complained to him about Apache outrages was going to get short shrift.

"My brother!" cried Geronimo in Chiricahua Apache, throwing his arms around Crazy Horse. A stern, harsh-faced man whose grim line of a mouth reflected a long series of tragic conflicts with the white invaders, he was happy to see an old friend and grateful for the appearance of even a few allies.

"*Goyathlay!*" Crazy Horse answered, using Geronimo's birth name.

Lozen, a confident, athletic woman in her thirties dressed in deerskins and armed with a knife and two revolvers, stood by smiling at the reunion and watching as the newcomers shook hands and exchanged greetings with the warriors of Geronimo's band. Their long crawl had taken them around a promontory that formed a barrier between them and the attacking soldiers, and the senseless firing continued to chip rocks and launch ricochets at what was now a comfortable distance.

Liam approached Crazy Horse: "Can you ask him what his plans are?" he asked.

Geronimo smiled, and answered Liam in Russian. "All of us speak enough Russian to get by," he said, "after all, they've been trying to force us to learn it ever since they took over from your people. As for plans, we were just trying to decide what to do about the mines when the soldiers landed in their airships."

"What do you *want* to do about them?" Chen asked.

"If there was any way to do it, we'd destroy them totally," said Geronimo. "Look at my friends there." He pointed to several warriors with hideous skin lesions, no hair, clouded eyes and other deformities that made Liam think of pictures of leprosy he'd seen in a freak show in Five Points.

"They're the only workers still living from the few who escaped the Russians before we drove them out. There is something in the rocks they were forced to dig out and bring to the surface that creates a sickness none of us has ever seen before."

Chen turned to his companions: "I've been thinking about the mines and I have a plan, but we have to be able to get close to the entrance without the soldiers turning us into mincemeat."

"We had been thinking about starting an avalanche," chimed in Lozen.

"That would be splendid," said Chen. "Can you show me where you were thinking of doing it?"

"Of course," said Geronimo. "Come on, let's go climbing."

⚷

For the next half hour, they continued around the promontory that separated them from the soldiers, moving steadily higher as they worked their way around, until in the end they found themselves on a tiny plateau overlooking the whole area from a height of four or five thousand feet.

Everything could be seen from here—in the distance, two Little Russian airships, moored next to a stream that wound through a narrow valley; then, a dirt cart track that climbed to the area where the attackers were entrenched, still firing madly away at uncomplaining boulders and greasewood bushes. And finally, several hundred feet above and a half mile or so behind the attackers, a dark hole in the side of the mountain, large enough even at this distance to suggest a substantial cavern that had been enlarged by human workers.

"That will do very nicely," said Chen. "It seems to me that if there were a decent-sized avalanche on either side of the invaders, it would be rather a long time till they could manage to extricate themselves. Especially if there were a few experienced marksmen to dissuade those who climbed too high."

"I think we could find those," said Geronimo with a small smile.

"I thought perhaps you might," said Chen.

"And of course," Custer said, "that would put the airships and all their contents on the wrong side of the spill as far as the soldiers are concerned. They'll be counting bullets once they realize they can't get more by sending a cart down the hill."

"Are you going to take the airships away?" Lozen asked a little anxiously.

"No," Custer said with a glance towards Crazy Horse and a somewhat ironic grin. "We have our own means of . . . ah . . . transport." Crazy Horse glared at him but stayed silent.

"Then we can keep the ammunition?" she asked eagerly. "That's why I came up north in the first place, my brother Victorio and his band have been staying south of the Rio Grande to avoid the Russians, but we're running low on ammunition."

"There should be plenty to go around," said Geronimo. He gestured towards the attackers: "At least those fools seem to think so."

"Good," said Chen. "In that case I'm going to do my part now." He knelt down and laid both hands on the rocks in front of him, closing his eyes and murmuring almost inaudibly in Chinese as he picked up handfuls of soil and pebbles, running them through his fingers and bathing his face with the dirt. After a couple of minutes there was a weird, liquid movement underfoot that lasted just a few seconds. Then at a point several hundred yards ahead of the area where the soldiers were entrenched, rocks started spilling down the side of the mountain—first small ones, then bigger and bigger ones till boulders were cascading down the side of the mountain, bounding high into the air when they struck larger stones, and then crashing into fragments when they landed.

For the first time, the soldiers stopped firing and milled around in a panic, trying to decide on their next move. At this point Chen stood up briskly and trotted back in the direction of the airships. When he had reached a point several hundred yards behind the attackers' positions he repeated the whole operation, and this time when the boulders started cascading down the mountainside the attackers fell into an obvious panic, though it was far too late to do anything about escaping.

Geronimo approached Chen and took his hand between his own hands: "I have never seen medicine that powerful," he said. "We thank you."

Chen smiled and gave him a little bow. "My pleasure," he said. "But I'm not quite done yet." And with that he trotted a little further along the path to a point directly above the entrance to the mine. "Now," he said.

Again, he knelt down and put both hands on the ground, this time chanting for several minutes until the strange liquid sensation was repeated. This time, however, the liquid sensation lasted considerably longer, until everyone around Chen started getting nervous. A moment later there was a strange shuddering movement all the way along the top of the plateau, followed by a low, grinding, crashing sound like the collision of half a dozen trains at once. Abruptly the earth under their feet seemed to sink a foot or so, and then there was total silence; below them, a huge cloud of dust arose from the mouth of the cavern.

"Great jumping Jehoshaphat!" Custer exclaimed after a moment. "If you never do that again as long as I live it will be just fine with me," he said feelingly to Chen.

"I think I can promise you that," smiled Chen, who was feeling more than a little bit wobbly on his pins after the effort of the spell. He turned to Geronimo: "The calorium mines have completely collapsed upon themselves and sunk to a point a good half mile below where they were previously. If anyone tries to re-open them he will face a bitter disappointment."

Geronimo wrapped his arms around Chen's skinny form and gave him a heartfelt embrace: "You are a great benefactor of the Apache people," he said, "and a brother to all Apaches. Whenever you are among us you will be welcome."

Chen bowed to him: "I thank you, sir, and I hope to see you again. For now though, the need to stop the threat of calorium is pushing us forward, and I regret that we must leave at once." He turned to Crazy Horse: "Unless you want to do the honors?"

Crazy Horse raised an eyebrow and said: "Hmmph!" Chen suppressed a smile.

"Very well, then," he said. "Mr. McCool?" Liam stepped forward curiously as Chen laid his hand flat on a huge boulder streaked with rose quartz. "Gentlemen?" he said to Custer and Crazy Horse, who stepped forward as Liam drew his katana from its scabbard. Chen gestured: "Now, Mr. McCool, if you please..."

Liam grinned. "Here goes nothing," he said, swinging the blade down in a two-handed stroke which had barely touched the rock when there was a blinding flash and the four men disappeared.

265

Chapter Twenty-Four

ecky and Tikhomirov were tiptoeing cautiously down the stairs leading to the basement that housed the central "brain" when she straightened up abruptly and laughed:

"What a pair of ninnies we are, Lev Alexandrich! If for some reason the fuse was just extra slow and is about to reach the blasting cap, we might as well stand up and meet our fate with a bit of dignity."

Tikhomirov chuckled, an eerie rasping noise that reminded Becky of a Turkish bass viol she'd once heard in a café in Istanbul.

"I wish you'd been with us in the People's Will, Miss Fox, Aleksandr II would never have had a chance."

Becky smiled, imagining herself in the pantheon of revolutionary women that included Sofia Perovskaia and Vera Figner and making sure to banish a slight tremor of uneasiness that tried to assert itself as she took hold of the doorknob. Then, once she had permitted herself to breathe freely again, she registered the infuriating fact that the fuse which one of their people had stolen somewhere was not—in the Russian phrase—"of the first freshness," and had simply gotten tired of burning half-way to the blasting cap.

"Damn, damn, *damn*!" she muttered, then—contritely—"Please excuse my language, Lev Alexandrovich, but really!"

"Let's use all these blasting caps and all the remaining fuse," he said, "we'll make sure that at least one of these sticks of dynamite blows up!"

"Wonderful idea!" she said (which would have made Tikhomirov blush with pleasure if he could have). "And we'll braid all the fuses into one long hank and light them all at once!"

The two of them set to work quickly and it wasn't long before the blasting caps were all inserted into dynamite sticks and the thick braid of fuses was ready to light.

"Let's drape it over something," she said, "so it gets plenty of air as it burns."

Tikhomirov grabbed a couple of chairs, set them up facing each other and draped the rope of fuses over the backs so that they'd be off the floor while they burned.

"Ready!" he thrummed.

Becky took a box of matches out of her jacket pocket and took a moment to make sure the fuses were all well alight. She grinned:

"Now, I think, we should run like blazes!"

"*Very* good idea," said Tikhomirov, and a moment later they were out of the room and off up the stairs.

Being in the basement had covered the sound of the Gatling gun fusillade from Yurevskii's automatons, but when they reached the upper level Becky and Tikhomirov were unpleasantly reminded by the sound of slugs caroming off the building.

"Come on," Becky said after a moment's hesitation, "I'd rather die outdoors than in here!"

She threw open the door, flattened herself on the courtyard paving stones and started crawling rapidly for the nearest cover. Tikhomirov opted for a low crouch and ran quickly after her, only to be hit a half-dozen times in succession and knocked over by the force of the impact. The crash of his falling body got Becky's attention and she looked back, horrified to see Tikhomirov down.

"Lev Alexandrich!" she cried.

"Stay still," he shouted back, "I'll shield you."

Scuttling forward on his hands and knees, he caught up with Becky in a moment and threw himself down with a *clang!* so that his huge metal body formed a shield between her and the Gatling gunners.

"Lev Alexandrich!" she screamed.

"Stay still!" he rumbled.

Now the gunners seemed to have gotten their range perfectly, and the slugs started hitting the ground around them with the persistence of a heavy rainfall. Becky closed her eyes tight and started repeating every childhood prayer she could remember.

о—т

A small knot of revolutionaries had collected around Plekhanov, who was staring towards the Central Control Station and grinding his teeth with frustration.

"Georgii Valentinich," one of them said, "do you think they'll be safe that close to the building?"

Plekhanov looked at him morosely: "Pray!" he said. "And hope that God listens to materialists."

Before the man could answer there was a brilliant flash and for a moment they all reeled blindly:

"We've been blown up!" screamed one of them. But as Plekhanov rubbed his eyes to get his sight back he saw a quartet of strangers standing in the street a dozen feet away, looking around a little dazedly. One of them—an athletic, good-looking young man with a mass of curly auburn hair—turned towards Plekhanov sharply:

"Hey, you!" he said in Russian. "Do you know Becky Fox? Do you know where she is?"

Suspicious and more than a little frightened, Plehanov said brusquely: "What's it to you?"

At that, the man leapt at him like a wolf, grabbed him by the throat and started shaking him:

"What's it to me?" he roared wildly. "Not much more than life itself, you schoolmarmish little son of a bitch! Speak up before I rip your liver out and stuff it up your nose!"

Plekhanov held up his hand and croaked desperately:

"*Stop*, damn you! She's over there!"

Plekhanov pointed towards the front of the Control Station and Tikhomirov's fallen body.

"She's sheltering behind the automaton!"

Liam let go of Plekhanov and looked back and forth from the metal body on the ground to the android Gatling gunners, who had kept up their fire without a pause. As Liam took in Becky's plight, he turned as white as a sheet, then so red with fury that he looked like he'd been parboiled. He strode out into the square in full view of the androids and bellowed at them in English:

"HEY! OVER HERE, YOU TIN PISSPOTS!"

The android gunners paused momentarily and swiveled questioningly in Liam's direction. At the same moment, Liam was raising his hands overhead and spreading them a little beyond shoulder width, feeling the heat of his fury and his fear for Becky swirling within him until he could picture them clearly, spinning and rotating like a sun, throwing off tendrils of pure flame as it grew bigger and hotter:

"THAT'S RIGHT," he shouted, "*HERE!*"

Now a weird sort of sparkling effect began to appear around Liam's spread hands, and then a ball of orange-white fire took shape in each hand, swelling until they were about the size of a cannonball. Suddenly, and without further warning, Liam flung both of them towards the Gatling gunners. The fireballs seemed to pick up speed and size as they flew, until—in the last seconds before they hit the gunners—they were each about a yard across, though no one could be quite sure later about any of the details since the moment of contact was so spectacular: it was as though someone had emptied a volcano on top of the shooters, a fountain of fire that spread among them instantaneously, incinerating them and their ammunition with thunderous explosions and a fire as intense and white-hot as the heart of a blast furnace. A few seconds later there was nothing left on the paving stones except a scattering of glowing metal fragments.

0—⊤

Stanton and Willie had been watching it from behind a curtain at one of the Palace reception room windows.

"Great God in Heaven," murmured Stanton. He turned to Willie: "Are you packed?"

Pilkington was nodding so hard he could barely speak. "Yes, sir. Oh, absolutely, sir, been packed since yesterday."

Stanton nodded, throwing a grim look across the room towards Prince Yurevskii, who was standing at another window looking downwards and shaking his head slowly.

"Come on," Stanton said. "Let's get to our airship while it's still in one piece."

He turned and strode rapidly across the room with Willie trotting at his heels muttering to himself.

"That's the limit," he was saying feverishly, "those people summoned the Devil! The *Devil*! That's *all*, I *mean* it. I quit. That's the absolute *limit* . . ."

As they neared the exit Yurevskii turned and yelled after them indignantly:

"Where do you think you're going? What do you . . ."

But the door was already closing after them. Yurevskii clenched his fists in a fury and shouted desperately:

270

"Boylan? Where *are* you, damn you!"

He waited for another second or two, realizing with a sinking certainty that his aide was long gone. Then he started across the room at a run:

"WAIT!" he bellowed after Stanton and Pilkington. "WAIT FOR ME!"

0—⌐

In the square below, Liam was running with equally mad energy towards the Central Control Station when suddenly it gave a sort of shudder and then settled in on itself with a slow, thunderous crunching like the sound of the calorium mines collapsing. Liam flinched, ducked, then saw that nothing more was going to happen and re-doubled his speed.

"Becky!" he shouted. "Becky! Are you all right?"

"*Liam?*" he heard her call faintly. "Liam, is that really you?"

A moment later he was through the gate, helping Becky to her feet, squeezing her so tight she cried out, and then kissing her and being kissed back with enough passion to make up for a lifetime of separation let alone a few days.

"How did you know I was here?" she asked finally.

Liam made a face. "I ran into Ubaldo in the Bear Flag Republic."

"In California? Really?" Her expression darkened as she remembered. "Did he tell you he kidnapped me? That's why I'm here."

Liam nodded and then grinned. "He's been punished. That's a *really* long story, and I promise to tell you. But first we have get out of here and get back to the East Coast."

Becky started to nod, but suddenly some part of her attention woke up and she realized Tikhomirov hadn't stirred. She dropped to her knees at once and laid a hand on the metal man's shoulder:

"Lev Alexandrich? Are you all right?"

The automaton continued to lie there without moving and a sudden awful intuition came over Becky. She reached out and took hold of him gently, pulling him slowly towards her so that his front was exposed instead of his back. Now it was all too plain to see: one of the massive .45-70 slugs had smashed into his left eye and the only sign that he had once been alive was a slow drool of blood and brain matter running down his metal face and pooling on the pavement. Becky burst into bitter weeping:

"You poor man. Thank you, thank you!" After a moment she looked up at Liam with a heartbroken expression: "He shielded me, you know? We placed dynamite charges on the brain that controlled the automatons, and when we came out there was so much gunfire that we had to lie there and hope the explosion wouldn't blow us up. He gave his *life* for me."

Liam pulled her to her feet and held her tight. "I wish there was some way I could thank him—if anything had happened to you I really wouldn't have wanted to go on." For another minute or two they just held each other, flooded with relief and gratitude that they were together. Then Liam pulled away a little:

"We've got to get going right now; Chen will tell you all about it. And Custer and Crazy Horse are here, too!"

There was a shout from the shopping arcade as the others saw that Becky was all right, and the others ran up to hug her and say hello.

"Some reunion, eh, Miss Fox?" Custer was grinning widely, and Crazy Horse took her hand and kissed it in his best Pushkin/Byron mode.

"Are you fellows going to stay in Petersburg?" she asked them.

Crazy Horse nodded: "We're where we need to be," he said. "It looks like Yurevskii has deserted his palace, and everybody who was working for him has disappeared into the underbrush. So we're already talking to Plekhanov about organizing a Grand Congress of the Peoples of the Trans-Mississippi West. With any luck the Russians and whatever Americans are out here and the People can come to a meeting of the minds and set up a government worth living with. And if you can do the same thing back in Washington, maybe we'll finally get somewhere worth going to."

"Mr. McCool!" Plekhanov was calling to them across the Square, approaching with a Japanese officer and a battalion of Japanese Aerial Navy troops who were goose-stepping smartly behind him. As they approached Liam and his companions, they came to an abrupt, precision-drill-team halt, and Plekhanov grinned a little awkwardly at Liam:

"These people would like to surrender, Mr. McCool, but their officer says they will only surrender to you!"

"Really?" said Liam dubiously. He turned to look at the officer, and as he did the entire detachment dropped to their knees and prostrated themselves in front of him. The officer's voice, muffled by his position, floated to Liam:

"No fire!"

Liam looked at Chen helplessly and Chen stepped forward and spoke to the prostrate officer in Japanese. After a moment a smile started to quirk his lips and he had to fight to suppress it:

"Evidently, Mr. McCool, they take you for a devil of some sort, and apparently a rather nasty one."

"Huh," said Liam, nonplussed. "OK, just tell him that I applaud his perspicacity, that I am most certainly the worst *kind* of devil and if they surrender now nicely and help out with some of the stuff this new Congress will be needing done around here, I promise to forgive them. If not, I will come back instantly with the fire and cook and eat every single one of them. Bones and all!"

Biting his lip hard, Chen translated all that into Japanese, and after a moment an involuntary chorus of apprehension arose from the prostrate troopers.

"We will obey to the letter, Mighty Demon, you may count on us."

"OK," said Liam, "now . . . uh . . ." he looked around at his friends, all of whom seemed to be equally at a loss. "Right, then! At *ease!*"

That seemed to do the trick. The officer got to his feet, bowing. Liam pointed to Plekhanov. "You report to him, all right?"

More bowing. Liam turned to Crazy Horse and Custer and hugged them both hard.

"We're going to miss you," he said. "Call us on the voicewire and tell us what's going on, we'll come through here on the way back to the Bear Flag Republic. Right now, though, we have to finish off this calorium business before there's a problem, and that means one more stop before New York. Ambrose, are you ready?"

Chen nodded and pointed to a spot twenty or thirty feet away from where Plekhanov had been watching the Control Station.

"Miss Fox, perhaps you should stand between Mr. McCool and me."

Liam took the ancient katana out of its scabbard and waved to his friends.

"*Dosvidaniia*, boys!" he called out.

Then he raised the sword overhead and swung it down towards the paving stones, and even as the blade met the ground there was an eye-wateringly brilliant flash of light and Liam and his companions were gone.

Camp Calorium—somewhere in
Loudoun County, Virginia
November 2, 1877

Chapter Twenty-Five

hiang Lee was enjoying himself. For one thing, that fat idiot Stanton had gone off to Little Russia for some kind of diplomatic haggle with Prince Yurevskii, which meant that Lee could take care of business without putting on a constant dog and pony show for his bankroller. For another, this whole Camp Calorium wheeze was strictly Lee's own brainchild and the marines and sailors who kept it running treated him pretty much like the Commanding General. Seriously, how bad could that be? If you considered that Lee had started out in life an orphan, grateful for his job as a cook in a Mott Street cathouse, this was a lot like dying and going to Heaven.

Lee checked himself in the laboratory's big mirror, spiffing up the set of his bow tie (navy, with white polka dots to accent a custom-made navy shirt with white stripes and a glittering white celluloid collar). Lee smiled complacently at his stylish turnout and then turned to stare out the window, enjoying the twilit peace here at the center of the Camp's 40,000 square acres. He was a little cross when a knock on the door jogged him out of his reverie.

"Dr. Lee? Should I bring this in now?"

It was one of his sailors, with a trolley-load of lead ingots for the smelter.

"Right over there, Seaman Oppenheimer, next to the conveyor belt. And if you don't mind, I'd like to have the thorium pellets right away."

"Aye, aye, sir!" Oppenheimer said, snapping him a salute and then rolling the lead away. As the sailor unloaded his trolley, Lee checked the instruments that controlled the temperature of the melted lead.

"Hm," Lee muttered, "running too hot."

He was just about to reset the temperature when there was a flash of light like a lightning strike and Lee almost passed out, thinking he'd made some mistake and the end had come. But before he could even get his eyes open he heard a familiar—and hated—voice behind him.

"Lee? What the devil do you think you're going to do with that lead?"

Lee had to fight to regain his composure, but he was absolutely damned if he was going to let Ambrose Bloody Chen see him ruffled. After a moment he turned with a smile and gave his trio of visitors a little half-bow.

"My dear Chen, what a pleasant surprise to see you here—still can't resist playing the showoff, eh? Nice materialization, and in company with two such famous faces!" He turned and half-bowed to Becky and Liam: "Miss Fox, Mr. McCool."

Liam frowned: "How do you know me?"

Lee laughed: "You must have been out of town lately—your "Wanted" circular is posted everywhere."

Seaman Oppenheimer spoke up, eyeing the newcomers suspiciously: "Do you need any help, Doctor Lee? Want me to call the Officer of the Day?"

"No, thank you, Oppenheimer. But if you don't mind standing by I'll be needing you to get some more supplies."

Chen's lips quirked with distaste: "*Doctor* Lee, is it?"

"Why not?" Lee said. "I have a friend in Great Neck who does some very artistic work with passports and diplomas and suchlike and he offered to make me a Yale graduate for a very reasonable sum."

"*Yale?*" Chen asked incredulously.

"It seemed a good idea at the time," Lee said with a cocky grin. "In any event, as far as I know there is no actual Yale, it's just something a bunch of wiseacre kids dreamed up to impress the girls." He gave his tie a superfluous tug and smiled at Chen: "Now, what can I do for you, Ambrose?"

Liam and Becky could see that Chen was having trouble overcoming an urge to read Lee the riot act, so they stayed silent, but there was a kind of underlying menace to the situation which was putting everybody on edge, something far bigger than the old enmities between Chen and his one-time protégé; finally, Chen mastered himself and got down to business.

"I have heard a rumor, Chiang, that you convinced Stanton to sponsor a process you came up with for refining calorium. Is this true?"

Lee jutted out his chin pugnaciously, but a hint of shiftiness in his eyes told Liam that he wasn't really sure of himself. It was starting to look like Chen had been right to worry.

"What if it is, old man? It's none of your business and if I were you I'd sling my hook and go where I was wanted!" Brave words, but this time Lee was definitely sounding like a schoolboy sassing his father.

Chen's jaw set and his voice hardened as he answered: "You were my pupil, Chiang. If you had been hard-working and honest you would have brought great credit on me, but now I fear you will bring nothing but shame to your teacher. Tell me at once what this 'process' of yours consists of!"

"I don't mind if I do," said Lee, "maybe you'll realize just how outmoded all your 'aligning with the Tao' and all the rest of that junk really are!" Adopting a slightly shaky professorial tone, he lectured his former preceptor: "After all, old man, all you really have to do is melt the lead and add powdered pitchblende to it. I've already taken care of that part, and now I've added carefully measured amounts of cinnabar and gold."

Chen recoiled as if he'd been struck. "Do you realize the risks you're taking? Do you have any actual idea of what's involved here?"

"You bet your tintype I do," Lee said, finally losing his temper. "What's involved is you old dinosaurs have lorded it over the rest of us long enough with all your Shaolin Temple la-di-da and all the rest of that magic bushwa. These are modern times, Granddad, wake up! Time is *money*, hadn't you heard? We don't have all day to sit around staring at our navels and getting in tune with the great principle of the universe or whatever it is, we have to hurry up and get in tune with the great principle of getting *rich* before some other clown beats us to it! There's nothing wrong with using a little magic, especially if it gives you a leg up on the other fellow, and I've certainly used some of what you taught me. But that's all I need, the rest of it is just a dead weight around my neck!"

Chen was turning dangerously pale again, but Liam couldn't tell if it was illness or anger. Either way, it looked like Chen was nearing a crisis of some kind.

"Do you even remember," Chen asked, "what the *wu xing* are, the five elements of wood, fire, earth, metal and water? Before you undertook this supremely dangerous experiment, did you make any *attempt* to understand the cosmological processes they represent in order to align your plan with the Tao, the energy of the universe?"

Now Lee turned red with anger, waving his fist at Chen as he spoke: "I remember what I need to and I understand what I need to. And part of what I understand is that you're just a pathetic, jealous old fool!" He turned to Seaman Oppenheimer: "Oppenheimer, go fetch me the thorium pellets, will you?" The sailor threw a brisk salute and exited.

Chen swayed, enough that Liam involuntarily moved to steady him. Then he closed his eyes and muttered under his breath in Chinese, but as he did, bands of blue-and-green sparks shot across the room as if someone had draped strings of electric lights from wall to wall. Chen's eyes shot open and he looked around with shock.

Lee sneered at him. "That's right, Ambrose, I did learn something from you. Everywhere in this building and on the surrounding grounds where it seemed like a good idea I set up the magical wards you taught me, and I've had time to make them strong enough that you won't be able to work a single spell to interfere with my experiment. What do you say to that, you moth-eaten antique?"

"I say goodbye!" Chen said flatly, and grabbing Becky and Liam by the sleeves he dragged them towards the exit:

"Come on," he said urgently, "we have to get out of here *now*!"

The three of them took off at a run as Lee jeered at them gleefully: "You'd *better* run, Grandfather Chen—if you don't, you'll have to stick around and see your despised dogs-body Chiang Lee become the rich and famous *Doctor* Chiang Lee, Master of Calorium!"

Lee's taunt echoed after them as they burst out through the front door. The twilit sky had already turned to the black-violet tint of early evening, suffused by the mellow light of a full moon, and all the Camp's personnel seemed to have gone inside somewhere. Chen was looking around desperately:

"A vehicle," he said tensely, "horses, bicycles, anything! We must get away from here as fast as we can!"

"There!" Becky cried, pointing in the direction of a group of outbuildings. "That looks like a steam lorry and it must be picking something up or delivering something, you can see the engine shaking it."

"Come on," shouted Liam, "I can drive one of those."

They tore away across the compound and jumped into the vehicle, Liam engaging the gears and swinging around in a circle till he was on the main road leading away from the laboratory.

A moment later sailors burst out of one of the outbuildings, shouting:

"HEY! WHERE DO YOU THINK YOU'RE GOING WITH THAT?"

"Hang on tight," yelled Liam, "I'm going to zig-zag in case they start shooting."

A moment later, as if they'd overheard Liam, the sailors started firing at the fleeing van, but between the darkness and Liam's driving they only got a couple of lucky hits.

"For goodness' sake, Liam," Becky said anxiously as one of the slugs punched through the back and out through the front window, "can't you get this thing to go faster?"

"Yes, dear," Liam said with a grin, stepping on the pedal that fed steam to the turbines, "just don't blame me if the boiler blows up!"

For long, tension-stretched minutes they drove through the moonlit night wordlessly, each of them plunged deep into clenched-jaw suspense, wondering desperately what Chen's experiment might be about to produce while the van went faster and faster, pushed to the extreme of its capacities, the engine shrieking with mechanical stress and the rubber tires screeching and jouncing as they hit unseen obstacles.

Behind them, the laboratory and its outbuildings and every other sign of human habitation had vanished an aeon or so ago, and they seemed to be lost in a fairytale forest of dark trees, the only light being the road lit by the moon, stretching ahead of them seemingly without end. Then, just when Liam was beginning to wonder if they'd ever get back to civilization, the moonlight showed a big sign lettered in phosphorescent paint that read: "APPROACHING MAIN GATE. SLOW VEHICLES TO 10 MILES PER HOUR!"

"Hurrah!" cried Becky jubilantly. "It looks like we finally . . ."

Before she could finish she was interrupted by a brilliant, blinding glare like ten thousand lightning bolts striking all at once, followed a split second later by a thunderclap louder than any they had ever heard. An instant later, the ground beneath the vehicle shook with that liquid earthquake feel, continuing to shake violently until a blast of searing wind picked up the lorry and spun it around as if it were a nursery toy, levitating it so that its wheels spun around crazily, screaming as the tires lost all traction, making the vehicle float like a feather and the engine shriek its death wail until the lorry suddenly slammed back to earth with a crash and the engine finally died for good.

The three of them stared out through the front window, hypnotized for a moment by sheer terror, until Becky broke the spell, pushing Liam's shoulder hard so that he opened the door and jumped out, followed by Becky and then by Chen. The three of them stood silently, involuntarily drawing together as they watched the mushroom cloud rising slowly, majestically, sucking up bits of debris and smoke as it climbed, its column roiling and billowing with flames and little bolts of lightning, the spreading cap silvered by the moon.

"I guess we were too late," Liam said at last.

"Maybe not," Becky said, "I imagine they'll have been pretty well shaken up by that in Washington."

Chen nodded slowly, thinking that over. "You may be right at that, Miss Fox," he said at last. "I expect Lee's wards end at the gate, why don't we get going?"

New York City and Environs
November 5, 1877

Chapter Twenty-Six

he Atlantic had always been what Liam thought of when he heard the word "ocean," but now, as he sat on the verandah of the Goodyear mansion wrapped in a borrowed greatcoat and scarf looking at the lowering November skies over Shelter Island and the chop on Little Peconic Bay, like furrows on a field of gray mud, all he could think of was the sparkling blue of Santa Monica Bay.

"Bah!" he said aloud.

"I quite agree," Chen said with a small smile. He was occupying a neighboring rocker and swathed twice as warmly as Liam. "I find it a useful position on most things. What was *your* 'bah!' about?"

Liam waved his hand in frustration. "We've been back three days, Mike can't take the time to come out since things are such a mess in the city, nothing useful's happening here, and I'm going cuckoo sitting around listening to these people *talk*. You'd think, everything they've been through, Stanton's persecutions and the exile in Canada and all that, they'd be wanting to get the bit in their teeth now they're on the threshold of taking over. But as far as I can see their idea of really getting to grips with things is staying up an extra couple of hours after dinner jawing about politics."

Chen's smile took on an edge of mild irony: "Be patient, Mr. McCool. I feel certain you'll have the opportunity to throw someone across the room or blow something up quite soon. Meanwhile, try to put yourself in President Lincoln's place! Think of everything the man has been through, and imagine what he must be feeling. No doubt all the talk helps soothe his anxieties."

Liam stared at Chen for a long moment with his own unreadable smile. "Here I thought when my old man got drunk for the last time and got himself shot for starting a riot I was finally going to be free of that whole paternal homily routine, but no! Providence sent me Ambrose Chen to remind me that There Is No Free Lunch, so if Providence thinks I rate a homily I'm going to get one even if I hide under a rock."

"Hmmph!" sniffed Chen. "I should have thought that any man who had a genuine longing to play the fool with impunity would have avoided involving himself with a woman like Miss Fox."

In spite of himself, Liam grinned. "You have a point there, Ambrose. Come on, let's go look for . . ."

At that moment, as if they had been listening and waiting for a good cue, Becky and President Lincoln stepped out onto the porch and came to join Liam and Chen, Lincoln's heavy automaton tread rattling the coffee cups at every footstep.

"Good morning, gentlemen," Lincoln said cheerfully. "Have you heard the latest? The mining and refining of calorium are going to be banned worldwide!"

Liam winked at Becky: "Looks like you and Chen were right—it wasn't such a bad thing that Lee blew up half of Virginia after all."

"Tut, tut, Liam," said Lincoln as he pulled up a special steel rocker that was kept for him on the porch. "No need for hyperbole, the reality was impressive enough. No one has been reckless enough to approach the blast site on foot, but surveillance from airships has shown a crater about a half mile wide and it's said that the entire area gives off a sickly glow at night. But more to the point was the fact that all the representatives of the world's nations who were present on government business in Washington saw the hellish fireball that rose from Loudoun County and felt the tremors and hurricane winds of the blast—after all, from there to Washington D. C. is scarcely thirty miles."

"There's going to be a giant convocation of world governments in Paris next month," Becky added, "and they'll be hammering out the details of a binding accord, but it's going to mean that everybody will have to start re-thinking their plans for endless industrialization and military expansion. Without calorium it will all be much more tedious—thank God, human soldiers and workers have voices."

"Of course," Chen said mildly, "some governments might cheat."

Everyone stared at him for a moment, until Chen spread his hands and shrugged, at which point President Lincoln sighed heavily, a deep pedal note of resignation.

"We'll all just have to take it one step at a time," Lincoln said. "Though it may seem a bit gloomy to say so in the midst of all the euphoria, human nature does have a stubborn way of sticking to old habits. Still . . ."

"It's a beginning," said Becky firmly. "Which brings us to the next order of business." She gestured to Lincoln: "Mr. President?"

Lincoln nodded his great steel head and turned to give Liam one of his inscrutable looks. After a moment he managed a very good approximation of a sheepish chuckle and spoke:

"Yet another request, Liam, though I expect you must be mightily sick of my 'requests' by now."

Liam smiled. "I'm not saying yet, sir, but just tell me this: does it involve sitting around Freedom Party Headquarters listening to a lot of palaver about the government?"

Becky beat Lincoln to an answer, which she underlined with tart emphasis: "No it doesn't, Liam McCool, and I'll tell you this for nothing—I'm going whether you come or not!"

Liam and Chen looked at each other and burst out laughing as Becky folded her arms on her chest and glared at them.

"Whatever it is, Mr. President," Liam said, "it looks like I'm on board."

○━

"All I'm saying, Gran, is I didn't *want* to be a magician or a sorcerer or whatever else you want to call it. I didn't ask for it, did I? Because I didn't *need* it. I was already the King of the Cracksmen and that should be good enough for any sensible man!"

If anyone had been near enough to overhear him, they might have been surprised to hear the frail old man's speech, and even more to see him addressing a considerably younger and sprightlier-looking old woman as 'Gran,' but she didn't hesitate to let him have it with both barrels:

"'Sensible man,' *phshaw*! Sure, now, Liam McCool," she said scornfully, "I didn't think ye were as big a baby as all that. Next thing I know ye'll be wantin' me to come check under the bed to make sure there's no monsters there!"

The other old lady in the party, who was walking next to Liam, giggled as she heard his grandma's rebuke and Liam turned and gave her an indignant look. But before he could say anything Gran picked up where she'd left off as the bushy-bearded old man next to her grinned his appreciation of the attack:

"It's been years now that I've known ye had the gift and I've said nothing since it wasn't time. Ye've had all the years any young lout might wish for, runnin' around the city havin' fistfights and robbin' rich folks down to their eye teeth and

292

makin' yerself look big! Well, now it's time to stop playin' the eejit and take up the mantle of the McCools, and ye'd best wear it with honor, or I'll box yer ears till you can't see straight!"

"Hmph!" Liam snorted.

Gran wagged her finger at Liam as they walked: "Ye can snort like a grampus and it won't change a thing. Like I said to Becky before, the times are changin' at last and magic's turning the tide against the doubters. But ye can be sure it won't all be *good* magic, some of it will be as black as Stanton's heart, and decent people will need their defenders. You hear me, Liam McCool?"

"Jasus, Mary and Joseph," he grumbled, slipping into her brogue, "I'd have to be deaf as a post not to!"

"Don't ye dare talk back to me, ye saucy blatherskite!" Liam sighed heavily. "Yes, Gran," he said.

"That's better," she said with a satisfied nod. "Now then, how far are we from where we're bound for?"

"Not far now, Mrs. McCool," said Chen through his pasted-on whiskers. "The ley lines brought us to the same spot where we began our travels—Central Park between the Reservoir and North Meadow, and from what President Lincoln told us it's in North Meadow that Stanton and Yurevskii have made a last stand. Right now there's a cease-fire while Stanton's forces and the rebel forces rest and re-group, and Stanton has announced that he means to have a giant rally today so that he can 'introduce New Yorkers to their new Mayor.' It's that rally that President Lincoln wants a report on."

"And we're just four nice old New Yorkers come to greet Hizzoner," giggled Becky, to whom being in disguise in enemy territory was meat and drink. Liam studied her appreciatively and then leaned over and kissed her neck.

"You're one bad old lady, Mother Fox," he said.

"Thank you, dear," she said with a curtsy.

Stanton had set up a giant tent—more like a pavilion from some medieval tourney—and made it the temporary head-quarters of two governments-in-exile, his own and Yurevskii's. The Prince, however, had drunk enough rye whiskey with Willie Pilkington that the two of them had finally staggered away to look for a brothel—which was fine with Stanton, who was heartily sick of Willie and his Russian "ally" both.

Meanwhile, he had important business to transact with the "new Mayor," banker and legendary financial bunco artist Jay Gould. Tall, dour and balding with a long, pointed nose and a face almost lost in thick black whiskers, Gould was a man who could play poker with wiliest of them and win. Now, how-ever, his emotions were openly on display and he was yelling at Stanton as if he were a clumsy subordinate.

"You promised me, Stanton, we had a *contract*! I advanced you a hundred million dollars to finance all the calo-rium development and you promised me a one hundred per-cent return. If there was a default for *any* reason New York City was your surety and you would hand it over to me lock, stock and barrel!"

"But, Jay . . ." Stanton began in a wheedling tone.

"Don't you 'Jay' me, you highbinder," thundered Gould. "I'm Mr. Gould to you and don't you forget it. Now! What is all this 'Mayor' folderol?"

Stanton took a deep breath and mopped his forehead with a handkerchief. "You know my forces have suffered some reverses, Mr. Gould. What we need to do if we are to regain the initiative is to rally the solid citizens of New York behind us, and that's why I asked you to come all the way uptown like this. You're a famous man," he said in his most flattering tones, "if I can present you to the audience as a great man who's willing to step down from his Olympus and help the good people of New York return to peace and prosperity, you can write your own ticket with them. For God's sake, man, they don't have to *know* that you own them now!"

Stanton could see Gould testing this idea mentally, biting the coin to make sure it was real, weighing its value. Finally, he gave a grudging nod.

"Very well," he said, "you may present me to them."

━○

There might have been a couple of hundred people in the audience standing on the grass in front of the make-shift stage, but as Liam looked around he realized this was not a group of political curiosity-seekers. Instead they were mostly poor and haggard-looking, twenty or thirty of them bearing signs reading: "FOOD!" "FEED US NOW!" "WE'RE STARVING!" and other angry complaints in the same vein.

"There's going to be trouble," Liam murmured to Becky.

"Look over there," she murmured back. Liam followed her eyes and saw a detachment of Johnnies drawn up in an area almost concealed by bushes and trees, clearly at the ready.

"Oh, oh." Liam said.

At that point the curtain parted and Stanton came out and stood in front of them, sweating profusely.

"Fellow New Yorkers," he began, but immediately he was interrupted by hecklers:

"Fellow horse biscuits," one shouted back. "You're from Ohio!"

"When are you planning on *feeding* your 'fellow' New Yorkers you swindling tub of lard?" shouted another.

One of them, a gaunt and feverish-looking woman, held a crying baby over her head:

"My baby hasn't had milk in three days, when are you going to feed *him*?"

Stanton looked around desperately until he hit on an out: "And now," he cried with plainly bogus enthusiasm,

295

"your next Mayor, the famous financier and philanthropist JAY GOULD!"

Without any further ado, he tugged mightily on a rope and swept the curtains open, to reveal Gould—who, gauging the temper of the crowd with his usual acumen—was backing away towards the exit at the rear of the structure.

One stentorian voice bellowed from the audience:

"GOULD, YOU CROOKED BASTARD! WHERE WERE YOU ON BLACK FRIDAY WHEN YOU STOLE OUR SAVINGS AND MY PAPA BLEW HIS BRAINS OUT?"

That was enough for Gould, who vanished so quickly through the exit that his presence might well have been an illusion. Stanton shook his head desperately, then snatched a police whistle out of his pocket and blew three short blasts on it, at which the Johhnies came out of their semi-concealment and started trotting towards the stage with their chromed weapons at port arms, their gear clanking and their heavy footsteps clomping rhythmically.

"There's going to be a slaughter," said Gran worriedly.

Liam's face grew dark as thunder: "No, by God, there *isn't*!" he growled, fueling himself with the picture of the gaunt and famished faces surrounding them. Then, raising his arms over his head and glaring at the corpulent, sweating figure of Stanton, fat enough to make three of any of Liam's skin-and-bones neighbors, he spread his arms wide and roared:

"*PIGS!*"

For a split second the picture held: Stanton with the whistle raised to his mouth and Johnnies double-timing towards the crowd with their weapons at the ready, then there was a colossal blinding flash, the biggest anyone there had ever seen, and a moment later as they all rubbed their eyes they saw, on the spot where Stanton had been standing, a hefty young pig at least three hundred pounds on the trotter, and next to the stage milling about among the dropped weapons and squealing in panic, a whole herd of nice, juicy hogs.

For another split second, the situation sank in on everyone, and Chen gave Liam a dubious frown. Liam held up a slightly shaky hand in defense: "You have to admit, Ambrose, I didn't take away, I *added*."

"Added *what*?" Chen asked dubiously.

As if in answer to Chen's question an ecstatic shout arose from the crowd: "FOOD!" someone shouted. And then a joyous roar: "*BARBECUE!*"

At which the crowd surged forward as one man and tore after the pigs, which fled across the North Meadow squealing hysterically.

Gran put her arms around Liam and kissed him on both cheeks. "Finn McCool would be proud," she said.

"Me too," said Becky, taking over the embrace and adding extras.

Gran poked Chen in the ribs with her elbow. "Don't be such an old fusspot," she said, "let's get back downtown and see if we can find something to eat."

"Oh, very well," Chen huffed. "But *no* pork!"

"Everybody ready?" Liam said. He raised a questioning eyebrow at Chen, who nodded and pointed towards a nearby rock. Stealing a quick look towards the pigs, now vanishing into the distance with their pursuers right behind them, Liam grinned, drew the katana and swept it downwards as one final brilliant flash lit the meadow and the quartet disappeared.

About the Author

Always impatient, Dennis O'Flaherty decided early on that it wasn't fair to have to wait a whole lifetime before trying his next life. As a result, he's been a U.S. Marine (rifleman, radioman, Corporal E-4), a historian of Russia (Harvard, Oxford, State University of Moscow on the U.S. Cultural Exchange), and a Grub Street hack in Hollywood (a shared Edgar Award for the script on Coppola's *Hammett*, many *Teenage Mutant Ninja Turtle* scripts, even a handful of cigar ads).

Now, after a lifetime of gypsying, he is happily settled in Arizona with his wife Mel, cats Smokey and Mickey, and legions of anonymous white-winged doves and collared lizards. But the anchor has always been his writing, and he still sees no reason to argue with W. B. Yeats' dictum: "Of all the many changing things . . . words alone are certain good."